SORIN

A JAMES THOMAS NOVEL

BROOKE SIVENDRA

Cover by Virtually Possible Designs

Ebook: 978-0-6480649-0-9

Print: 978-0-6480649-1-6

PROLOGUE

ERIC

Eric looked down upon her pale body. Maya slept now, heavily sedated, while the chorus of the Gods played through the sound system. Eric lit the candelabras beside Maya's bed. He wondered how long he'd have to wait for James Thomas to arrive, with Makaela. *Not long*, he thought. If the man was as good as Eric thought he was, he wouldn't take the chance that Eric was bluffing. And he would've known what was in that vial. It was unfortunate for Maya that she'd become a pawn in the game, but such pawns were sometimes necessary.

"How is your patient?"

Eric turned to face Lucian. "Well. Taking a nice, long nap."

The corner of Lucian's lips turned up as he sat down in one of the chairs beside Maya's bed. He moved with the grace of a God—fluid, lithe, as if floating across this Earth. Lucian had been touched by the Gods, blessed by them, and Eric wanted the same. He wanted it so badly.

"Has there been any response to your message?" Lucian asked, crossing one leg over the other.

"No official response, no, but I didn't expect one. There will be movement in their camp, though, of that I'm sure. He'll be drawing up his tactical strategy, designing a plan to fool me—but not this time. We know this building better than anyone. This," Eric said, holding his arms out, palms turned toward the ceiling, "is just a small piece. The tunnels have protected Saratani for as long as it has existed, and they'll protect us again."

Lucian's nod was slow, thoughtful. "How are the new security teams?"

"Better than before. I made the mistake of underestimating James Thomas. A mistake I will not repeat."

Lucian narrowed his eyes slightly. "His alliance with Biskup continues to concern me. They provide a brute force that is unparalleled. If Biskup were to dedicate all of his men to the rescue of Maya, and the subsequent capture of you, it will be a battle that you cannot be certain you will win." Lucian held his gaze. "You are the son I never had. I love you like my own blood, and that's why I want you to listen to what I'm about to say. This is not about your wife Makaela, so do not let your personal feelings get in the way. This—she," he said, dropping his eyes to the bed, "is a means to eliminate Makaela's security, and thus destroy the relationship with Biskup and eliminate the threat and distraction he poses. You need to have all of your attention focused on Liam Smith. He, and he alone, is your key to the Gods. Success in capturing him will ensure your passage to be an Elder—the youngest ever—and you will earn a level of respect never seen before. A level of respect greater than I even have. They believe you are a son of the Gods, Christos, and now it's time to show them you are."

Eric looked into the gray abyss of Lucian's eyes and he felt an energy swirl in his body. Lucian could do that—it was one of his gifts. Lucian had the power to create that dynamic shift within the soul. Without Lucian's guidance over the years, Eric knew he'd never have become the man he was today. He owed Lucian everything. After all, it had been him who had introduced Eric to this world and had taught him what was possible.

"I will show them, and I will make them believe in me again. This will be my redemption for the worship ceremony," Eric said.

"I know you will. I've never had more faith in anyone than I have in you," Lucian responded as he sat up, as if he were ready to depart. "Where is Marianne? I thought she was going to be the one to care for Maya."

"She is and she'll be here in a few minutes," Eric said as his phone began to ring. He drew it from his pocket, noting the number. "Yes."

"He's awake," the man replied.

Eric looked to Lucian and Eric wondered if it was the sparkle in Eric's eyes or the smile on his lips that piqued Lucian's intrigue.

"I'll be there soon," Eric said. "Which tunnel is he in?"

"Cera Six."

"Warm him up for me. I'm on my way." Eric hung up. The tables had turned in his favor. "The man we captured from the Nic House, the one sole survivor of the explosion, has just woken up."

Lucian flashed a grin, showing two rows of perfect white teeth. "Thank the Gods, for they are looking out for you—guiding you. I'm very interested to hear what he has to say. Shall we?" Lucian stood.

"We shall," Eric said, looking toward his new head of security. The men swooped in and accompanied Eric and Lucian down to the cells. The remaining security stayed with Maya.

Eric set a fast pace, excitement effervescing in his chest. His exterior, though, was calm and controlled. He made sure of it. He had to be extra cautious around Lucian.

It wasn't just the prospect of gaining knowledge that would help them when James Thomas arrived, it was the prospect of potentially finding out who he was. Lucian's warning was at the front of his mind, but Eric couldn't deny this was personal. He wanted Mak to himself, and once he found out who her boyfriend was, he was going to dig up every dirty secret the man had and expose him. He would destroy their relationship, initiate Mak into Saratani, and then his mind would be free to focus on finding Liam Smith. The Gods always had a plan, however testing it seemed at times, but Eric felt like the tide was turning. James Thomas was a very powerful man, but he didn't have the favor of the Gods. Eric had the upper edge—he'd had it from the start.

Eric stood beside Lucian as the wall turned one-hundred-and-eighty degrees, revealing a tunnel that led to the cells. Security went in first, followed by Lucian, and then Eric, with more security at the rear.

Lucian kept up the fast pace, much to Eric's delight, and the only sound was the echo of their footsteps.

They came to a stop at the cells and security entered a code before ushering them in.

Eric's fingers tingled and his body pulsed. His heartbeat whooshed through his ears. Lucian entered first but stepped aside, letting Eric take control.

The man laid cuffed and strapped to a gurney. The attending nurse looked up at them and then quickly finished what she was doing. She scuffled out.

Eric sat down on the edge of the bed. "I'm very glad to see you...awake."

The man remained stone-faced but Eric knew, without a doubt, this man knew who he was.

"As you're aware, your employer and I have a troubled past. But I'm not concerned with that, and that's not what I'm here to talk to you about."

The man stared straight ahead.

Eric angled his head, forcing the man to meet his gaze.

"I want to know about James Thomas. I want to know everything about him: what he looks like, where he's from, what his skills are."

The man's pupils dilated at the mention of the name James Thomas, and that told Eric everything he needed to know. The man knew who he was, and he'd likely worked with them on the attack at the worship ceremony.

"I am going to kill you," Eric continued. "I saved you only so that you could tell me what you know. But there are multiple ways of killing someone, and some are much less painful than others."

"You're a traitor," the man spat at him.

Eric smiled. "On the contrary. I am very loyal, but only to those worth being loyal to. Alexandr Biskup is a greedy, manipulative man with only his best interests at heart. I was never on his team, and therefore I never betrayed him. He should've seen it coming—it's not my fault that he didn't."

"You're insane is what you are," the man said with burning eyes.

"You only think that because you don't know our world. You don't know the gifts available to us if only we trust in the Gods."

The man scoffed. "James Thomas... He's better than you. You outsmarted Biskup, and Kovalenko, but Thomas is different. We believe in him, Biskup believes in him. He'll get you, Eric, and then you'll pay for everything you've done."

"What makes you so sure about that?" Lucian injected coldly.

He looked at the other man before returning his wild eyes to Eric. "Everything. Everything about him. You should be scared, Eric. He's smart and he's skilled, but it's not just that—it's the way he works, the focus, the determination...you can see it in his eyes. Black, consuming wells."

Eric's heart lurched into his throat. "Black eyes?" he said casually. "No one has black eyes."

It was what the man didn't say. He drew back, reserved, like he'd somehow known.

Could it be?

The whispers of a chill that spread through his veins told him not to let this go. There could be more than one man on this earth with black eyes, but Eric thought, perhaps guided by the Gods, that this was the one he'd been looking for.

And, if so, he'd been under Eric's nose this whole time.

Liam had come for him in Amman, but who had he come for? Eric?

Or Christos?

And if he'd come for Eric, how long had Liam known they were the same man?

Eric raised his eyes to Lucian's and for a moment he lost himself in the stormy, swirling clouds in his eyes. He knew Lucian had come to the same potential conclusion—a conclusion that made everything make sense. It would've been how they'd been able to so effectively protect Makaela. And how James Thomas had been able to form the partnership with Biskup.

His blood began to heat up. A slow simmering sensation filled his veins as the shock wore off and reality sank in.

Liam Smith is sleeping with my wife.

"Pass me a knife," Eric said, holding out his hand, his eyes cold, penetrating his captive.

Security passed one to him, and Eric brought it to the man's ear. He was going to talk, and he was going to tell him everything he needed to know.

This changes everything.

1

JAMES THOMAS

The whiteboard was once again a blank canvas. Over and over, they'd drawn strategies made up of dots and lines marking entry and exit points. And over and over again they'd wiped the board clean.

James stared at the board, chewing on his cheek as his mind churned. It looked impossible. Every way he looked at it he saw defeat. But he was not ready to be defeated. He would not be defeated.

Defeat meant failure.

Failure to rescue Maya.

Failure to secure Mak's safety.

There is always a solution, James told himself. It was the phrase he'd used so often in his career and he was holding on to the hope it promised now.

James checked his watch. Five hours until Mak arrived in London. Five hours until he needed to be at the hangar with a plan.

He rubbed the palms of his hands over his face, pushing aside the fear and worry.

This is your fault, James thought. *You should never have allowed Maya to take that trip.*

He cursed under his breath and reeled his mind in. He needed to focus.

Think, James, think.

"Okay," he said to Deacon, who was rocking back and forth on his heels with his arms crossed, staring at the whiteboard. "Eric knows that we know this building. And he knows that we saw him exit via the tunnel. So all of those entry points have to be ruled out. But are there any other tunnels? We need to investigate this further because without alternative entry points we might as well walk in the front door."

Deacon nodded, thoughtfully. "The question we didn't answer from the worship ceremony was how that many people got into the building unseen. Samuel reviewed all of the footage again, and no one went in via any of the known entrances."

"I think there's at least one other tunnel that only Eric knows about," James said. "Yes, we created hysteria that night, but for the crowd not to move toward that door has to mean that they didn't know about it—and I bet he has another secret escape route as well."

Deacon held up his hand. "Let's not get ahead of ourselves. We need to get Samuel to review the footage that came through via our cameras again. That way we can see where the crowd *was* running to. It won't tell us how to get into the tunnels from outside the building, but it might somehow help identify an approximate location," Deacon said, pulling his phone from his pocket.

James tilted his head. "Samuel also needs to do a match of every face he can pull from the worship surveillance feed. I know he's already doing that, and trying to identify them, but let's see if he can get a CCTV footage match. Maybe we can see them entering a building nearby," James said. Samuel was going to be insanely busy.

While Deacon made the phone call, James took a moment to eat a sandwich and wash it down with juice. He wasn't going to be sleeping tonight, so he needed something to give him energy.

Why did I approve Maya's trip? James had tortured his mind with that question over and over since he'd received the news from Samuel.

He'd known the risks. He'd known the danger Mak's entire family was in. James had increased the size of Maya's security team substantially, but she would've needed a security team the size of Mak's to stop the breach. She should never have gone on the trip—that was the truth, and James couldn't escape it.

James shook his head, groaning under his breath. He couldn't undo his mistake, but he could fix it—as much as it could be fixed.

He needed more time, but the longer they delayed rescuing Maya, the more severe her addiction would be. And James didn't trust Eric not to do anything else to her—particularly if they didn't play his game.

I can't let Mak down, James thought. *I can't fail her now.*

He had to figure this out—he had to create a plan that would work.

"You look worried," Danny, one of Biskup's men, said as he came to sit beside James at the folding table. It had been one of their many makeshift dining tables for the past few weeks.

"Wouldn't you be?" James said, his eyes lingering on the blank whiteboard.

"Sure, I'd be freaking out... But you've been so collected until this point, it's a surprise to see any emotion on your face," Danny said. "That makes *me* worry."

"I'm worried because we don't yet have a plan. Once that's in place I'll feel a million times better," James said, searching the man's eyes to see if he believed him.

Danny gave a nod that indicated he did. With everything falling apart, he needed these men to continue to believe, and it was his job to make sure they did. James couldn't let his guard slip now.

"Fair enough. Can I do anything to help?" Danny said.

"Yeah, get some sleep, because as soon as we do have a plan you'll be on your feet, and I don't know for how long. It's time to finish Eric off once and for all," James said, noting that brought out a vicious smile from Danny.

"I'll be ready." As the man stood to leave, James stood too, returning to his brother.

"Samuel's on it," Deacon said. "How close do you think we need to get Mak?"

James bit his lip, sighing. "Eric needs to see her entering the building. She needs to walk through a known entrance, and then—somehow—we need to create a distraction so that Cami and the team can get her out while we surprise Eric. If we can access those tunnels that we think exist, it could actually be possible."

"I agree, I think they're our best shot," Deacon said. He inhaled deeply. "I don't want to be negative right now, but what happens if something goes horribly wrong and we can't get Mak out? You need to prepare yourself for this, James. You can't be next to her, not if we're going to try and keep your identity concealed. Kayla told Samuel that she gave a sketch of my face to Eric, so we're going to have to send someone else in with Mak—someone pretending to be you."

"I know," James said. He didn't want to think worst-case scenario —he couldn't bring himself to—but he needed to prepare for it. "My only consolation is that I don't believe Eric will kill her. God only knows what he has planned for her, but he won't kill her. And that means there's always a chance to get her back—provided we get out of there alive."

"Do you think it's time to call Haruki?" Deacon asked, pulling his lips to the side.

"I'm planning to as soon as we have the plan in place. I want Haruto and a team here on standby in the event that Mak gets out but we don't," James said, struggling to swallow.

It wasn't death he feared, for he'd faced it before—he'd seen its shadows waiting for him. But it was the fear of what would happen to Mak if they weren't around to protect her. And it was the fear of saying goodbye, something he was not ready to do.

Deacon nodded, and then cleared his throat. "Let's get back to business," he said, drawing a circle on the whiteboard. "If, hypothetically, there are multiple tunnels leading into this building, then if Eric didn't already, he'll have cameras in there now. We need to find a way to either loop that footage or, failing that, take down his system."

"So where is the control box?" James asked, glad to have something else to focus on other than entry and exit points, even if just for a few minutes.

"I think, if it's the right box, that it's in the room adjacent to the back entry—where we came in. It looked like a control room of sorts. It's a guess..."

A vague strategy began to form in James' mind. "Eric needs to see Mak there. If he sees us first, and he doesn't believe Mak's there, I think there's a good chance he'll kill Maya before we can get to her—as punishment for not playing his game. So if we can get Mak in the front door so that Eric can see her, and then disable all surveillance and power—total blackout—it will give us a window, albeit very brief, to get her out again before he realizes what is going on."

A surge of adrenaline woke up James' body, and his mind. It was the first time he'd felt even slightly hopeful. James picked up a whiteboard marker, drawing up another plan. They continued to refine it hour after hour. Until they could get further information a lot of it was hypothetical, but at least they had some form of a plan.

James sat in the back seat of the car, cracking his fingers as he looked down the runway. Any minute Mak's plane would land and with it her security team—a team James had to rely upon to keep her safe. He'd trained them, he'd mentored them, he'd coached them for years. But would it be enough?

He pressed a finger against his pulsing temple, trying desperately to relieve the hammer that was banging inside his skull.

James lifted his eyes when he heard the familiar sound of jet engines. His heart rate elevated and with it his body temperature. This was it. It was real. The woman he loved had arrived and he was going to take her into the dragon's lair and pray they all got out alive.

The whirl of the engines subsided and James and Deacon exited their vehicle, stepping onto the tarmac. James watched as the door opened and the stairs were lowered. In proper protocol, the team began to exit, huddling Mak in the middle. James couldn't see her amongst his tall, well-built men until she was on the bottom step. She raised her eyes to meet his, and her composure cracked.

James stepped forward, enveloping her small body in his arms. He closed his eyes and held her tight as she wrapped her arms around his waist.

He didn't speak, because he couldn't offer her any comforting words. He just held her and vowed to himself that he would make sure she got out alive, along with Maya. If he had to die to do that, then that was his fate.

James leaned back, looking into a pair of bloodshot eyes.

"Let's go," he said, wanting to get to the safehouse as quickly as possible.

She inhaled a shaky breath and nodded.

He took her hand, leading her toward the car.

"Deacon, what happened to your hair?" Mak asked, her voice a few notes higher than usual.

Deacon gave her a charming smile. "James gave me a haircut. Do we look more like brothers now?"

James saw Deacon give her a wink, and he knew his brother was trying to ease some of the worry and tension he knew Mak would be feeling. She seemed momentarily distracted, but it didn't last long. Her face grew somber once more.

James reluctantly let go of her hand as she was ushered into the back seat and Cami and Tom took their positions beside her. He wanted to sit with her, but he needed to be in the front passenger seat. He was done taking chances, and if they were somehow ambushed, he wanted to have the best seat in the house.

He closed his car door and laid his pistol in his lap.

Mak cleared her throat. "Where are we going?"

James angled his body to look back at her. "To our townhouse. We're going to stay there for the next little while until we finish refining the strategic plan. Once that's done, Deacon and I will head to the warehouse to train the men. And then it's time to get Maya back." James took her hand, squeezing it.

"How long is all of that going to take?" she asked.

James hesitated. "I don't know yet," he said. "It's worth taking the additional time to get the plan right. We won't make a move until that's done. We can't. Training the men won't take too long—they've done this kind of work before and they've been training for weeks."

Biskup's men weren't trained in hostage retrieval—they were usually the ones taking hostages. But, James needed Mak to be as confident as possible, and if he had to lie to her to do that, then so be it.

"Have you eaten?" James asked, and Cami was quick to answer.

"No, she refused to eat all flight."

James squeezed Mak's hand again. "You need to eat, we all do. The next forty-eight hours are going to be intense and you'll need the energy."

"I feel sick," Mak said, shaking her head.

He sighed—he felt ill, too. "I know, but you need to eat anyway," James said.

James checked the mirrors even though he knew Deacon was looking constantly.

"What are we going to say to my family?" Mak asked. "When Maya's fiancé can't get hold of her, he's going to worry."

"They've been escorted to your apartment as a precaution. Deacon and I are going to have a video conference with them in a few hours."

Mak met his gaze. "I want to see the video from Eric."

James had known this conversation was coming, and he didn't know if showing it to her would be a good thing. He couldn't predict how she would react to it and that made James fearful. The video would make her angry and that fury could give her the strength to face what she needed to do. But her fury might not only be directed at Eric. When Mak saw her sister in the bed, she might look at James with a look he'd never wanted to see in her eyes. He'd failed her to protect Maya, and he wouldn't blame Mak for being furious with him, too. James' stomach clenched and his legs felt weak. He'd failed her.

James nodded. "When we get to the townhouse."

"Good," she said.

James checked the mirrors again. No tail.

The car was silent for the rest of the journey. When they arrived at the townhouse, all three security cars pulled into the underground garage and they ushered Mak into the stairwell. James led her past the basement bedroom that housed their weaponry and up two flights of stairs to a spare bedroom. He closed the door behind them and drew her in.

"I just...I feel like this isn't real...that this can't possibly be happening," she said, her breath catching.

"I know. It's a nightmare, but we're going to get her back," James said.

"But you can't promise me that."

Mak searched his eyes and he wondered what she was searching for. Fear? Doubt? Nerves? They were all there, but he didn't let her see it.

"No, I can't, but I believe it," James said.

A tear slipped from her eye and ran down her cheek. She looked away quickly, but James cupped her cheek, guiding her eyes back to his.

"I don't want you to do this," Mak said. "If you can't get her out, then I'm going to lose both of you. How am I supposed to live with that? This is my *husband* who has done this!"

"Hey...stop. Don't torture yourself over this. He stopped being your husband a long time ago. Eric isn't the man he was when you knew him—of that I'm certain. He's a very different, very dangerous man living in a completely delusional world. You're not to blame for any of this."

I am, James thought.

She took in a shaky breath. "I want to see the video," she said.

James sighed, and then drew his phone.

He sat down on the edge of the bed and motioned for her to sit beside him.

He pressed play.

2

MAK ASHWOOD

Mak sucked in a breath as she saw her husband for the first time in thirteen years. Nearly fourteen. It was like seeing a ghost, and perhaps that's what it was, because when he started talking she didn't recognize him as the man she'd been married to. His voice sent a chill floating across her skin as she squinted to see her sister. Maya's eyes were closed as she lay in the bed, white blankets drawn up to her waist.

This is not happening, Mak thought. But it was. It was very real.

"I don't appreciate your new relationship with Alexandr Biskup. Nor do I appreciate your relationship with my wife. Because that's what she is—*my wife*. And so, unfortunately, things have come to this."

I am not your wife, Mak thought through gritted teeth. *I would rather be dead than be your wife.*

As Eric drew up the heroin dose, anxiety gripped her. She wanted to stop him, to protect her sister, but she could only watch on. That wasn't even the worst part, though—it was the haunting smile he gave to the camera. The smile that indicated he was enjoying it, like it was some kind of game.

Mak couldn't tear her eyes away.

"Oh, and one more thing. I'd like you to bring my wife with you. Our reunion is long overdue. I'll see you both soon."

When the video finished Mak leaned forward, resting her elbows on her knees, burying her face in her hands. She fought to keep her resolve, to keep from breaking.

She let out a sigh that bordered on a whimper.

James gently took her hands, guiding her eyes to his.

"We're going to get through this—all of us." His eyes flared with pure determination.

"What was the attack on him? What happened?" Mak asked. She wanted the truth.

James looked torn and she wondered if he was holding back information. "Eric is the leader of a radicalized religious cult. They have regular 'worship' ceremonies—sacred events. We ambushed one of them recently. Eric managed to escape, but not before recognizing one of Biskup's men."

Mak shook her head, pinching the bridge of her nose. "A religious cult? When were you going to tell me about this?"

"My strategy has not and will never change—not for you, and not for any of my clients. You are on a need-to-know basis when it comes to intel."

"What harm comes from knowing that?" Mak said, raising her voice.

James shook his head. "The point is that underestimating Eric is a very bad idea. He's changed in the years since he's been gone, Mak, and not for the better. He's insane, he's brainwashed, and he's dangerous. He loves to play games, as you can see."

"What happened to his hand?" Mak asked.

"Someone shot it," James said, his expression indicating he didn't feel badly about that. Neither did Mak—she just wished that person had been a better shot.

James looked down to his watch. "We need to eat and I need to get back to work. The sooner our plan is finalized, the sooner we can go in."

Mak nodded. *Go in.* She felt like she'd been transported to another world, another reality. It all felt surreal.

"Okay," Mak said with a sigh. She didn't know how much she could eat without it coming back up, but she was going to try. She wouldn't be the weak link in this operation. She would be strong— for Maya, and for James. She didn't want him worrying about her— Mak wanted him laser-focused on getting Maya out.

Mak didn't believe in the death penalty, she didn't believe that another human should get to decide when another's life is up, but if a bullet landed in Eric's chest at some point in this rescue operation, Mak didn't think she'd mind one bit.

She stood up to leave, but James tugged on her hand.

"Wait," he said quietly, before he stood and wrapped her up in his arms.

He looked down at her, and his expression was unreadable. James lifted her chin and brushed his lips over hers. Mak closed her eyes, her skin tingling. Their mouths pressed together in a kiss that wasn't hungry, but was beautifully intimate.

James drew back, his lips searing her forehead as he held her for a second longer. "Let's go," he said, weaving his fingers between hers.

They took the stairs down one level where her security team was eating from a spread of food on the dining table. James passed her a plate and she looked over the selection, trying to find something that she thought she could keep down. She settled on a banana muffin and some water. It was a start.

Deacon was talking on the phone, and as he turned away, a fresh onslaught of nausea hit Mak.

"What really happened to your head?" she asked, stepping forward to take a closer look. She couldn't believe she hadn't seen it in the car—she'd been too busy focusing on James and trying to read his body language. Deacon turned away from her, but not before she got a good look at the dark brown scab of the healing wound. *That is why James had cut his hair—if that's even the truth,* she thought.

"I slipped up in training and fell backward. It's all good," Deacon said.

Mak's eyes flickered to James, but his calm exposure didn't fracture. Mak knew Deacon was lying, though. Were they present at the attack on Eric? Was that when Deacon got hurt?

Both of them are injured, Mak thought. James' arm couldn't possibly be healed yet and Deacon had a wound the size of a small apple on the back of his skull.

"I don't believe you," Mak said, but Deacon was too distracted by the phone call.

Deacon's eyes darted to James'. "Where? ... Good, good," he said and then hung up. "Samuel thinks he's found three entry points based on the CCTV footage."

James sprung up from his seat like it was on fire and strode toward the adjoining lounge room. Mak followed him, her muffin in hand.

James rolled out a large map and then, looking at his phone, drew three separate red circles on the map. Deacon kneeled beside him.

"Three entry points is a damn good start. We can get a lot of men in there," James said, sitting back on his heels.

"Samuel's not keen on trying to disable the security from the box," Deacon said, giving James an odd grin.

Mak watched the brothers keenly.

Deacon continued. "If we block off all entrances," he said, marking crosses on the map, "and then enter through their tunnels, they're not going to be able to get out very easily, if at all. Samuel's been looking at the power grids—he thinks he can take out this entire section."

A smile grew on James' lips. "That would be damn helpful," he said, nodding. His eyes glided as they seemed to roam the map. Mak wondered what he was searching for, or what he was thinking.

James looked over his shoulder. "Come here," he told her, shuffling over. Mak knelt between the brothers. "This is the building Maya is being held in," he said, tapping the marker on the map. "We need Eric to believe I'm bringing you in—otherwise we're worried he'll kill her as punishment, before we can get to her, for turning up without you—so we're going to walk you in the front door, blow the power circuit, and then take you straight back out the front door. By the time Eric realizes what happened, you'll be in a car heading back to this house, the one we're in now. The rest we'll handle, and then we'll meet you back here."

It seemed so simple, but most things were simple only in theory.

"I'm going to walk in on my own?" Mak asked. Eric had managed to take down Maya's entire security team, so how did James plan to keep her safe?

"No. You're going to have security teams in the background, covering you from every angle, and I'm going to send one of your security team in with you...pretending to be me," he said, his eyes searching her.

"Why?" Mak said, sure there was a very interesting answer to her question.

"I don't want Eric to recognize me, Mak. He's formed some relationships with men from my past, and if they realize that James Thomas is that same man, things will be a lot more difficult."

"And who is that man?" Mak asked, one eyebrow raised.

James didn't hesitate. "A man you're better off not knowing."

3

JAMES THOMAS

Mak hadn't spoken a word as they'd continued to throw strategies back and forth, keeping some and ruling out others, but James knew she was watching and listening intently to every word. As much as it pained him to have her involved, he felt powerless to change it now. All he could do was to make sure she lived—at all costs.

James looked to Cami, and then to Deacon. "Any last recommendations?"

Deacon shook his head. "I think it's the best we're going to get."

Cami nodded in agreement.

They'd been able to locate five different entry points into the worship building and Samuel had confirmed he'd be able to take out the power for a few minutes at minimum. That should give them enough time to get into the building, and then to get Mak far away from it before Eric's security teams could react. There were many smaller details that still needed to be confirmed, but they weren't plans that James wanted Mak to hear.

They'd only taken one break in the last seven hours, and that was to have the teleconference with Mak's parents. James wondered what they thought of him now. They were justifiably terrified, and James had needed to inspire enough trust in them for her family to realize that going to the police wasn't an option. He'd shared a few details of his past—details he had never intended on sharing with any member of her family—but it had been necessary. He needed them calm, or as calm as they could be under the circumstances. And he needed Mak not to be worried about them while she was to play her role—a role he hadn't disclosed to her family.

"Let's go and train the boys," James said, standing up, stretching out his stiff legs.

Deacon nodded and rolled up the plans.

James caught Make's eye and nodded toward the stairwell. He wanted—needed—a moment alone with her.

She followed him, and he reached back, taking her small hand in his. He'd been desperate to have a plan detailed out, but he'd known that for every step they got closer to confirming it, it was a minute less he'd have with her. There'd never been any guarantees in his career, but this mission felt like a death sentence.

He closed the bedroom door behind them.

"How long is it going to take to train them?" Mak asked.

"I don't know. I need them to practice the training drills until every single one of them is confident and knows their role. And then we need to practice substitute drills, in the event the plan changes, which it likely will. I'll be gone a few hours at least, perhaps even the night," James said, taking her hands.

"Can I do anything in the meantime?" Mak asked.

"You should eat something and try and sleep for a few hours. That will do you more good than you can imagine."

"You expect me to be able to sleep?"

"Not really, but you should rest at least," James said. "I'm going to take Cami with me, seeing as she'll be leading one of the teams. Tom and the rest of security will stay here with you."

"And then we go in?" Mak asked, visibly swallowing.

James nodded. "Then we go in," he said quietly.

She placed her palms on his chest, looking up at him through her long lashes. "How did Eric's men breach her security team, James?

You're always so careful; you don't take risks with clients. So how did this happen?"

"It happened because I made a mistake. I should never have allowed her to take the trip—that's the bottom line," James said. There was no way to sugarcoat it, and his chest tightened as he waited for her response.

She looked away, rubbing her lips over each other. Was she mad? Was she disappointed in him? He focused on his breath—he had to stay strong. He had to keep his mind straight.

"I should never have married him," she said, her jaw grinding. "Marrying Eric was the catalyst for this entire situation..." She looked back to him. "I don't want you to do this. I don't want you to risk your life—I don't want any of you to. I feel like my heart and mind are in a constant tug of war, like I have to choose between you or Maya. I couldn't live with myself if we didn't try, but how am I going to live with myself if you don't walk out of this? If Deacon or Cami don't? I don't want you to have to do this."

"I have to do this, Mak. Not just for Maya, but to end the threat that Eric poses. You'll never be free of him while he lives. He takes what he wants, and I still don't know why he's waited so long to come for you, but he has now. And he'll continue to, over and over, until he gets what he wants. This needs to end, for all of us—me included."

Sadness crept into her eyes like a misty fog. "It seems like a situation where there won't be any winners."

She looked down, shaking her head softly. James tucked a strand of hair behind her ear and tilted her face up to meet his.

"There are never any winners in a war. Only survivors. And *we* will be the survivors," James said.

It was time Eric reaped the consequences of his actions. Not just for what he'd done to Mak and her friends and her family, but for what he'd done to every innocent and every non-willing participant in his mad cult.

Eric had slipped through his fingers twice, but not a third time. James couldn't let that happen—the price was too grave.

James held Mak to his chest, letting the fresh, citrus scent of her perfume intoxicate his mind for a moment. "I would do this for you a million times over, Mak," James whispered.

She squeezed her arms, pressing her chest against his. "When this security threat first started, I had no idea how much I would end up needing you. And how hard I would fall in love with you."

His skin tingled, and his body flushed warm. Never in his life had he felt like this and he'd never felt less like he deserved it than he did right now. "Neither did I, Mak. But meeting you was the best thing that has ever happened to me, and I don't say that lightly. We were fated to meet—I know that for sure."

James wondered yet again if it was going to be a love story cut short.

Not if I can help it, James thought, and that star of hope in his chest sparkled once more.

Never give up.

Never.

"I need to go. The sooner we have the men trained, the sooner we get your sister back and end this," James said. If only it were that simple.

Mak pulled back, resting her hands on his hips. "I'll eat, and I'll try and sleep." James saw the conviction in her eyes and he knew she was determined to do what she could, however small her part in the plan was.

James gave her a small smile. "I love you," he said, kissing her forehead. "I'll call you when we're on our way back."

She nodded, letting her arms drop to her sides. He wished he could stay in her arms forever; but while fate had brought them together, now it was trying to rip them apart. Yet James was ready to defy his fate—he was ready to control his future. A future he was not ready to say goodbye to.

He turned and left, taking the stairs down to the basement. Deacon and Cami were waiting in the car.

James got in the passenger seat and buckled up. "Let's do this," he said as Deacon started the ignition.

The drive would give them time to finalize the plans, but James needed to make one phone call first. He dialed the number.

"James Thomas...another unexpected phone call," Haruki answered.

"Unfortunately it is. The time has come sooner than expected. I need Haruto and a team in London in twelve hours. Can you do it?"

"I can make anything happen, but I want to know why. And I want your word that my boys will be kept out of your mess. I won't drag the Tohmatsu name into this war," Haruki said, his words as hard as steel.

"Eric has taken Maya Ashwood hostage," James said, noting again how Haruki's sigh sounded more like a whistle. "Mak's in London at our townhouse. We're going in to get Maya, so I need Haruto to stay at the townhouse and wait. If he gets the instruction from Samuel, he's to get Mak on the jet, take her to Tokyo and wait for further instructions. That will be his only involvement. You have my word."

"I want the information," Haruki responded, all business.

"I'll have Samuel send it to you now," James said, knowing Samuel would be listening in on the conversation.

"Then I'll get the boys on a jet. Good luck, James." Haruki sounded as genuine as James had ever heard him.

"Thank you. Someone will be in touch soon—hopefully me," James said, ending the call.

"Okay," James said, turning in his seat. "What are everyone's major concerns?"

"Who are we sending in with Mak?" Cami asked.

"Tom came up to me and offered. I think he's the best choice, and Mak will be most comfortable with him." James looked to Deacon. "What do you think?"

"I agree. He's taking a huge risk, though. God only knows what Eric wants to do to James Thomas," Deacon replied, his eyes never leaving the road.

"I know. And Tom knows that," James said. If the plan went to plan, which plans rarely did, then Tom would be fine. But if and when it didn't, James had no idea what Tom's fate would be.

They continued to refine their strategy, making additional notes as they went. When Deacon pulled up James was surprised at how quickly the time had passed. Time seemed to be escaping him lately.

"Get ready to meet the boys, Cami," Deacon said, looking in the rearview mirror.

Cami scoffed. "I've listened to enough surveillance to have a good idea of what they're like. I'm with Samuel, the sooner this is over, the better. They're not my idea of good company."

James agreed, but they served their purpose well.

He opened the door, stepping out with the plan rolled up under his arm.

Make this work, James.

James watched each of the men like a hawk, his mind focused on the present moment and only that. He wasn't thinking about the conse-quences, he wasn't thinking about Mak. His mind was consumed with the plan.

When his cell phone rang and he saw it was Samuel, he wasn't expecting good news.

"Samuel," James answered.

"Go outside." Two words that carried as much power as a gun to the head, and Samuel's tone was darker than he'd ever heard it before.

James' eyes met Deacon's and as James turned, in his peripheral he saw his brother move toward him. "Cami," James said, his voice hushed. "Keep training them."

"Sure," she said, but he saw the change in her eyes. He didn't know if it was fear or confusion, but she knew something was up.

James left the door open as he exited the warehouse and when he heard it close he knew Deacon was behind. James put the call on speaker.

"Go ahead," James said, scared of what was coming next.

"We've got another problem. Nine problems, to be exact," Samuel said.

Fear blossomed in James' chest like black mold.

Samuel continued. "Nine deaths, all linked to you. Pavel and Eric have set their plan in motion."

James' eyebrows creased together. "What are you talking about?"

"God, I feel sick," Samuel said, and he sounded it. "They know everything about your past, James. Everything. More than one person at the CIA has been talking. The dark net is in a flutter—videos of brutal murders are going viral. I can see the victim's faces, and they're all people of your past."

James' heart skipped three beats. "Who are they?" he asked with difficulty, his throat seizing the words.

"The first one I watched was your ex-CIA boss, Marie," Samuel said and James leaned back reactively.

How did they get to her? When James visited her in Paris not long ago, he'd taken note of her security measures, and she was no easy target. And she was smart—she knew how to protect herself.

James closed his eyes. "How did she die?"

"They slit her throat—but judging by the other wounds on her body, they had her for a few hours at least," Samuel said delicately.

"Who else?" James said, unable to lift his eyes from the ground.

Samuel listed them off. The army general that had helped James transition into the CIA. The colonel that had honed his sniper skills. Two of the friends he'd had in the army before they'd staged his death and he'd left it all behind for a life in the agency. James sank to the ground. They were all innocent people. And they were all dead now because of him. James didn't need to watch the videos to know that they weren't given a quick death.

He ran his hand over his head as he leaned forward, resting his elbows on his knees. He let his head drop down as waves of nausea rolled in, one after the other.

As Samuel continued, James waited for one name to come, one name that would hurt more than the others. When Samuel stopped talking, James realized he'd lost count.

"Is that all of them?" James asked.

"That's nine," Samuel replied.

James tried to think, to break through the slush of emotions overriding his mind. Samuel hadn't said the name, but Eric had dug back far enough into his past that James didn't believe he hadn't come across this person, nor that he'd missed the relationship.

And James knew Eric well enough to know how much he liked playing games. The fact that the name hadn't been said worried him.

"Samuel, check on Sister Francine," James said quietly, closing his eyes once more.

The one woman who had believed in him, the woman who'd come closer to a being his mother than he'd ever had. The first person who taught him anything about love. She was an angel on Earth.

"I already have," Samuel said. "I can't find her."

4
_____

JAMES THOMAS

I can't find her.

That told James that the worst-case scenario playing out in his mind was real. Eric had her. Or Sokolov had her. One of them did, and James cringed as he thought of what they would do to her. She was the kindest, most gracious person James had ever met, and she was going to meet a horrible death.

They were going to use her as bait, James knew. They were going to draw him out by torturing her. It would be the next video on the dark net, and one James didn't know how he was going to bring himself to watch.

Perfect timing, Eric, James thought.

If the video came soon, it would force him to make a choice. And James already knew who he'd choose. He couldn't go for Sister Francine now, not with the situation they were currently dealing with. He'd choose Mak—it wasn't even a choice—but it would haunt him until the day he died. He'd always said he never lived with regrets, but he had harbored one since that fateful day in Paris. And this was going to be his second.

James put his phone down on the dirt between his feet. He wanted to pretend that phone call had never happened. He wanted to pretend that Maya wasn't being held hostage. He didn't want the responsibilities his life was forcing upon him. If one situation hadn't been enough, Eric had added another capable of giving him a nervous breakdown. James gave a sigh that sounded like a cry.

Deacon sat down beside him. "Breathe for a minute. They're not going to kill Sister Francine until she serves no use."

Until they have you, was what Deacon didn't say.

"No, but they'll hurt her," James said.

"Yes, but the body has a remarkable way of forgetting pain in time, we both know that. She'll cling to her faith—it will serve her well."

Where is God now? James thought. *Why is this happening to her?*

James looked up to the night sky. The stars were back—a sparkling blanket wrapping around the earth. The stars brought him no peace now, though. He couldn't stop his mind from spinning.

"I can't deal with this," James whispered, scared to voice his fears. Fears he could only ever share with his brother.

"No, but we can. We do it together, just like we always have. One problem at a time," Deacon said.

"I can't think straight," James said. "How am I supposed to focus when this is on my mind, too? We can't afford any mistakes, we can't afford to be distracted, and yet I don't think I've ever felt less in control. Everything is slipping away, I'm going to lose everything—"

"No, you're not," Deacon said, his stern tone cutting through the hysteria James had slipped into. "We're not giving up now, and we're not changing the plan. Everything stays as it is. We get Maya and Mak back in safe arms, and then we'll deal with this."

"And if it comes to a head at the same time?" James said, looking at his brother.

His lips pressed together. "Then the plan stays the same and you can't punish yourself for making that choice. I would've done it for Nicole, and you'll do it for Mak."

Somehow, Deacon's mention of Nicole calmed James down. He needed to get his mind straight—he couldn't let what happened to Nicole happen to Mak.

"How long have we been out here?" James asked.

"It doesn't matter," Deacon said, not even looking at his wrist. "Cami can keep training them as long as we need. You need to get back in the right frame of mind—that's the most important thing."

And James knew he would have to keep that frame of mind when the next video came. *And it will come in the form of a video,* James thought, because Eric was so fond of the lens.

James picked up his phone knowing there would be consequences for the words he was about to speak.

"Samuel, if Eric posts a video showing Sister Francine, before the mission at the worship building is complete, don't show it to me. Don't even mention it."

There was a pause before Samuel answered. "I understand."

James knew Samuel would—James wouldn't be able to keep focused and deal with the video simultaneously. He couldn't be distracted; he didn't want to put himself in a position that would weaken the rescue mission. He'd made his choice, a choice that could ultimately sacrifice Sister Francine, and he would deal with the consequences later. If he lived to see that day.

Deacon nodded, and James assumed he agreed he'd made the right call—however ugly it was.

"Let's finish training these boys," James said standing on legs not yet fully recovered from the anguish of Eric's brutal plan.

James pulled out the bulletproof vest they'd had custom-made to fit Mak—a vest he'd hoped to never have to use. It looked too small, too inefficient to protect her. And it partly was—the vest would stop a bullet from landing in her chest or abdomen, but it couldn't fully protect her. Nothing could. Including James.

James closed the trunk of the car, grabbed his kit and took the stairs into the townhouse. He'd spoken to Mak on the drive back, so he'd expected her to be waiting. And she was. She was dressed in jeans, a light sweater and trainers. Shoes she could run in—as they'd instructed. James gave her a smile, hoping it hid the storm of emotions he was feeling inside. The boys were ready. Samuel was ready. Mak and her team were ready. James wondered if he was the only one who wasn't ready. But then he would never feel ready for this moment. How could he, when the consequences could be so devastating?

"Did you eat?" James said, kissing her cheek.

"I did. Two meals. Are we ready?" Mak asked.

No. "Yes, we're ready. Come upstairs with me," James said.

In the bedroom, he put his kit down on the bed.

"How are you feeling?" James asked.

"I don't know what to feel. I'm trying not to feel anything at all," she said.

James nodded. "That's the best strategy. I have something for you." James held up the vest.

Mak paused, biting her lip. A bulletproof vest was a stark reminder of the grave situation they were going into.

"Take off your sweater and your bra," James said, wishing he were saying those words in an altogether different scenario.

Mak hesitated, but then quickly did so.

As James stepped forward to strap on the vest, he cringed internally, shuddering, but he refused to show it. He'd known this day could come, under a number of plausible situations, but he wasn't prepared for it.

He strapped on the vest as Mak held her arms out and a small sigh slipped through his lips as he made the last adjustment. "This is harder than I thought it would be," James said quietly, resting his forehead on hers. "I only ever wanted to protect you, to shield you from this mess, and now I'm leading you into it."

Mak cupped his cheek. "You've done everything to protect me— more than I think I will ever know or understand. This is Eric's fault, and his fault alone." The conviction in her words helped to ease his mind, but he didn't miss the words she hadn't said. He hadn't done everything to protect her sister. If they all got out of this alive, James wondered if that would have repercussions down the road.

James sighed. "I love you, Mak. I love you more than I knew it was possible to love someone. No matter what happens, I want you to know that."

"Are you saying goodbye?" she said, pulling back.

"No," James said quickly. "Never. I will never give up. But I think it's easy to take for granted the people closest to us. My life has constantly taught me not to do that. I should tell you every day how much I love you, even though there are really no words to describe it." James paused, mindful of the time. He had to get back to business. "The plan might change tonight, you know that, but I don't want you to panic if it does. We're used to this—to re-strategizing mid-mission. All you need to do is to follow Tom's instructions. Do exactly what he says. No improvising, not even if another option looks better at the time. He'll have information—via an earwig—that you don't. Promise me you'll do exactly what he says. Your safety, Maya's safety, and the safety of everyone on this mission depends on orders being followed."

"Yes," she said without hesitation, and James knew with one look at her eyes that she would.

"Good." James turned back to the bed. He needed to put on his own protective gear, but he'd left most of his weapons in the car. He didn't want Mak to see what he was taking in.

James stripped off his sweater, tossing it on the bed before he strapped on his vest. He felt Mak's eyes on him, but he had no idea what she was thinking. He strapped on a holster, loading his pistol into it, and then slipped his sweater back on. James pulled out a few more items before he zipped up his kit and slung it over his shoulder.

"These are for you. Keep them in your pockets and use them as Cami's trained you to do—under Tom's orders. Knife," James said, passing it to her. "And your own pistol." He lifted her sweater enough to strap a holster on. He passed her the gun, observing how she held it and how her chest rose. It was one thing to practice with one, it was another completely to intend to kill someone, or even seriously harm them. "You're a good shot, an excellent shot—don't hesitate to use it. But just remember, if you somehow end up shooting at Eric—don't kill him. He needs to survive, because without him, we don't have the code and then we have a very big problem with Biskup."

Mak blew out a long breath. "Got it," she said, putting the pistol in the holster. "Anything else?" she asked, and James thought he heard some trepidation in her voice.

"No, that's it. Just follow instructions—that's all you need to do. I'm just preparing for the worst-case scenario. It would be foolish not to," James said.

He put his hands on her waist, holding her for what could be the last time. She tilted up onto her tiptoes and wrapped her arms around his neck. "Thank you," she whispered, her lips not an inch from his. "Please be careful, James. I can't lose you."

"I will, I promise."

This is what I'm fighting for, James thought. *For this woman, for this life—for our life together.*

His chest fluttered as she kissed him and he closed his eyes.

A kiss he had thought would be bittersweet had a surprising effect on him. It gave him confidence, it gave him determination.

He kissed her back, hungry for anything he could take in the next minute. His heart raced wildly and his body heated, as it always did around her. His hand slipped down to the arch of her lower back and he drew her in, needing to hold her, to feel her for as long as he could.

When he heard Deacon's voice penetrate the walls, yelling to Cami, James knew it was a subtle hint that it was time.

James drew back, looking deep into her eyes.

"Let's do this."

5

ERIC

Eric looked at his watch. Sokolov would arrive in thirty minutes.

It's time to show them who you are.

Eric went to the fridge and pulled out a vial, tourniquet, and a fresh syringe.

He still couldn't believe it. Liam Smith was dating his wife. The bitterness lingered like a pill stuck in his throat. A pill he'd tried to swallow day after day, but it remained, lodged, choking him.

"I don't know why this has happened the way it has, Gods, but I trust you," Eric said as he drew up a fresh dose.

Liam Smith had a skill set that he couldn't rival, but Eric had one thing the other man didn't: the power of the Gods.

Eric sat down on the couch, applied the tourniquet, and then pressed the tip of the needle into his skin. He rarely self-injected anymore, he normally had some whore do it for him, but he wanted to be alone right now. He needed to be in control, and focused. And in a few minutes, with the help of the Gods, he would be.

He leaned back as he felt that familiar tingle and the rush of power. He breathed deeply, in and out, increasing the amount of oxygen available to mix with the alchemized blood. When the plunger hit the end of the syringe he pulled it out, setting it on the floor. His reflection stared back at him from the mirror across the room.

You will be an Elder. You will be loved like none before. This is your time; to be the greatest leader they have even seen. They will bow and pray at your feet for all eternity. It is time.

Eric stood, moving toward the exit. He knocked, and then waited for security to move the painting.

"Is Maya awake?" Eric asked.

"Yes, although barely coherent, apparently. Marianne is adjusting her dosages now," Seth, his new head of security, responded.

"Good. We'll go down and see them," Eric said, waiting for security to move first.

They took the elevators and when Eric stepped out, the music of the Gods welcomed him. *That's right,* Eric thought.

He strode toward the center of the gallery where his wife was sitting beside Maya. Eric stopped at the foot of the bed.

Maya's eyes were slow to focus, but they did. A look of disgust followed.

Eric smiled. "How are you feeling?" he asked.

She didn't respond.

Eric raised one eyebrow. "Do we want a repeat of this morning?"

Maya's chest heaved, with fear, and perhaps anger, Eric thought.

"How are you feeling?" he repeated.

"Good," Maya said with a croaky voice.

"You share your sister's strong will. Unfortunately it will do you no good now. When I ask you a question, you respond. If you don't," Eric said, flashing a pocketknife, "I'll cut you again. Now, tell me about Mak's boyfriend, the man with the black eyes."

Eric saw a flicker of emotion in her eyes. Was she surprised?

He gave her a wider, more arrogant smile. "That's right, I know who he is. I also know all of his dirty secrets. But I want to know what *you* know about him." Eric sat down on the edge of the bed.

Maya tried to shift, to move away from him, but her movements were too slow. Eric put a hand on her leg, holding her still.

He looked to Marianne who sat calmly beside the bed. She

showed no emotion—no fear, and no sympathy for Maya. Marianne understood why it was all necessary, and that's why she was his perfect partner in this organization. Together they would rule the world, he thought with a sadistic smile.

"Answer me," Eric said, returning his gaze to Maya.

"I don't know him," Maya eventually said.

"You must know something about him."

"He runs a security company. He has a brother. That is all I know."

Eric couldn't tell if she was lying or not, but he doubted she was. Not because he didn't think her capable of it, but that he thought Liam Smith had been much too careful to disclose any details of his past. He wondered again what Makaela knew about him. Very little, Eric suspected.

"Did he tell you he's a wanted criminal? Or that he's such a liability that the CIA don't even want to admit he was one of them? What about his penchant for torturing his victims with a scalpel—did he tell you about that?"

Her eyes widened, but her response remained the same. "I don't know him."

Eric shrugged. She was useless, then.

He looked to his wife again. "Put her back to sleep."

"No! No!" Maya said, fighting against the restraints.

Marianne paid her pleas no attention, instead letting her struggle against the restraints as she loaded a syringe into the intravenous line in Maya's arm. It didn't take long for the drug to take effect. Her movements slowed before her eyes closed and she was motionless once more.

"Keep her under. I have a feeling they're going to be here soon and I don't want her causing any problems," Eric instructed.

"Of course," Marianne said. "How do you feel about what is going to happen?"

"I'm ready. I've been ready for a long time. And I've got the upper hand now. Everything has come together. The Gods have rewarded us," Eric said, moving toward her.

She stood, touching his arm. "They have. And Sorin is going to reward you, too. The Gods are always with us, even when they test us. No one could've achieved this but you, Christos. You were born for this role."

He smiled. *That's right. I was born for it, but not for this role—I was born for even greater things.*

"You're the most amazing wife and mother. Speaking of which, where is our daughter? I know you don't like leaving her."

Marianne gave an elegant shrug. "She's with one of the nannies. No, I don't like to leave her, but this is important. I want to be by your side, supporting you, when this happens."

And it's going to happen soon, Eric thought.

We're so close. I can feel it.

6

JAMES THOMAS

James stood in the garage, watching as Mak's car pulled away. He couldn't see her through the tinted glass, but he could feel her eyes.

Please, God, if you exist, keep her safe.

Samuel's voice interrupted James' prayer. *"The Tohmatsu boys are five minutes away."*

"Copy," James said. He'd wanted Mak out of the townhouse before the boys arrived. If he had to explain why they were there, it wouldn't fill her with confidence that this mission was going to be a success.

Mak's car was headed toward the worship building, but they would remain a safe distance away until James gave the command for them to move in. How he was going to be able to force those words out of his mouth he didn't know.

"Full kit," Deacon said, passing him a bag. James nodded his thanks, opened the car door and put it on the passenger seat. He unzipped it and began strapping the weapons onto his body, ready for battle.

Samuel hadn't said a word about Sister Francine, and as much as James tried to push it from his mind, he couldn't help but wonder if that was because there had been no contact from Eric, or if it was because James had told him not to.

James blew out an anguished sigh.

"Open the garage," Samuel instructed.

Deacon hit the button, standing against the wall as three cars pulled up—the back-up team of gangsters.

"The Thomas brothers," Haruto said as he swung open the passenger door.

"Good to see you." James shook his hand first, patting his shoulder. "Boys..." James nodded to each one as they all gathered around.

James continued. "We're leaving in a few minutes, so listen up. As Haruki has instructed, you're to do nothing but wait here. If this mission fails," James said—a gentler way of saying, *If we're dead or so incapacitated that we can't contact you*—"Samuel will issue the command. Mak will be brought back here and you're to get her on the jet immediately and take her to Tokyo. Secure her in Haruki's compound and await further instructions. Any questions?"

No one had a question.

"We've got you covered," Haruto said. "We brought plenty of weapons, you supplied the fast cars, and so we're good."

James took one last look at the men, searching for any doubt. Any fear. He couldn't see any. If anything he saw disappointment. The Tohmatsu boys apparently weren't too keen on being left behind.

"Target at first point. Car secure," Samuel said.

James grimaced. The "target" was Mak.

"We'll be seeing you all soon. Sean's inside—he'll sort you out," Deacon said, getting into one of the cars.

Sean was a member of the team they were leaving with the Tohmatsu boys. He knew the house and he could fit them all with communication devices.

The Tohmatsu boys went inside and James got in the passenger seat. He strapped himself in as Deacon put his foot down, moving the car in reverse.

It was time to meet with Cami and the crews.

~

James said little as Deacon steered the car through the traffic. He was using the time to get into Liam's head.

You're can't be James Thomas anymore, he told himself. *You need to be Liam Smith.*

Liam showed no mercy.

Liam felt no guilt.

Liam never gave up.

Never.

"Target at second point. Car secure."

"Copy," the brothers said in unison.

"Cami, check in," James said.

"We're in the vans and waiting. What's your ETA?"

"Seven minutes," Deacon answered.

James looked to the ink-blue sky. Daylight was fading, but the night had not quite settled in. *But it will be dark soon,* James thought, and he found comfort in that. He'd always loved the dark. He felt more comfortable, more secure in it.

They pulled up next to the vans and James turned to his brother. It could be the last time they saw each other—and they both knew it.

A somber moment was followed by a moment of solidarity.

Deacon gave a smile. "Let's get this fucker."

James smiled despite the circumstances, despite the fear, despite the worry. This was what they did best.

James closed the car door behind him and jogged across the street toward the van holding his crew. It felt good to move, to breath in the ice-cold air. He could feel his mind transitioning in sync with the night sky. The darker it got, the closer he felt to Liam.

James slid open the van door, striding in. "Boys," he said confidently, earning a round of smiles. "Are you ready?"

Biskup's men hollered in response. "We've been ready for years!"

"Let's go."

James' team was moving in on foot and he was glad he'd made that decision. With each step and each pulse of his heart, his confidence grew and his mind began to settle for the first time it really had in days. The lure of the field was pulling him in and he let it.

James looked over his shoulder, counting his men as they strode the pavement. Danny was backing up the rear. He was no replacement for Biskup's main man, Maksym, but he was good. And he was hungry for blood and violence—just the way James liked his men.

"Target secure. Ready and waiting," Samuel confirmed.

Each team then gave their estimated time of arrivals.

"Two minutes."

"Three minutes."

"Six minutes," James said, looking at the GPS on his phone. He picked up the pace, moving with long even strides. His body was flowing now, his muscles relaxed. He was Liam Smith.

"In position," Cami said, and James noted the time.

Deacon's confirmation came in shortly after. Mak's position was already confirmed, so now it was just James' team.

Even though he wanted this over with, he slowed down the pace now that they neared the entry building. His eyes roved looking for snipers, for watchmen, for security of any type. He didn't see any.

"Danny, hold back," James said as he entered the restaurant. His men had scoped it earlier and had found additional security cameras, which Samuel had managed to manipulate. It was a separate system to the one inside the worship building, and likely the tunnels, but James knew Eric would have a tap on it. It was working in their favor now, though.

"Samuel, I'm in," James said, keeping his head down and moving casually toward the bathrooms.

"I can't see you. Confirm footage remains looped."

"Team, move in," James said.

They had a reservation for a large table at the rear of the restaurant. It gave them an excuse for being in the restaurant, but they would only be at their table long enough to order a round of drinks. Those drinks would never touch their lips.

It didn't matter if the restaurant staff were on Eric's books. By the time they realized, the power would be down and Eric would know they were there anyway.

James used his foot to swing open the bathroom door, striding toward the last cubicle. It had taken his men ages to find the entry point, but if one particular tile was removed, it revealed a handle for the sliding door into the tunnel.

"Team seated," Danny confirmed, and James counted the seconds until the bathroom door swung open and he appeared in front of him.

They pulled out their pistols, their fingers on the triggers. James removed the loose tile, his eyes setting on the small white handle no bigger than a fingertip.

"In position," James confirmed.

As Samuel's words came next James kept his eyes on the handle, his finger on the pistol trigger, and his breathing steady.

"Sending the target in."

7

MAK ASHWOOD

Mak's pulse was thick and hard in her chest and her hands began to sweat. The waiting was agonizing. She tried not to think of the bitter-sweet goodbye with James. She tried not to think of what Maya was going through. She tried not to think of Deacon and Cami and that they were also risking their lives to save her sister. She did think of Biskup's men, and although she didn't want anyone to die tonight, she cared less for them.

"Confirm," Tom said from beside her.

Her eyes snapped up to him and he nodded. "They're ready," he said.

Tom got out of the car and held out his hand for her. She wiped her hand on her jeans, removing the slick moisture, and then took his. They had six blocks to walk and she counted each one.

"You're going to be fine," Tom said as they passed the fifth block. "You may or may not know this, but those brothers are the best I've ever seen. And I've seen more than most."

More than most.

Mak's mind was suddenly distracted and then she wondered if that was a tactic. She wouldn't have been surprised if the whole street could hear her heart thundering in her chest.

Tom continued to hold her hand as they came to a stop at the building.

You can do this. Do this for Maya. Do this for James.

As instructed, Mak looked up to the top corner of the building where she'd been told there was a camera. She stared straight into the lens, but she didn't smile. She imagined Eric behind it, looking back at her, and her eyes narrowed and her jaw set.

"Hello, Makaela."

Mak recognized Eric's voice and it made her spine tingle. It wasn't a good feeling.

"We're here," she said, resisting the urge to clear her throat. She would not show weakness—not to him.

"I can see that. Do you want to see your sister?" Eric asked.

Mak heard something in his voice. Joy? Pleasure?

"Yes, I do," she said. She'd been briefed on what to say and how to respond, so she followed those instructions instead of voicing what she really wanted to say: *Fuck you, Eric.*

"I'm excited to meet your boyfriend. James, isn't it? Or should I call you something else?"

Mak looked straight ahead as Tom answered with an unwavering voice. "You can call me James."

"Well, come in, then."

Mak took a deep breath as she heard a clicking noise indicating the door was open. Tom squeezed her hand, and then dropped it, and Mak felt a rush of adrenaline so severe her legs felt weightless beneath her.

They took a step inside, and everything went black.

8

JAMES THOMAS

"Go!"

James pulled the handle and lunged forward as the tunnel opened up. A fist came pummeling from the right but James had been anticipating it, and he incapacitated the security guard with a hit to the temple. He dropped to the ground and James jumped over him.

"In!" James called as he began to sprint.

"In! ... In!"

All teams were in the tunnels.

So far so good.

James pushed his legs faster, counting each second that passed until he heard Tom's voice via the earwig. When he did he almost tripped over with relief.

"Target secure, car en route."

However, the relief was short lived.

James heard the gunfire before he saw the man. James fired a running shot. It was a better shot than the man's and it hit the intended target. James hurdled over the man's body, Danny's footsteps following his. And then James began to hear more footsteps as the rest of his team followed in.

James couldn't see the end of the tunnel, but he continued to fire into the darkness as he ran. He wasn't going to get to the end just to be welcomed by a security party.

He heard screams, and then what sounded like a door opening.

Gunfire lit up the tunnel and James heard Danny howl behind him. James didn't stop, he didn't slow down. He pulled out his second pistol and fired back. His mind was on autopilot now. Mak was out, and that was the part of the mission he cared about most. Now he could enjoy himself—now he was completely free to be the man who'd earned such a reputation. A man he never wanted his girlfriend to meet.

A jarring cry echoed and James recognized the thick accent. The Russians were here. It was going to be one big get-together.

Six down.

Seven down.

James counted the men on the ground as he jumped over them. The tunnel was becoming an obstacle course. He slowed down as the end came in sight. James had no idea what was waiting for them on the other side, but he wanted to get through that door before the power was back on.

Stay in the shadows, in the darkness. Always.

James looked over his shoulder, surprised to see Danny running with the other men. By the way one arm was limp and flopping around, James knew where the bullet had landed.

"In position," James said.

If their calculations were correct, this tunnel would open up to the south side of the gallery. James didn't know what Eric was doing with Maya, but he knew one thing—Eric liked to put on a show. James had no doubt he'd have her in the gallery, maybe even on the stage. James hoped so—if they kept the bullets low, it would keep them away from Maya.

"In position," Deacon confirmed.

James held his breath until Cami answered. "In position," she finally said.

"I haven't got any surveillance. Good luck, teams," Samuel said.

Samuel could use their trackers to keep location tabs on everyone, but that was as much help as they were going to get. They were going in blind, but they had no other option.

James pushed down on the door handle, not surprised to find it was locked. He took a step back, preparing to fire at it.

"*Code 633,*" Tom's voice came through his earwig.

James felt the air knock from his lungs.

No!

9

MAK ASHWOOD

Mak grabbed for the seat in front of her as Tom abruptly swung the car around a corner.

Code 633—what does that mean?

The energy in the car changed—snapped—and if Mak hadn't been able to feel it she would've been able to see it. Her companions, a second ago relaxed yet cautious, were now alert and poised, ready to react.

"Confirm. Two tails and overhead surveillance," Tom said.

"Confirm four tails now," the man in the passenger seat said as his head arched to look behind them.

Four tails?

This was not part of the plan, Mak thought. *Eric knows that I'm not in the building—and he's coming for me. No, please, no.*

It wasn't even her life that worried her—it was what would happen to next.

Where is James?

What is going through his head right now?

Where is Maya? Is she okay?

The questions came, one after the other, gathering momentum like an avalanche.

A sharp impact came next, so severe that a shot of pain hit her neck like the crack of a whip.

Mak cried out, her head spinning from the pain.

"Hold her," Tom commanded and strong arms grabbed her arms.

"We're going to be okay, Mak," Tom said. "Right now everyone just needs to stay calm. No matter what happens, stay in the car."

She'd heard similar words from James in a similar situation, but James wasn't here this time.

He can't protect you now.

Mak's wild eyes looked around, frantic.

"Samuel? Tell me you've got eyes on them!" Tom said and Mak desperately wished she could hear Samuel's response.

James had given her protective gear and weapons, but he hadn't given her an earwig—and Mak knew that he'd never intended to.

"Copy," Tom said and there was little Mak could deduce from his answer, so instead of letting panic rule her, she tried to think.

Last time Samuel had cleared a path for Deacon, and Mak started noting the traffic grid. She observed the lights—they'd turned green just in time, every time. Samuel was working with them.

Mak took note of their location—the street names and the landmarks. If something calamitous happened, Mak at least wanted to be able to know where she was. She didn't know London very well, but she was getting a crash course in geography. Mak found the task helped to ward off the panic—until bullets began hitting the car.

Mak ducked instinctively and her heart slammed into her chest.

"Hold on!" Tom said, swerving the car in a snake-like pattern. Mak didn't know if he was dodging bullets or cars.

Mak dared to lift her eyes. The man in the passenger seat—she realized she didn't even know his name—had his seatbelt off and his body angled like he was ready to fire.

The passenger-side window opened and, as Tom took another sharp turn, the man did fire. He jerked back as another bullet hit their car, but he angled his body again, unharmed, returning fire.

Mak heard a thunderous crack and a second later Tom screamed an obscenity as a ball of flames blocked their path. The sound of screeching tires followed and the car came to a hasty stop.

"Reroute!" Tom shouted as the car lunged into reverse.

Panic seized Mak with a deathly grip. She fought to stay calm, to think with her head, to use the mental training Cami had taught her. As part of her "training," Mak had been thrust into simulated situations like this time and time again. But theory never held up to real-life experience.

They were moving forward again, racing through the streets. The buildings blurred into one another, a row of colored streaks in her peripheral. Mak kept her eyes forward, so as to avoid the nausea—another lesson in her training. It seemed to work, although her body was prickling, a response to the adrenaline perhaps, and it made it hard to know for sure what she was feeling.

Whatever was said next caused every person in the car—excluding Mak—to crane their heads up to the sky.

"What?" Mak asked, her body pulsing with fear.

"Drones," the guy next to her said. "A lot of them."

Drones. Helicopters. Cars on the ground.

Mak's stomach churned as she realized the odds of outrunning all of them were significantly less than she'd even thought—and she hadn't thought they were good to begin with. The only thing she did have confidence in was Tom's driving. If he were to challenge Deacon, Mak wasn't sure who would win.

The car came to another screeching halt as a truck blocked their path. Mak was thrust forward, her seatbelt the only thing keeping her from becoming airborne.

"Motherfucker!" Tom said, lunging the car into reverse once more.

"Samuel, reroute. They're controlling our path. Break it," Tom said.

Controlling our path? There was no doubt that the fireball had been Eric's move, but the truck, too? How did Tom know? What other intel was he getting?

Mak's thoughts flickered back to James, but she blocked them quickly. She knew that whatever was going through his mind wasn't good, and she couldn't afford to let those assumptive thoughts cloud her mind any further.

"Tom, nine o'clock!" the man in the passenger seat barked. Amidst the chaos, his voice had been calm—until now.

Mak jerked her head, looking at the man's nine o'clock, but she didn't see anything sinister. But then she didn't know what she was looking for.

Silence followed—a silence that was unbearable. Mak's heart walloped against her rib cage so violently Mak thought she might crack a rib.

"I see it," Tom said. "Samuel?" Tom shook his head dubiously. "Let's try it."

Mak wondered if it was Samuel, Deacon or James giving support on the other end—or all of them.

But aren't they inside the building?

Mak couldn't keep her thoughts straight any longer. She had no sense of time, of how long they'd been dodging traffic and bullets and fireballs. How much time had passed since the first tail was confirmed? How long had it been since she'd been on the doorstep of Eric's building, and had spoken to her husband for the first time in thirteen years?

Tom sped through another intersection, his front wheel over the white line before it had turned green. They were pushing it in every sense: the car, the traffic, their fates.

Mak held her breath as they narrowly avoided one collision after the other. *How long can this go on for?* Mak thought, trying to swallow, but her mouth was as dry as crusty bread.

"Hold on!" Tom said, taking a sharp turn so narrowly they rode up onto the sidewalk and then bumped down again.

Mak wiped the sweat from her hands so that she could get a better grip on the seat in front of her.

Her neck snapped as a van appeared from nowhere and they drove straight into it. Stars blinded her vision, but it only lasted a second. A raw, gutting rush of fear brought her back to reality.

Tom reacted first, trying to reverse again but the car wasn't moving. "Come on, come on," he willed it, but it still didn't move. "*Fuck!*" he screamed, hitting the steering wheel before resuming conversation with Samuel. "We're down. Code 719. Moving on foot."

All three of them, now armed and ready, reached for the doors at the same time as Mak heard the screeching of tires. Tom's head snapped up, and darted around the car. Mak saw it then—the fear in his eyes.

He turned to her. "Draw your weapon, follow my lead. If I tell you to shoot, do it like we've trained you to." His words were delivered quickly with a strong, steady voice. "Worst case, they'll take us. If that happens, stay calm and do whatever they tell you to."

Words escaped her so she nodded. Her hand trembled as she drew her weapon. It felt heavier in her hand than it ever had and she wondered for a moment if she could actually shoot it. But she had to, and she would—if it meant getting out of this situation and giving everyone else, her sister included, the best chance at surviving.

10

MAK ASHWOOD

Mak tried to recall everything she'd been taught in training. Now was not the time to panic—now was the time to breathe and focus on the task. Block everything else out, they'd told her.

Concentrate, Mak. You can do this. You are going to do this.

"Code 22, on the count of three," Tom said. "Mak, keep you your head down until I tell you otherwise. Three, two, one!"

The doors of the car swung open and a deafening shower of gunshots followed. Her ears began to ring and when she lifted her head just enough to look at Tom, she gasped. He was firing back, but the man in the passenger seat was crumpled awkwardly. Mak didn't need any other information to conclude he was dead. Her hand went to her mouth as she fought the retching reaction that followed.

Hold it together, Mak. Don't you dare buckle now.

The man next to her cried out in pain and was abruptly pulled from the car. Mak screamed, her lungs burning as a man she didn't know looked at her. He smiled, a smile that made the bile in her throat rise, before a bullet landed in his forehead. Mak screamed again.

"Use your weapon. Shoot!" Tom shouted.

It took a moment for his command to register in her mind—a

moment too long. Mak drew her pistol, but hands had already reached in, grabbing her forearms and yanking her from the car. The pistol dropped to the ground, and, as if in slow motion, she saw the man who had her kick it with his foot, sliding it underneath the car.

Mak tried to fight him off and when that didn't work she tried to wriggle out of his grasp, but his hands held her so tightly her skin burned. She tried to kick him, aiming for his kneecap but missed as she was passed to another man.

"Get her in the car! I'll get him!" the man who'd taken her shouted.

Tom?

A black cloth was brought down over her head and she screamed again, trying to get her arms out of the tight hold. Instead of getting loose, her arms were jerked behind her and cuffed.

Mak felt like she was suffocating. *Calm down, breathe.* The thought seemed to come from nowhere, but it must've been buried in her subconscious after all of those hours of training.

Her body shook. She listened around her, noting her environment: how many voices? She noted the accents—Russian. She listened to the background noise, the slowing of gunfire, the revving of the engine. And she knew when they had Tom in the van by the loud thud followed by a groan. He said her name—perhaps to comfort her—and then Mak heard another noise, one that sounded like a kick to the abdomen. The man beside her banged his hand— Mak assumed—on the metal behind her. "Go, go!"

Mak didn't question where they were going, she knew. They were going back to the worship building. She swayed as the van rushed off, but she kept upright. There were no strong hands to hold her, to keep her safe. Mak guessed that her companions didn't care if she ended face down on the floor of the van.

Concentrate.

Mak wriggled her fingers, keeping her movements small, not wanting to attract attention. She was cuffed tightly and she couldn't reach the knife in her back pocket. She wasn't entirely sure what she would've done with it anyway. She'd counted the voices of six different men in the van and knew her chances of making a getaway were negligible.

They came to a stop and she became airborne, falling forward. She hit her head against the cool metal. Her husband's instruction might've been to deliver her alive, but that directive certainly hadn't included making sure she arrived without any bruises.

Arms grabbed her again, hauling her out of the van. Her feet dragged against the ground as she was carried along. The temperature warmed and she knew instantly she was inside a building. She was lowered to the ground and a hand pressed on her back, pushing her forward.

Mak walked stubbornly and deliberately slow. She had no idea what plan James had since devised—if he even had one—but she was determined to give them as much time as possible. One might think a few seconds didn't matter, but as Cami had told her time and time again, in their world, a few seconds could be everything.

"Faster."

Mak ignored the command, but was given no choice. She stumbled forward as she received another, more forceful push.

She heard it faintly at first, and then more clearly as they walked toward it. It sounded like church music.

This is it, he's going to be here, Mak thought, taking a deep breath and steeling herself.

"Stop," the man behind her said as he grabbed her forearms, pinching them. He pushed her to her knees.

The music faded, but continued to play in the background. The cloth was ripped off of her head. The sudden light left Mak blinking, unable to see.

When her eyes finally focused, she saw him. She wanted to look around, to get a sense of her bearings, but she couldn't draw her eyes away from her husband. Rage, hate, and anger swirled within her.

He pulled his lips to the side in an amused grin. "If looks could kill," he said with a chuckle.

"Makaela, it's been far too long," Eric said, standing. He walked toward her like a lion stalks its prey. It made Mak's skin crawl. He lifted her chin with his index finger. "I've missed you," he said.

Mak's jaw was set tight, the words slipping from her seething throat. "I haven't."

His backhanded slap made her recoil and left her cheek stinging.

"Things have changed since we were together last," he said. "I'm not just your husband anymore. I'm the leader of Saratani, the organization that is going to change the world. You will respect me," he said, a self-assured smile on his face, "in time. And you will love me like they do."

"I'd rather be dead," she spat at him.

He laughed. "Oh, that won't happen." He kneeled in front of her, whispering, "But I can make your life hell, and if you continue to disrespect me, I'll do exactly that until you learn who you obey now."

"Obey?" Mak asked incredulously. "You're out of your fucking mind."

He stood, crossing his arms over his chest. "I'm going to show you now just how much of a nightmare your life can become." He looked to the right. "Bring him in."

Mak couldn't breathe. *No, not James.*

When Tom was pushed to his knees, beside her, she felt a guilty surge of relief.

Eric looked to Tom. "It's James, I believe?"

Tom looked straight ahead, his face as blank as a marble statue. "That's correct." Tom's voice didn't waver; it didn't show any sign of the emotions he had to be feeling inside. Mak was impressed.

"James Thomas," Eric stated. "A very skilled man, a very dangerous man. A very elusive man..."

There was something in Eric's voice, an underlying tone, a hint of malice, that caused Mak's pulse to peak.

"How long have you been dating this man, Mak?" Eric returned his attention to her.

"Months," she answered simply.

"He doesn't really look like a James to me," Eric mused as he drew a blade. He held the tip of it to his finger, twirling it.

He knows, Mak realized. She kept her face straight, as stony as Tom's. She didn't know what to do, or what to say. She thought doing nothing and saying nothing was the best option at this point.

Eric looked between them, his eyes darting back and forth. He was enjoying it, tormenting them—it was as obvious as a neon sign.

"No, you definitely don't look like a James to me," Eric said lightly, before slashing the blade across Tom's throat.

Mak screamed as Tom's eyes widened and he made a gurgling sound as he tried to breathe. She squeezed her eyes shut, turning her head away as her chest heaved.

"That's what happens when people lie to me," he said harshly, before smiling that same relaxed smile again. "Let that be a lesson, Mak. Now, where is the real James Thomas? I know he's here. I know he's watching and waiting to make his move. Oh—do you want to know *how* I knew that wasn't James Thomas?" Eric asked, his eyes mockingly wide.

Mak opened her stinging eyes, but she couldn't bring herself to look at Tom's shuddering form.

"He didn't have black eyes." Eric's smile was chilling. His eyes then looked behind her, his head moving in an arc.

Mak made the mistake of glancing toward Tom's now still body. His lifeless eyes seemed to stare at her. *Oh, God,* Mak thought, diverting her gaze, trying not to fall apart.

"What has your boyfriend told you about his past?" Eric said, returning his attention to Mak. When she didn't answer he pressed on. "Very little, if anything, I'm sure. Do you know why that is? Let me tell you," he continued. "It's because he doesn't want you to know. You're a criminal prosecutor, and he's a man that is such a fucking liability that even the CIA has wiped their records of his existence to avoid being associated with him. A man gone rogue, a man known for slaughtering and mutilating people. His favorite weapon of choice: a scalpel."

Ignore him.

Eric seemed to enjoy taunting her, Mak realized, and she wasn't going to give him anything that would provide satisfaction.

"You see, you know him as James Thomas. The rest of the world knows him as Liam Smith, amongst other names. Did he tell you he and I met a few months ago in Amman, in Jordan? Did he tell you he launched an attack on my home, killing all of my security men and putting my wife and daughter's lives at risk?"

He was in Amman? He'd been that close to Eric? Eric has a wife—another wife—and a daughter?

That poor woman, and child.

"This is all news to you, isn't it? I can see it in your eyes," Eric said. "What I'm about to tell you is for your own good. I know what you stand for, Mak, the values you uphold, and beyond the charming façade he's used to lure you into bed, there's an ugly, despicable monster. I'm going to take a guess now, a wild stab in the dark, and say he's told you that he can't tell you about his past because it will put you at risk. Am I right?"

It took all of Mak's self-discipline not to react.

"I asked you a *question!*" Eric said with a hard voice, before taking a deep breath and smiling again, though his eyes remained steely. "And when I ask questions, I expect answers. I won't be lenient simply because you're my wife. Don't make the mistake of believing that."

One of your wives. Mak refused to react, or to speak.

Eric took a step toward her and she fought the instinct to recoil. *Don't react, Mak*—that's what he wants you to do. James had told her little about her husband, but it had only taken Mak a few minutes to conclude many things about him, including his love of power.

Eric crouched down so that he was at eye level. "There are things he could tell you, more about his past—like his real name: Joshua Hart—but he chooses not to. I'm going to tell you, though. I'm even going to show you some things, and I'm going to enjoy every minute of it." He paused, looking into her eyes, his own strangely devoid of emotion. "You don't love him," he said, his voice almost a whisper now. "You can't love a man like that."

Rage welled within her, rage and hate for the man standing in front of her. "All I know is that he's a better man than you'll ever be."

Eric pressed his lips together tightly, his chin jutting out. Mak immediately regretted the slip in self-control when he brought a blade to her neck. "Let's see, shall we?"

Mak hissed in a breath, closing her eyes as the blade pressed into the soft skin of her neck. The same blade he'd used to sever Tom's throat. Her breathing became short and labored, her focus blurring.

Then, lightly, only scratching her skin, Eric drew the tip of the blade across her throat. "The next one will be a little longer, and it will hurt a little more!" Eric spat, raising his voice, almost shouting the words. He looked behind her, his head sweeping from side-to-side, his eyes searching. "If you think I won't kill her to get to you, Liam, you're very wrong. That was never my intention, and it would break my heart, but if it is a sacrifice I need to make, then so be it. I know you're here—and the sooner you give yourself up, the better this will be for Mak."

Mak listened for any movement around her, but the only thing she could hear was the soft, barely audible, gospel music in the background.

Eric shrugged. "While we wait for him to join us, Mak, let me tell you what he did to one of my men in New York recently... I heard about my grave—the one you supposedly buried me in. I was curious to know who you'd buried instead of me, if anyone, so I sent two of my men to check it out late one night. Now, what happened to one of those men is still a mystery—he seems to have disappeared. But the other man"—he paused, Mak thought, to add some drama to his story—"Liam did quite a job on. The man was tortured for hours and then delivered to me, faceless, his skin sliced and peeled off. It takes quite some skill and practice to do it so well, but your boyfriend is a master with his scalpel. Now, what does he tell you when he's gone all night? Does he tell you he's working late? What does it feel like to know that a man can do that to another man and then, the very next day, possibly hours later, after he's showered and washed the blood from his hands, kisses you and holds you with those very same hands?"

Eric's words made the hairs on the back of her neck prickle and as she thought back over the nights James had been in New York—there were some he'd worked late and then slipped into bed beside her.

Could James do that to someone? Not the man she knew, but she'd always known there was another side of him. A side she knew would kill to protect those he loved, or clients, even. But to torture someone so violently?

He smiled at her discomfort.

Stop, she demanded of herself. *He's playing with you!*

Eric flicked his wrist, looking at his watch. "Time is ticking, Liam," he said in a voice that seemed to echo.

"But it's not just men he kills... Your man is a self-serving, cold-hearted killer. He'll do anything to get what he wants—to win. Including killing innocent women and children.

"I'll do anything I need to." James had said those words so many times, but he couldn't have done that, he couldn't have killed innocent people. She shook her head. *He couldn't have.*

"I'm not lying, Mak," Eric said, correctly reading her thoughts. "But I don't expect you to entirely trust me—not yet—so let me show you something, because nothing beats cold, hard evidence, does it, Mak? Nothing convinces a jury like photographic proof—or, in this case, a nice little video that came from one of my new friends in the CIA." Eric drew his cell phone, tapped the screen a few times and then held it in front of Mak's eyes.

She fought off the urge to look away and kept her eyes forward. Eric would make her watch it one way or another—the latter certainly involving pain.

She saw what looked like a church, or some kind of religious building. People were on their knees, praying. Youths. It looked like some kind of youth center.

James came into view and issued a command—one that wasn't spoken in English.

Chaos broke out and people began screaming and running in all directions as shots were fired. A group of boys drew weapons.

Gunshots followed and Mak struggled to keep track of James on the camera view. But then the image suddenly changed, as if there were a segment of time missing, and James was front and center of the camera. He had a gun pointed at a young man, a man who looked no older than thirteen or fourteen at best—although it was impossible to know for sure.

The man looked around him, frightened, searching for a way out. But James stalked toward him, backing him into a corner.

Mak didn't need to speak the language to know that adolescent was pleading for his life.

James didn't stop. A moment later his gun was pressed against the man's temple and he was dragged toward one of the pews. One of James' men tied him to it, and then it began. Torture. James spoke in the foreign language and when the man didn't respond James removed his ear lobe first, and then the other. The young man screamed, but he didn't appear to volunteer any information. James untied his wrists and held one flat against the pew. James seemed to ask another question, and when he didn't get an answer, James brought a knife down over the man's hand, slicing off his fingers one by one.

Mak drew in a wheezy breath and looked away. "You've made your point."

"How old do you think those kids were in that church?" Eric asked, and Mak thought he couldn't wait to tell her the answer. "How old do you think that that boy was?"

When she didn't respond, he said, "Thirteen. The young man your boyfriend tortured for information was thirteen years old... His life was just beginning."

She swallowed, lifting her eyes to meet his. She said nothing, but her silence was an answer in of itself.

"He fooled you, as smart as you are. But you shouldn't blame yourself; he's fooled other women, he even fooled the head of the CIA into thinking he was the best agent they'd ever had, and then—when he was ready, when the time suited him—he decided to leave, killing everyone that had enough power to stop him."

Eric crouched down again. "Do you feel like a fool?" he asked, his lips turning up at the corner.

He brought the blade to her neck, but she refused to answer. He pressed it in, slicing the other side this time and she winced in pain.

"That's enough!"

A loud voice came from behind them and Mak recognized it immediately.

No!

Eric's head jerked up, his face transforming with delight.

A commotion that sounded like scurrying feet and guns being prepared for battle followed. Eric held out a hand. "Let him through."

Mak dared to look over her shoulder. She saw James walking toward them and his eyes met hers for a splinter of a second, but if there was a message in them, Mak didn't get it. He was completely unreadable to her.

With Eric distracted, Mak's eyes quickly darted around the room. It was a good thing she was already on her knees because when she saw her sister, asleep in the bed, her body began to shake. Two of the people she loved most were at the mercy of her husband.

She looked to the woman sitting beside Maya, her demeanor calm and at peace with the situation. Mak despised her immediately.

"Well, well, well, Liam...so, we meet again," Eric said with a cocky grin.

James stopped four feet from Eric at an angle that allowed Mak to watch him without turning her head. She wondered if that was intentional—so that he could see her.

What are you doing, James? Don't do this. Get my sister out and leave —even if that means without me.

But Mak knew he'd never do that.

"Check him," Eric said. James held his arms up in surrender and four burly men rushed in, patting him down.

"He's clean," one said, taking a step back, but staying close to Eric's side.

"Imagine," Eric said, "that after all of these years looking for you, that when I finally found you, I found you *fucking* my wife." Eric's jaw set tight.

All of these years? What is he talking about?

"Perhaps you shouldn't have walked out on your wife, Eric," James replied, his voice calm, steady, cold.

"I did what the Gods needed me to do, and now I'm being rewarded for it," Eric said.

Gods? Mak couldn't fathom what kind of God would reward Eric for his behavior.

"I had no idea that kidnapping Maya was going to be the best move of my life—my career... It couldn't have worked out any better if I'd tried," Eric gloated, and Mak wanted to slap him.

"It's a little early to be singing your victories just yet. The upper hand can change in a second—you know that too well," James said. He still hadn't given another glance in Mak's direction and he looked as calm as if they were discussing what to order for dinner.

Eric scoffed. "I have Mak on her knees, blood trickling down her neck. I have your friend here"—Eric nudged Tom's lifeless body with his foot, a gesture that made Mak's stomach churn—"making a mess of my fucking floor. I have Maya up there, well on her way to being a heroin addict, and I have you standing in front of me, unarmed. I think my odds are looking pretty good, don't you?"

James raised one eyebrow, as if considering it.

"Get on your knees," Eric said.

James dropped to his knees and Mak willed him to look at her, but he didn't. His eyes never left Eric's.

Eric's men rushed in, binding his hands together, and then his feet. James didn't even try and fight it.

Why is he doing this? And where was Deacon? Was this part of some plan?

Eric leaned in and whispered something in James' ear. Mak strained to hear, but her own blood whooshing in her ears ruined any chance.

Eric stepped back. He seemed pleased with whatever torment he'd just delivered, even though James continued to show no emotion.

"I know your brother's here, too," Eric continued. "And we'll get to him in a minute, along with the surprises I have for you. But first, let

me finish introducing Mak to the real man behind the many masks
you wear. Did you enjoy what I've told her so far?"

"You're very good at embellishing the truth," James replied.

"Embellishing the truth? Hardly. You know, I could sit here for
days, telling Mak various stories about you—but, alas, we're on a
deadline. So, I thought I'd cut to the chase and tell her the most
important one, the one that's going to make her despise you…"

Mak's pulse spiked and she held her breath, trying to keep her
face as impassive as James'.

Eric looked to her, a smile shining on his face.

You bastard, Mak thought.

He looked back to James. "What happened in Paris?"

Mak watched James carefully. His expression didn't falter, but she
thought she saw a tightening of his chest so minute she couldn't be
sure she hadn't imagined it.

"No, I didn't think you'd told her about that," Eric said. "Do you
want to tell her now, or should I?"

James didn't respond.

"Cat got your tongue now, Liam?"

"Your death, when it comes, is going to be extremely painful,"
James said slowly, and Mak knew he meant every word.

Eric gave a taunting laugh. "On that you're very wrong. My death,
when it eventually comes, many, many years from now, will be a tran-
scendence to the Gods. Your death, however, *will* be extremely
painful, and it is coming soon. But not yet. I don't want you to die
before you watch your girlfriend's heart break. I do believe you love
her, otherwise you wouldn't be on your knees right now—but she
doesn't love you, she can't, because she could never love someone
who murdered their own child to protect themselves."

Mak's heart cracked, a jagged crevice opening. *His child?*

"You can't even deny it, can you?" Eric said. He sighed, a display of
faux sympathy. "I'm sorry to have to be the one to tell you this, Mak,
but you need to know. Liam, here, had a girlfriend in Paris. An ex-CIA
agent.

"They'd been together about six months when he found out

something he didn't like... She was informing on him, giving the CIA information about him and his whereabouts. So, what does a man like Liam do to eliminate the risk? Eliminate the person—at all costs. She was pregnant, Mak, with his child. Five months pregnant when he took her life, and the child's, to save his own."

Mak looked to James, needing him to do something, to give her a sign that it wasn't true, but he didn't. He stared straight ahead, ignoring her pleading eyes.

Eric seized the moment. "Don't bother looking to him for answers. His silence should tell you all you need to know. Her body is still missing, but it's confirmed he was the last one to see her alive... the week after she telephoned him to tell him the happy news." He paused. "You don't believe me? Shall we watch another video? This is one you'll really enjoy."

Mak couldn't look away even though her heart pleaded her to.

She saw a woman walking through a house. A woman wearing a simple, tight-fitting black dress. A woman that, even via the surveillance footage, had a clearly defined bump—one she rested a hand on as she walked through the hallway. The camera changed, showing her in a bedroom. She pulled an oversized sweater over her head and then returned to the hallway.

James entered the hallway, his pistol raised at shoulder height. He fired two shots into the woman's chest and, as she fell to the floor, he callously stepped over her body, walking out of the frame of the camera. The video went blank. Mak squeezed her eyes shut, knowing she'd never be able to forget the images she'd just seen.

That's why he's so adamant about birth control, even knowing I'm on the contraceptive pill, Mak realized.

Her heart cracked wide open.

11

JAMES THOMAS

Breathe. Breathe. Breathe, James told himself, but he felt like Eric had put a plastic bag over his head, suffocating him. Even without looking directly at her, in his peripheral vision he could see her breaking. He could see the strong, careful façade she'd displayed slipping.

He didn't know how Eric had gotten hold of that video, but he knew what Mak had just watched. *That's what Eric and Sokolov were looking for,* James realized. He'd missed a camera somewhere. He'd done a full sweep of the building, but that had been after he'd learned the truth. He'd been an emotional wreck, and he must've missed it.

"I'm going to destroy you." They were the words Eric had whispered to him, and it took him all of a few minutes to do it.

James had never told Mak about Paris because the shame had been too crippling. And also because his greatest fear was exactly what Eric had said: that she couldn't love a man who had done something like that. But now wasn't the time to defend himself or to contradict Eric's embellishments and lies.

Deal with your emotions later. Get her out of here—alive.

Eric turned back to James, and James had never had a more powerful urge to rip someone's throat out.

Eric leaned in again. "It hurts, doesn't it?" he whispered before he landed a blow on James' injured arm. James' body contracted, but he managed to stay upright as he wheezed in tight breaths. A fire burned in his shoulder, scorching his skin, but the physical pain was preferable to the emotional pain.

James straightened, preparing for another blow, but it didn't come. James knew it was only a matter of time, though.

"Now that we all understand who you really are, I've got a surprise for you," Eric said, waving his hand. "Bring her out, Pavel."

With every second that passed, the situation got worse—and as James waited, not daring to look over his shoulder, his skin began to tingle. In a moment of clarity, Eric's plan flashed before his eyes, and when the old lady was marched forward, James was not surprised to see it was Sister Francine. James felt his resolve crumble, his shield slip before he could pull it back up. Eric saw it too.

"I wondered what it would take to finally make you break," Eric said with the sly smile of a madman.

James looked past Eric, his eyes meeting those of his longtime enemy. Sokolov didn't grin—he wasn't as arrogant as Eric. Instead, James saw focus in his eyes: a determination to end what had started so many years ago. To end the threat that Liam Smith had always presented.

"It's been a long time, Liam," Sokolov said, his thick accent giving his words a brutal edge.

"Not long enough," James replied. He didn't want to look at Sister Francine, he didn't want to see the fear and pain that he knew would be in her eyes, but he needed to take stock of the situation.

Her composure crumbled as their eyes met. "Josh, please…" she said with a whimper that didn't hide her strained voice. James wondered how many times she'd screamed in the past few days.

"Please give them what they want. Please!"

Pavel's hand tightened around her arm and she sucked in a breath.

Sister Francine's eyes, visible through the clear-lens glasses that sat on her nose, were red-rimmed, and her long, gray hair was wet on her cheek. He held her gaze for a soul-breaking second and he did his best to give her a reassuring look, however false it might be.

Breathe, James.

He took stock of her injuries. She was shivering, small jittering movements—most likely from adrenaline and fear. Her left cheek was clouded in purple, a bruise that, judging by the color, was a day old at least. Her bottom lip was cut. The anger boiled fresh in James' chest. Sister Francine would hardly have been a match for one of Eric's men. They'd hurt her to hurt him, and it was one more reason to find a way out of the hell they were in.

Don't give up. Deacon's still free and moving men into position.

Deacon and his team had retreated from the building upon hearing Tom call the codes. But they'd be in the building again by now, entering via one of the upper levels, and crawling through the vent space. Cami's team should also be inside, weaving their way into position. James' job now was to buy them time to get as many men into position as possible.

James pulled his gaze away from Sister Francine.

"Beating on innocent, old, fragile women, Sokolov?" James asked. "Or did you not want to do the dirty work yourself, giving it to your men instead?"

James focused on engaging Sokolov—who was clearly more rational than Eric. And by doing that, he was more easily able to connect with Liam Smith. The man who would treat Mak and Sister Francine as nothing more than hostages. A man who would not be emotional.

"I've got to tell you, Liam, I'm surprised...I can't believe you were stupid enough to get yourself involved in a relationship of any kind. You created a little family, fell in love...presumably." He raised an eyebrow coolly. "You built yourself a nice life, but people like you know that you're better off alone in this world. Any relationship you have gives your enemies leverage. The Ranger learned that the hard way, didn't he? Where is he, your brother Deacon?" Sokolov said, the hint of a smile on his lips.

James knew what Sokolov was trying to do, and he hoped Deacon was able to ignore him—if he was close enough to hear him, which James hoped he was by now, or their situation was looking grimmer than he'd even thought possible.

"He's busy," James said, mirroring Sokolov's smile.

"It is his fault that she's dead—everyone knows that. How many men raped her while he did nothing?" Sokolov said, slowly, savoring each word.

He heard a slight cry, and he knew it had come from Sister Francine. They were going to hurt her in a bid to distract him and blow his focus. James didn't look at her, he avoided her desperate gaze, and he hated himself for it.

"It's hard to do anything when you've been tortured and beaten so badly that you can't even stand, isn't it?" James said, raising one eyebrow. "But while we're on the subject of women, Sokolov, what-ever happened to Marissa?" James asked sardonically, pausing for effect. It was a minor blow compared to the one he'd given to Deacon, but it was the best James could do. James smiled before he continued. "At least the women we choose are loyal."

James saw the flash of anger and humiliation in Sokolov's eyes. "That's right," James said. "I've been gone a long time, but I'm not dead—I see and hear everything."

"The entire world wishes you were dead, Liam," Sokolov said, his voice dangerously soft, and while that wasn't entirely true, James knew there were more people that wanted him dead than alive.

Eric seemed amused by the conversation, and he seemed completely relaxed. James didn't think there was a shred of doubt in that fucked-up mind of his that the tables couldn't turn.

That might just be your mistake, James thought.

James stole another sneak peek at Sister Francine then, despite telling himself not to. Her hands weren't bound, which indicated they didn't think she was a threat. In no way did she appear to be one, but people were capable of almost anything under the right circum-stances. And, if James could get one of his men to her, it was a hell of a lot easier to run without your hands tied behind your back—James knew that from experience.

He looked away, but he knew she hadn't—he could feel her watching him. Her eyes pleading to a man that couldn't help her in this moment.

James wanted to look at Mak, too—to give her a reassuring look and tell her he was sorry, to tell her he still believed they could get out of this alive, but he was scared that the small thread of composure he was still managing to hang on to would shatter.

Instead he looked to Eric's security men. He'd been watching them discreetly, focusing on the man closest to Eric—his head of security. He noted where the man's eyes looked, how often he checked his watch, when his lips moved—likely responding to security checks. He looked calm and confident, and that did nothing to ease the pit of anxiety deep in James' stomach.

"Well, this has been a lovely reunion, but the sooner we wrap things up the better," Eric said, interjecting once more, taking back control of the situation.

James wondered if he'd ever met a more power-hungry man. Even Sokolov didn't match Eric.

Come on, Deacon.

James didn't know how much longer he could stall them, and he wanted Deacon and Biskup's men to launch their attack before Mak was out of his sight. Now that Eric had successfully shattered Mak's image of who James Thomas was and had potentially destroyed their relationship, as well as forcing James to give himself up, James thought he'd want to separate them as soon as possible. That would be James' next move, if he were Eric.

James thought to the other player in the room, the one he thought had more power than she had ever displayed: Eric's wife, Marianne. James had been watching her when Mak was brought in, and when Tom was murdered. She didn't flinch and she didn't look surprised. She either knew Eric's plan, or she simply expected as much from her husband.

Marianne was also the one stationed next to Maya. Maya appeared unconscious, which James thought was actually a good thing. A half-lucid person on a drug high was generally uncooperative and difficult to control—the last thing they needed. Sure, she wouldn't be able to run, but she could be carried out.

Eric continued. "But before we go, I'd like to meet your brother. Where are you, Deacon Thomas?" he sing-songed.

Silence filled the room and James saw Eric's men looking, their eyes darting from point to point, as they had been since James had walked in. But not one of them had moved that James could see, and that was potentially a good sign—they hadn't worked out Deacon's plan yet. Eric's men would be looking for him on the ground; but he wasn't on the ground, he was in the ceiling. Or should be. James really wished he still had an earwig.

Come on, Deacon.

James didn't want him to rush, and he didn't want him to make a move until he was sure they were in position and could make the shots. But he didn't want Eric to retaliate by hurting Mak, or Sister Francine.

In a last-minute plan devised out of desperation, the brothers had chosen to use their favorite strategy, one that had never failed them. It was simple, but sometimes simple was best.

Don't fail us now, James prayed.

James looked to Eric's head of security again. His eyes were diverted upward, but James didn't think he was praying to the Gods. James wanted to follow his gaze, but he didn't dare—he couldn't risk revealing their plan.

"He's always useless when you need him most, isn't he?" Sokolov said, returning to his taunting ways.

But as a smile stretched his lips, blood sprayed from his forehead.

"Get down!" James yelled to Sister Francine and from the corner of his eye he saw her drop to the floor as gunfire erupted around them.

Deacon had arrived, and bedlam had come with him.

James looked to Mak at the same time Eric did. Eric kicked her in the stomach, temporarily incapacitating her, and she fell forward.

The cries of a man, or possibly two, sounded behind him—James guessed they'd been shot. Deacon was buying him time and James didn't waste another second as he wriggled his body into a necessary yet painfully awkward position.

Come on, come on, James thought as he struggled to find the blade he kept in the inside of his shoe. His fingers grasped the blade and he pulled it loose. His heart was pounding and his pulse raced. A hand grabbed his shoulder—but the hold suddenly weakened and then James heard a thud behind him as the man presumably went down.

The gunfire was so loud that it made James' ears ring but the familiar sound helped him to focus.

His eyes flicked up, noting the bodies piling up around him.

Breathe, James told himself as he worked the lock with shaking hands. Mak was so close to him, but he couldn't get her. Not yet. The lock clicked and he ripped his wrists apart. The cuffs fell to the floor.

Eric's wide eyes met James' and he knew the predicament Eric was in, because he'd been in it before. Eric couldn't kill James, and given that Eric could no longer shoot with his right hand, and he wasn't trained with his left, James didn't think Eric trusted himself to deliver an incapacitating shot without killing him. Eric's eyes were blazing.

Men continued to approach James, all getting to be a foot in front of him before they fell to their knees, taken down by a bullet.

James sawed the blade across the rope binding his feet. His conscience tugged at him, telling him to look for Sister Francine, but he didn't.

His ankles fell apart—he was free.

Now! James thought as he lunged toward Mak, but a blow to his back bungled the attempt. James fell forward, landing on Tom's still-warm body. Another disabling blow came, this time across the back of his head.

Despite seeing double, James pushed himself up only to take a third blow, this one to his jaw. James tasted blood.

When security tried to tackle him, James lifted his knee, pummeling it into the hard chest of the man. It was enough to take the man's breath away and James landed two more angry blows—hard and fast—before the man went limp. James rolled him to the side, ignoring the fact that his own shirt was soaked with Tom's blood.

Mak.

James jumped to his feet but a command froze him in place.

"Don't fucking move or he'll pull the trigger!" Eric shouted above the noise and tilted his head toward the man behind him.

A security guy had an elbow wrapped around Mak's neck and a gun against her temple. Mak's body trembled.

"I'll kill her if I have to," Eric said.

James held his hands up, surrendering once more as his pulse peaked at a new high. A swarm of men moved in and cuffs were slapped back on his wrists. A gun was pressed against the curve James' spine.

"Move!" Eric commanded.

Fear made James' legs weak.

He couldn't see Mak.

He was losing her.

James tried to peer over the wall of burly men that encircled him —desperately searching for her—but each time he tried he received a blow to his face.

As he was forced to take one step forward after another, his mind raced, figuring out a plan to stall them until Deacon or Cami could get to them.

He didn't come up with one quick enough.

Mak's scream filled his ears and he fought wildly against the men holding him. He strained, lifting his head and saw her hair, coated in blood, before the world went black.

12

MAK ASWHOOD

Thick, warm liquid coated her face and a scream wailed from her throat. A scream that made her throat burn.

Mak's mouth tasted like rust and metal and she leaned forward, retching onto the man now limp at her feet.

More blood. More death.

Her legs gave way and no one caught her.

Her hands were still cuffed behind her and she landed in a pool of blood. Another tidal wave of nausea rolled in and she heaved as she tried to find a piece of floor that wasn't stained red.

Her body shook and a rough hand grabbed her arm and pulled so hard she thought her shoulder might come out of its socket. She was halfway to standing when the hand let go and she fell back to the floor. But she'd barely landed amongst the dead bodies when a gentler but still firm hand gripped her. He kneeled in front of her and Mak looked into Deacon Thomas' eyes.

"Come on, we've got you," he said, taking only a second to reassure her.

He had her wrists free before she knew what he was doing, and Mak's eyes pooled with hot tears as she stood on shaking legs. If not for Deacon supporting most of her weight, Mak didn't think she would've been able to move.

They ran. Deacon fired shot after shot, taking down anyone that approached them. With each step forward, and Deacon's steadying support, her body began to recover. Her legs, although shaky, felt less like lead weights—and Deacon must've realized this too, as he dropped the hand around her waist, taking her hand in his, and guided her forward.

"Cami—left exit, Tunnel 6A!" Deacon shouted.

Mak looked around again, horrified by the bloody scene that surrounded them.

Where is James?

She looked frantically, but she couldn't see him.

"Deacon, where are James and Maya?" Mak shouted.

Deacon didn't slow down, and his focus didn't deter from the path in front of them. "Maya is out!" he yelled above the noise.

But where is James?

The answer escaped her as they hurdled over two dead men on the floor. Mak fought the urge to vomit again and vowed to keep her eyes up.

They were running faster now, sprinting, and Mak realized bodies were dropping all around them, but the bullets weren't only coming from Deacon's gun. Someone was clearing a path for them. *Cami?*

Mak's lungs began to burn, but she could see a door ahead and she pushed her legs faster. Deacon responded, increasing his pace another stride and pulling her once more.

Two men stood by the door, but when they didn't react as Deacon and Mak ran toward them, she assumed they were on their team.

"Close it!" Deacon yelled as they ran through and into the tunnel. He didn't stop running.

Inside, there were blood-splattered walls and more dead bodies to dodge, but they sprinted on regardless.

Mak wondered how long she could keep going. She ignored every aching, burning muscle and instead focused on her breathing as she'd been taught to do.

"One minute," Deacon said and Mak wondered if he could tell the agonizing pain her body was in and he was talking to her, or if he was communicating via his earwig. Either way, she didn't have enough breath to respond, so she just kept running.

Deacon slowed down only to open the door, and then they ran up a flight of stairs, through an office building and into the bitter-cold night.

The air was like pouring gasoline on a fire in her lungs and despite her best efforts, her legs slowed down.

"One more block," Deacon said, almost dragging her now.

Mak took a deep breath, forcing herself to keep going.

One more block.

It felt like hours had passed before they reached the corner. A black van sat waiting, its engine purring, and as they approached the door it slid open.

"Come on," Deacon said, helping her into the van.

Once inside, Mak's legs gave way. She hardly noticed the other men already inside.

"Go!" Deacon instructed, to whom Mak wasn't sure. He turned his head back toward her and crouched down, his eyes scanning her from head to toe.

"Are you hurt anywhere else?" he asked her, looking at her neck.

"No," Mak said. She didn't think she was hurt, or at least she couldn't feel it if she was.

"Good. You're in shock. Just sit for now. Everything's okay. I'll clean your wounds when we get to the townhouse," he said, squeezing her hand before looking over his shoulder. "How is everyone?"

One man responded. "Danny's arm's not good."

Deacon crawled over to the man. "Pass me the kit," Deacon said, swaying as the van turned a corner.

Deacon pulled out one item after another, passing them to the man behind him, who then held up a small flashlight. From her position, she could see ripped, hanging flesh on Danny's forearm.

Deacon swabbed over the wound, and then said, "Samuel, location?"

Location of what?

In an effort to distract her mind from the horrors of the night, Mak watched Deacon clean, anaesthetize and suture a wound with the skill of a surgeon.

Deacon is my doctor. James had told her that once, and she'd thought he was joking. How little she knew about the Thomas brothers, she realized, sadly.

Eric had wanted to break her, and he had.

"Heart rate?" Deacon asked.

Mak looked to Danny, who was watching Deacon keenly. And not for his suturing skills.

What am I missing?

Deacon placed a bandage over Danny's wound as the van pulled to a stop.

Mak twisted her neck, but she couldn't see through the front window of the van. Men began jumping out as Deacon gave his orders. "Refuel, rest for thirty minutes, and then prepare your kits. Wait for my call," Deacon said.

Deacon and Mak were alone now, excluding the driver.

"We're going to meet everyone back at the safe house. Maya should be there already," Deacon said, kneeling on the floor in front of her again.

Mak looked at him as steadily as she could. "Where is James, Deacon?"

Deacon hesitated. "Eric has him."

Any feelings of exhaustion were washed away as waves of guilt and fear rolled in. "He's going to kill him," Mak said with a heightened voice. He'd kill him, Mak knew, but not before he tortured him.

"We're going to get him back," Deacon said, determination laced through every syllable.

"What happened?" Mak said. Everything had happened too quickly.

"Basically, once the situation got out of control, Eric started moving toward an exit. He allocated a security team to you, and the rest of his men to James."

"Could you have gotten him out?" Mak asked.

"No..." Deacon let out an exasperated sigh. "He was surrounded by walls of men and they moved fast. Eric had an underground escape route a few meters from where he'd been positioned. A section of the floor lifted, exposing a tunnel, and they disappeared in seconds. The hatch was lined with metal—we couldn't get through it, not without risking James' life. A second team was simultaneously working on taking down the men around you. They created a gap in your security and I moved in."

Mak shook her head, her thoughts jumbled like a tangled ball of knitting wool. The plan had failed.

"We'll get him back, Mak. Samuel's tracking him and we'll reassemble and go in for him. Eric's not going to kill him immediately, so we've got some time, but we'll need to move quick."

Mak nodded, words escaping her.

"What was said tonight, Mak... James is a good person. He doesn't kill innocent people. Eric was playing games with you, just like he does with everyone in his life. He's insane. What happened in Paris was an accident—"

"I want to hear it from him," Mak said, wiping away the hot tears that stung her eyes.

Deacon's lips puckered, but he let it drop. "Maya's at the townhouse now. We've got a doctor there and he's going to take care of her treatment. We can't be sure what Eric has been injecting her with, or the dosages, so he'll make sure her system is cleaned and detoxified correctly. She's going to need you when she wakes up, Mak. For the next twenty-four hours at least, you need to focus on her. I'll focus on getting James back, and when we do, you'll have the opportunity to ask him whatever you want and move forward from there. But until that time, do your best to focus on Maya."

Mak nodded.

"What if you can't get him back?" Mak asked, her voice flat, exhausted, scared to hear the answer.

"I will. I won't fail him," Deacon said.

Mak wondered if Deacon believed he'd failed Nicole. If he believed her death was his fault, as the Russian man had said. What had happened with Nicole had been used to torment him tonight.

It was a cruel world they were living in.

"I'm sorry you got dragged into this mess, too. I'm sorry for what happened to Nicole," Mak said.

Deacon looked at his hands. "So am I."

"And Tom..." Mak couldn't bring herself to say the words. He'd died for them, and right in front of her. That memory would plague her forever.

"Tom was a good man," Deacon said with solemn eyes. "We'll grieve for him when this is all over."

Mak nodded. "Who was the elderly woman?" Mak asked. When Deacon responded, he confirmed her suspicions.

"That was Sister Francine," he said.

She forced the next question from her mouth. "What happened to her? Did she get out?"

"I don't know. We're still trying to confirm."

From the look on Deacon's face, though, he was worried.

If James survives, how will he live with himself?

13

ERIC

"Cerah zalû," Eric whispered as he looked down on the battered face of Liam Smith.

Praise the Gods, and you shall be rewarded. And rewarded Eric was.

The man lying unconscious, at his mercy, was Eric's salvation. For years, he'd been under relentless pressure to find Liam. And his failure after failure would've destroyed any other man, but Eric had known all along that the Gods had a greater plan for him. Capturing Liam Smith had been a test, one he'd passed in many ways thanks to his wife Makaela.

Who would've ever guessed that Liam Smith would sacrifice himself for a woman. Eric smiled, a chuckle slipping through his lips. That was the power of the Gods—they made things happen that were unfathomable, inconceivable. The Gods had an organizational, universal power that humans rarely understood. But Eric understood it, and that's why he'd refused to give up or crack under the pressure. There were moments of self-doubt, of course, but somewhere in the depths of his soul he'd known he'd be successful.

Eric ran a finger over Liam's warm cheek. "You, bastard son, are going to give me more power than I have ever dreamed of." More respect, more authority. Anyone who doubted Eric before would no longer—he was the son of a God.

"Show them who you are," Lucian had told him. And Eric had done just that.

It was a shame that he didn't have Makaela, too. But that gift would come later, and now that he'd fulfilled Sorin's wish, Makaela would be his wife. Everything was working out just how he'd planned.

Eric's daydream, however, was cut short by an incoming call—one he'd been anxiously awaiting, one he couldn't wait to take.

"Lucian," Eric said.

"My son, never have I been so proud," Lucian responded and Eric tilted his head back, closing his eyes.

Lucian continued. "I want you to bring him to my estate. They will come for him, we know that, so the sooner we hide him the better. Bring him to me and we'll keep him in the catacombs—where they'll never find him—until we receive further instructions from Sorin."

Eric had scanned him and found no tracking device, which surprised him. He'd made the men repeat the procedure another three times. They found nothing. Regardless, Eric agreed with Lucian —it was best to take Liam somewhere that they had the advantage. They'd already started laying traps for the Ranger and Biskup's men.

"Of course," Eric said, his voice smooth and controlled.

It was only a matter of time until Eric joined Lucian's ranks as his equal. It was a goal Eric had set when he'd first been inducted into the organization. It had taken Lucian himself thirty-two years to be crowned an Elder. It will only have taken Eric nineteen by the time his ceremony would take place. The fastest progression in history.

A story fit only for the son of a God.

"I'll see you soon," Eric said, ending the call, only to make another to his head of security.

"Prepare the plane. We're going to Romania," Eric said, looking down once more on the face that was the key to his future.

"Sleep well, Liam. You'll need all of your energy when you wake up," Eric said.

~

It was an hour until the plane was ready and Eric didn't leave Liam's side. No, he would not let the man out of sight until they reached Lucian's compound. Liam was strapped to the bed, a rigorous system no man could get out of, but Eric knew what jealousy did to other men. Someone in the organization might try and sabotage him, and Eric wouldn't let that happen.

Eric had called his wife and ordered her to pack enough belongings for them, and their daughter, and to meet him at the hangar. Eric would need Marianne by his side now. Liam would need a nurse—Marianne—to heal the injuries he would sustain over the coming days, only to be tortured and mutilated again. It was a brutal cycle—one Eric couldn't wait to participate in. And one that he didn't have to share with the Russians now that Deacon Thomas put a bullet in Sokolov's head. Eric smiled—he couldn't have planned that better, either.

Though what Eric really wanted, more than anything, was to see what Sorin was going to do to Liam. That would be a performance Eric would not miss for anything.

"The chopper is ready," Seth said as he walked into the room with an additional security team. "Let's take him up to the rooftop."

Eric wasn't taking any chances. He wouldn't risk transporting Liam by car. It was a long enough drive to the hangar that, even with a convoy of cars, they would risk being attacked. No—they would transport him by chopper, wheel him straight onto the tarmac and then the plane and take off. There would be no downtime, no chance of interception.

Eric pushed on the plunger of a loaded syringe, delivering a second dose of sedation into Liam's intravenous line. Having Liam wake up mid-flight was not something Eric wanted to deal with.

Eric threw the empty syringe into the basket by the bed and

stood back as his security team wheeled Liam out of the room and toward the lift. Eric followed them, his strides confident, calm, and powerful.

One day, Eric would replace Sorin.

Eric would be the Dumnezeu: The Lord of All Mortality.

The breeze blew the lapels of Eric's jacket open as they walked toward the chopper. A sprinkling of rain fell over them and Eric looked up to the sky.

Thank you, Gods.

But he spent only a second thanking the mighty powers.

Liam was loaded into the chopper and Eric climbed in, signaling takeoff immediately. He sat beside Liam, barely able to draw his eyes away. Eric wanted to wake him now, he wanted to see Liam's face when he realized where he was, how powerless he was, and he wanted to see how he'd react when Eric told him that he also had Mak. It was a lie, of course, but Liam would have no way of knowing otherwise. It would be just one of the tortures he would endure. Just one.

Eric knew failure wasn't something Liam Smith was familiar with —they had that in common. But Liam would die thinking he'd failed Mak, and that was the icing on the cake.

The pilot began his descent and Eric gave his instructions once more. There were to be no delays.

"Have Marianne and my daughter boarded?" Eric asked.

Seth responded. "Yes, they're strapped in and ready. We'll carry Liam on board and take off as soon as the doors are closed."

Eric smiled. It was a seamless operation. "Very good."

Although it had been a shame to lose Frankie in the worship ceremony massacre, Eric had to admit that he preferred Seth. He was a man with a hard edge and a no-bullshit attitude, and he was unforgiving when rules were broken. He instilled fear in others, but he also instilled respect in them. It was a delicate balance, but one Seth had mastered. And one Eric needed his head of security to have after that humiliating night.

The process of transferring Liam onto the plane was as swift and fluid as Seth had promised. Eric boarded and was welcomed by Makaela's cherubic face.

"Daddy!" she said, waving at him. She was strapped in beside Marianne.

"Hello, princess," he said, kissing her cheek, and then Marianne's. He sat opposite them, fastening his safety belt.

"Mommy said your friend is sick and we have to take him to Papa's to see the doctor," Makaela said, never short for words.

"That's right. Mommy, daddy, and the doctor are going to take very good care of him," Eric said, smiling at his wife.

Eric sat in the recess of the window, watching the streaks of rain run lines down the glass pane. The jet had landed on the private runway at Lucian's compound and Liam had been transferred into the medical ward.

Flawless, Eric thought to himself, grinning at his own achievement.

Marianne was settling Makaela in her bedroom, Lucian was on a conference call, and Eric was waiting patiently for Liam to rouse. He checked his watch, knowing Lucian would be done soon and would want to talk with him. Eric looked back to Liam—he didn't want to miss seeing him wake up.

Eric tapped his fingers on the glass window, formulating the plan in his mind. *Perhaps I'll help him to wake up*, Eric thought. He bit his lip, drawing a knife from his pocket, and walked slowly toward the sleeping man. He unfastened only one of the restraints, just enough to pull the blanket down, revealing Liam's chest. His fingers tickled with excitement as he brought the blade to Liam's skin.

"Cerah zalû," Eric chanted as he made the first cut. He watched Liam's response—the man remained still.

He pressed the blade deeper, and as he carved one letter after another, Liam began to wake. Blood pooled on his chest, and when

Eric finished the first word, he wiped his palm over his artwork—revealing his masterpiece—roughly tearing the skin in the process.

Liam Smith's eyes opened and he inhaled sharply. He blinked several times, his eyes appearing unfocused until they landed on Eric.

Eric grinned, and began carving the second word.

Liam groaned through clenched teeth as he tried to fight the restraints. But Liam wasn't going anywhere. He was completely, utterly helpless.

When Eric was done, he repeated the chant as he stared into those big, black eyes. "It means *praise the gods*," Eric said, using the voice he knew could chill a room. "Welcome to hell, Liam. Your time here is limited—ended only by your death—but Mak's is not."

Eric gave it a minute to settle in, watching with glee as Liam's eyes widened.

Eric nodded. "I have her. And I have you." A grin spread across his face. "As I said... Welcome to hell."

The door opened and Marianne walked into the room. Her eyes fell to the bed, seeming to note the bloody chest, but she showed no adverse reaction. One of the many reasons she was the perfect wife.

"Father is ready for you," she said, walking toward him. She kissed Eric's cheek. "I'll sit with him."

Eric turned back to Liam—motionless, except for his eyes, which were flickering between Eric and his wife.

"Liam, meet my wife Marianne. The two of you are going to get well acquainted. Think of her as your private nurse, without the perks," Eric said, chuckling as he turned his back.

"I'll see you both soon."

14

JAMES THOMAS

The latch closed and James felt only a sliver of relief. He had to get out of here—he had to find a way.

He heard Mak's scream again in his mind and he looked to the ceiling, fighting to keep some composure. He wouldn't let her suffer at the hand of that maniac. She deserved so much more and James hadn't been able to protect her when she'd needed him most.

James felt like he might finally understand how his brother felt, and now he knew why Deacon had never forgiven himself. How could he?

"I need to clean your wounds," Marianne said, pulling James' attention from his frenzied thoughts.

Focus, James, focus.

James didn't want her to touch him, he didn't want her anywhere near him, but he knew the restraints he was under and he knew that unless someone undid them, he was powerless.

James didn't respond, but only stared at her. She didn't flinch. And that icy demeanor she wore so well didn't falter.

"They'll get infected if I don't—you know that," she said, turning her back to him. He listened to her footsteps, to the sound of running water, and then her returning footsteps.

She sat beside him and when she reached out with a wet cloth, he wanted to scream. He wanted to kill the woman that aided Eric, the one that had been injecting Maya, the one that would now be his nurse.

This can't be the end, James thought.

"It's antiseptic wash. It's going to sting," she said and James wondered why she even bothered to tell him.

James didn't waste any energy trying to figure out the answer and instead went back to his training, doing his best to mentally remove himself from the situation. He'd been tortured before, mutilated even. And he'd had more wounds cleaned than he could remember. But still, when she dabbed the cloth over his skin he hissed in a breath. He couldn't control his mind—all he could think of was one person: Mak.

What had happened?

What had stopped Deacon and Cami from getting to her?

Every minute they'd spent on their plan had been a waste.

I can't live with this pain, James thought, and he wasn't referring to the physical pain. The wounds on his chest, the piercing pain in his skull, the throb in his injured arm—it was nothing compared to the ache in his heart.

If he couldn't get out of these restraints, he was going to die without seeing her again. Without telling her how sorry he was. Without telling her how much he regretted Paris—that he didn't know about his child.

James stared at the ceiling, not even flinching now as Marianne injected something into his chest. *Anesthetic*, he realized, as the numbness set in. Eric had obviously cut deep enough that it needed sutures. James knew, though, that this was just the beginning of Eric's torment.

"I'm a trained nurse," Marianne said, as if that might relieve some of his concern. It didn't.

James rolled his head to look at her. He cleared his throat. "A nurse? Nurses care for people. They have compassion. You heal people so that your husband can cut them open again."

She met his gaze, unfazed.

James continued. "I watched you at the worship ceremony. I watched you sit beside Maya Ashwood. Do you know what I think?"

"What do you think?" she asked, seeming genuinely interested in his answers.

"I think you're a perfect match for your husband. I don't think I've ever seen a better suited pair." His words were scathing, hot in his throat. He was furious—furious at himself for failing Mak, furious that Eric seemed to have won, and furious at Marianne for her role in Eric's grand scheme. Marianne was the one he could release any anger toward and so he vented.

"Your first impressions are good," she said, not refuting it.

James rolled his eyes—the only part of his body he could move other than wiggling his hands and toes.

Marianne stood, leaning over him as if she was inspecting his chest. She whispered, in a voice James strained to hear, "But looks can be deceiving. Eric doesn't have Mak, James, your brother does. The cameras are watching."

He stilled and he swore his heart stopped beating.

Is she lying? Is this part of Eric's torture? To fuck with my mind?

He wanted to believe her, but he had no reason to.

She sat down beside him and drew the blanket up to his chin.

James' eyes darted around the room, searching for the cameras. He saw two, and if they were the only ones, Marianne had positioned herself such that when she spoke to him, her face was at an angle that wouldn't have shown her lips moving.

What is she up to?

"You should try and sleep. You're going to need your energy," she told him in a voice that was nothing like the one she'd just used.

15

MAK ASHWOOD

Mak sat in a quiet corner of the room, holding Maya's hand, but it was the flurry of activity around them that held her attention. What appeared to Mak to be a remote, makeshift surveillance operation was happening in the lounge room of the Thomas brothers' safe house.

Two large televisions were being used as computer screens and Mak couldn't see that they were linked to computers, so she assumed that Samuel was somehow feeding the data through. One screen showed a sprawling castle-like estate in Romania, the other displayed the data from James' tracking device. Mak was amazed at how much data such a small chip could provide.

Apparently, no one felt the need to hide the situation from her anymore. Eric had cracked open the vault of secrets and they were continuing to spew out one after the other.

There was so much James hadn't told her. Things he should've told her. Only an hour ago had Deacon given her the truth about James' situation. Her world had been tipped on its axis.

Each time James' heart rate spiked, her soul fell into turmoil. Sympathy for the man she loved—the man she had thought she'd known—and anger at his deception, and all of the things he'd hidden from her, things she could no longer ignore.

Mak recalled all of the strange phone calls and all of the so-called "client case" emergencies that had taken him away for sometimes weeks at a time. The client had been her. Or him. Both related back to Eric.

Of course Thomas Security had other clients, but Mak didn't think that's what James had been spending most of his time working on these past few months.

And Paris...Mak couldn't get Paris out of her mind. Deacon had said it was an accident, but it didn't look that way. If it was an accident, then he couldn't have known she was pregnant and Eric had lied—which was highly probable. But on the off-chance he hadn't been lying, if it hadn't been an accident...then Mak couldn't even begin to reconcile the James she knew and the James she had seen in her mind.

Her eyes lingered on James' heartbeat graph. It had settled again, and although neither Deacon nor Cami had said it, Mak concluded that when it had been jumping around he'd been in pain. Someone was hurting him, and Mak thought it very likely that someone was Eric.

How long did Eric plan to keep him alive? Judging by the intensity of activity in the lounge room, Mak didn't think anyone believed it would be for long. They had surveillance images of the estate and blueprints, but thus far no one had managed to find a way to get past the security—let alone get to James and get him out again.

Deacon was hunched over the blueprints now, his back a mass of strained muscles visible through his white T-shirt. He was in charge, and this would be one of the most important missions of his life. Mak knew he would die trying to get James out.

Along with Cami and the usual security team, the Tohmatsu boys were also present, huddled around the blueprints. That had been another surprise when they'd arrived at the townhouse.

When Mak had asked Deacon if that was the reason for the business meeting James had attended in New York, the night of the wedding, he'd admitted that was what he was doing—meeting with Haruki Tohmatsu. And James hadn't planned to speak a word of it to her. Did he think she couldn't handle the truth?

Her nerves were raw, her emotions high, and she knew now was not the time to search for the answers to her questions. There was only one person that could answer her questions anyway, and he was currently on borrowed time.

Maya's hand jittered in hers and Mak's attention shifted. Her eyes fluttered, and Mak squeezed her hand. "Maya," Mak said softly, watching her carefully. The doctor had a number of patients to treat, so Deacon had been playing the role—rather successfully, Mak thought—when the doctor had been busy.

"Maya," Mak repeated, a little louder this time, and Deacon appeared by the bed. Deacon wanted Maya in the same room so that he could work and monitor her simultaneously.

Deacon flushed her intravenous line with clear fluid. "She'll wake up soon. Keep talking to her—she'll recognize your voice."

"Where did you get your medical training, Deacon?" Mak asked.

"Some of it I received in the military, the basics really...the rest James taught me," he said, meeting her gaze.

"And how did he get his medical training?"

"Life experience, mostly. When your job means that you have a high probability of getting shot or stabbed, you must quickly learn how to treat yourself, and therefore others," he said.

She nodded. She'd always assumed James' past was as such, but being confronted with it last night, seeing so much blood and violence, it was still a harsh reality to face.

Maya's eyes fluttered again as she tried to open them.

"Maya, wake up, Maya. It's Mak, you're safe." Tears pooled in Mak's eyes as she said the words. She'd seen the cuts on Maya's chest when Deacon was examining her injuries. *Eric did that to you, I know he did,* Mak thought. *And I'm so sorry.*

Deacon put a hand on her forearm, squeezing it, rustling her a little. "Open your eyes, Maya. It's time to wake up."

Her eyes opened again and then closed. A pattern she repeated over and over as Mak continued to talk to her.

When her eyes finally stayed open, they looked around the room, hazily, before settling on Mak's.

Mak did her best to give her sister a big comforting smile. Maya looked to Deacon, and then her nose blushed pink as tears began streaming down her cheeks. Deacon stepped back as Mak got up from her chair and sat on the edge of the bed, folding her sister into her chest.

"It's okay," Mak said, unable to control her own tears. "It's okay now."

Maya's sobs grew louder and all Mak could do was hold her tight, and rock her back and forth like a child.

And if it wasn't for James, Deacon, Cami, and their teams, that moment wouldn't have been possible. Mak thought again of Tom, but pushed it from her mind before she fell apart. She had to take care of Maya now—she would process the rest later.

Slowly, Maya's sobs slowed and her heaving settled. She cleared her throat and wiped her tears away as she lowered herself back against the pillows.

"You're okay?" Maya asked, her eyes looking Mak up and down.

"I'm okay. I'm sorry, Maya. I'm sorry for what he did to you," Mak said, squeezing her sister's hands.

Maya shuddered as she seemed to recall the past few days. "There's something wrong with him. He's..."

"I know," Mak said, not needing her to finish the sentence—they all knew what Eric was.

"Where are we?" Maya said, taking in her surrounding, her eyes settling on the surveillance operation underway beside them.

Deacon returned to her side, flashing that poster-boy, charming smile of his. "Welcome back," he said. "How are you feeling?"

It took a few moments for Maya to answer. "Confused. Tired. Nauseous..."

Deacon nodded. "That's to be expected. I'll give you something for the nausea, though." Deacon loaded up another syringe.

"What happened? I don't remember getting here..." She looked to Mak. "Eric kept telling me that no one would come for me. That James wouldn't risk it—not for me. He said he was going to turn me into an addict and then...then sell me." She exhaled a shaky breath.

"Eric likes to torment people. He likes to play games," Deacon said. "We were always coming for you. *Always.* That wasn't even a question. We just needed some time to formulate a plan that would work."

But it didn't work, Mak thought. One person got out, but another was taken. And Mak wondered how many would die, or become captive, during the next rescue mission.

"Thank you," Maya whispered with red-ringed eyes.

"Deacon!" Cami yelled out and Mak peered around him, immediately looking at James' charts—they looked steady and Mak released the breath she hadn't realized she'd been holding. "The plane is ready."

"Load up," he said without looking at Cami.

"What's happening?" Maya said.

Deacon didn't respond immediately and Mak wondered if he was weighing between telling Maya the truth or fabricating another lie. Mak's mind was pure suspicion.

"James didn't get out. But he's okay," Deacon said quickly. "We're going to get him now."

"Oh no, Mak," Maya said, her voice cracking.

Tears that refused to subside flooded Mak's eyes again. She nodded, unable to speak.

Deacon continued. "There's a doctor here that's been treating you. He's a friend of ours and he's worked with us for years. You can trust him. And the Tohmatsu boys are going to stay with you and Mak until further notice. We'll either meet you back here, or in New York at Thomas Security."

Haruto, whom Mak had met ever so briefly at the Tohmatsu wedding, swaggered toward them, his stride casual and relaxed. "I'll bet you've never had such fun babysitters," he said, grinning and pulling out a packet of cigarettes. "Want one?"

Deacon shook his head. "Maya is medicated and is not having anything. Mak..." He hesitated as he looked at her. "Go for it, if it'll help."

Mak waved her hand. "I'll pass."

Haruto shrugged and sat down on the spare chair beside Maya's bed, leaning back and crossing his legs over.

How can he be so relaxed? Mak asked herself. Did he not care about the situation James was in? How well did he know James?

"Are you leaving all of that on?" Mak asked, looking toward the television screens.

Deacon hesitated. "Mak, it's best you don't watch it."

"I'll decide what's best for me going forward, and I want it left on," she said with a sudden ferocity, her tone sharp.

She saw Haruto look between them, an odd smile on his lips.

Deacon shook his head. "Okay," he said, checking his watch.

The table had been packed up and Cami walked toward them. As it had turned out, Cami had been the one firing bullets and clearing a path for Mak and Deacon to get out. She'd also been the one responsible for getting Maya to an exit.

"Good to see you again, Maya," Cami said without a line of worry on her face.

"Thank you," Maya said. "I can't thank you both enough. But I feel horrible..."

"James is going to be fine," Cami said and Mak was amazed at how confident she sounded. Mak knew, from watching her and Deacon huddled over the plans, that everyone knew the reality was a very different story. "Now, let's rock 'n roll, partner." Cami tapped Deacon's shoulder.

Mak watched them leave and heard the door lock behind them. She then looked around the room at who would be her company for, possibly, the next few days.

When James' heart rate spiked, all eyes turned to the monitor.

16

JAMES THOMAS

Mak!

James awoke drenched in sweat and fighting against the restraints as the sound of her scream echoed in his mind. His labored breathing was the only sound in the room. He looked around desperately.

Find a way out, James.

He didn't find an exit, but he did find Marianne, sitting beside his bed.

"Nightmare?" she asked coolly.

James closed his eyes. Nightmare or not, he was still in hell.

Marianne's phone rang and James watched her carefully as she answered it.

"Hello," she said, looking past James.

"Yes, he's awake... I'll see you soon," she said before hanging up. Nothing about her expression changed.

No sympathy.

No pity.

No concern.

She stood, washed her hands, and then gloved up.

What is she doing? James asked himself.

His eyes followed her as she went to a table that was now set up with medical supplies.

She must've done that while I was sleeping, James thought.

He was surprised he'd been able to sleep and he wondered if she'd given him a helping hand.

"You have visitors coming," she said.

James didn't respond. He couldn't work her out. If she wasn't just playing with his mind, what did she have to gain by helping him? What did she think he could do for her?

She removed the bandage on his chest, leaving it open.

Oh God, James thought. Eric was coming back and James was helpless.

What will he do this time?

It doesn't matter, James told himself. *Deal with it, survive, because you need to get out of here and find Mak.*

Marianne was still wiping his chest when the two men walked in. Eric first, and then the man James had seen in the photo with Marianne.

Now, this is interesting, James thought.

Eric stopped by the bed, looking down on him like a cat playing with a mouse.

I can't wait to kill you, was James' first thought despite how the odds were stacked.

James turned his attention to the second man. His steely gray eyes were powerful—piercing. He was in charge, James realized, or at least he was close to the top. This man knew why James was being hunted.

The man looked to Marianne. "The cell has been prepared. We'll move him shortly, but we want you to stay close—to watch him."

James couldn't pick the accent precisely, but the man was definitely European.

"Of course, father," she said, and James almost recoiled in response.

Father? James looked between them, still not seeing the resemblance. *She must take after her mother,* James thought.

But that one word changed everything. Marianne was married to the leader of Saratani, and her father was someone higher up.

"That's right," the man said, looking down on James once more. "My name is Lucian. This is my daughter, Marianne. And you've met my son-in-law, Christos, on several occasions now." His voice turned hard. "The time has come to pay for your actions—the turmoil and disgrace you have caused our organization—and the actions of your family. When your father, and mother, betrayed our Lord, they did so knowing the consequences. Your father has paid his, and now it's time for your mother to pay hers. Unfortunately for you, you share their blood, and therefore you will also pay the consequences."

James still had no idea what they were talking about, but he recoiled in shock at the idea that his mother was indeed alive.

He wasn't expecting a happy reunion.

"Your mother is being prepared now," Lucian continued, confirming James' assumption.

James wondered what exactly "preparing" involved, thinking he was likely going to be subjected to a similar tradition. His mind flashed back to the worship ceremony. He really didn't want to be tied to a cross.

"Any questions?" Lucian asked with a mocking grin.

James returned the expression. "Can I please go to the washroom?"

Lucian broke out into a full smile. "It's a real shame that we can't indoctrinate you. You would've been a valuable asset."

"There's still time to change your mind," James said. He looked to Eric again, noting how reserved he was with Lucian present.

Lucian chuckled. "I have some business to attend to, so I'm going to leave you in the capable hands of my two favorite people. They'll take very good care of you."

Lucian had a steely, composed resolve that was reflected in his eyes, but James wasn't fooled. Lucian was more dangerous than Eric. Far more dangerous. Suddenly Eric's company had become appealing.

The moment the door closed Eric flashed that gloating, maniacal grin. "And soon, we'll be Mak's new family."

Eric tilted his head to the side, but James didn't give him the expression he so obviously wanted. James didn't give him anything.

"We're going to take you down to the cell now, but first I need to check your injuries. This bullet wound..." Eric paused, pressing his finger against the wound. "I just need to make sure the bullet is actually out."

James' eyes followed Eric as he retrieved a scalpel from the medical table Marianne had set up.

"Not so much fun when the scalpel is in someone else's hand, is it?" Eric said.

James drew in rapid breaths, clenching his entire body. The blade felt like a searing iron as Eric dug it deep into his wound, twisting it.

~

James awoke, bolting upright. No restraints, no light—darkness. His arm burned and it was wet and sticky. Blood. Eric's latest torture session flashed in his mind. He'd dug a gouging hole, looking for the bullet.

He'd then repeated the same procedure on James' left arm.

Forget the pain, James told himself. *Use the time you have alone.*

He extended one arm, reached his fingertips out, searching for anything. He touched the rough brick of a wall.

I must be in the cell they had mentioned, James thought. His muscles protested as he stood, but he ignored the pain—he was finally free to move.

He ran his fingers along the bed, which felt too small to hold him, but it obviously had. Eric certainly wasn't providing any luxuries. James used the wall as a guide, trailing his fingers along it until he reached a corner. He continued along the adjoining wall. It was sparse. Neither his fingers nor his body touched anything but the bricks. James reached another corner—it was hard to be sure, as darkness could confuse the mind—but he thought it was either a square or rectangular cell.

James' foot kicked something that made a hell of a noise. It sounded like a metal object tumbling across the concrete. James had been in enough cells to know it was probably a bowl to urinate in. How kind of Eric.

James paused now, listening. His ears pricked. He braced himself for bright, shining lights to blind him, but they never came. He heard nothing, not even the breath of another person. James could've heard a pin drop it was so deathly quiet.

He moved again, slower now, careful with his feet. He reached a corner, but he didn't find an adjoining wall—he found metal bars. He was in a cell. But at least he could move again.

Never give up.

James ran his fingers up and down each bar, trying to locate the door—and the lock. When he found it, a lead boulder dropped in his stomach. He knew the lock, and he was not getting out. Not unless someone let him out.

Or unless he forced someone to let him out.

James moved toward the bed, running his hands underneath it. What could he break that he could use as a weapon?

It was a typical prison bed, but James assessed it anyway, looking for a weak spot. He tested the legs, pushing and pulling them as best as he could with one hand, but they remained steadfast. He knew it was hopeless, but he kept trying. What else did he have to do? His fingers searched for the joins, finding the legs welded on. No bolts. And unless he could break the weld, he wouldn't get one of the legs off.

The mattress was a single layer of foam with no bedding laid over a single metal slab. The bed was a bust.

Keep looking.

James had no idea of how many hours passed, or for how long he ran his hands up and down the walls, searching for anything he could use as a weapon. Anything at all that might help him. He found the bowl again and picked it up. It was metal, but it was lightweight and would hardly serve as a weapon—especially since Eric had considerably reduced the strength of his arms with his mutilation.

James knew that had been his intention. If James had a gun in his hand right now, he wouldn't trust he'd even be able to hit a target.

He continued his search, not even sure at what point he realized he could see the shadows of his hands.

Daylight.

James could see the bars now and moved toward them, twisting his neck to see the side wall. There was a tiny window outside his cell, barred and secured. There would be no getting in or out of it, but at least he could see now. He turned around, surveying his environment with the gift of light. It was exactly as he'd mapped out during the night. Four bare walls. One prison bed. One metal bowl. Hopeless.

The sound of a door caught his attention and he spun on his heels, stepping away from the bars.

"Good morning," Marianne said, carrying a plate. "Breakfast. I suggest you eat it."

In a different circumstance, James might've worried that the food had been poisoned—at least enough to make him ill. But in this case he knew it wasn't. Eric wouldn't let him die that easily, nor was it his method of choice—it wouldn't give Eric enough enjoyment.

James' wondered how many hours or days had passed since he'd eaten last—and since he'd seen Mak last.

Marianne passed the tray through the slot. "Eat," she encouraged, and he saw the look in her eyes—the message. "You haven't eaten for twenty-four hours, and we don't want you faint for the service."

Twenty-four hours.

James could've assumed that by the daylight cycle, but then he had no idea where he was or how long he'd been sedated for. They could've moved him at any point, to any location around the world. He'd been unconscious for several periods, which would've given them ample opportunity.

Twenty-four hours too long.

The one thing Marianne didn't know, that Eric didn't know, that Lucian didn't know, was that James had a tracking device. Eric's men would've scanned him, for sure, but they must not have found it, otherwise they would've cut it out. Unless they *wanted* Deacon to come for him—whatever building James was in, he knew it was one of theirs and that gave them the advantage.

And Deacon would come for him, if he could. But James had no idea if his brother was alive and able. He had no idea what had happened to the ones he loved. And he couldn't trust what Marianne had told him. James had to assume he was on his own. He wasn't going to buy time and wait to be rescued—he had to find a way out.

There's always a solution.

James set the tray down, taking the plastic lid off the small plastic bowl. An omelet. James wondered if Marianne somehow knew his favorite breakfast, or if it was just a coincidence.

The smell wafted into his nostrils and his stomach growled in response. He was hungry, and he knew he would need energy for whatever would come next.

James picked up the plastic knife and fork but first took a sip of the orange juice accompanying his eggs. The cold, sweet liquid eased his parched throat.

He put the plastic cup down, his stomach hungry for food. He cut the omelet, taking the first bite. Whoever the chef was knew how to make eggs. James wondered if this was his last meal, like a man on death row.

The second bite was just as good as the third, and so on. As he made another cut into the omelet, he almost paused, but his mind was quick enough to keep his hands moving—concealing the surprise. He fed another forkful into his mouth, casually keeping his eyes down, reading the note that had been placed underneath his eggs. A square, laminated note typeset in a tiny font.

You will die at midnight unless you can escape. I can get you out, but there's one condition: you take me and my daughter with you. You don't need Eric, because I have what you need: I have the code.

If this was a mind-fuck game, Marianne was playing it brilliantly. James continued to eat his eggs, although he tasted nothing now.

It's a risk to trust her, to believe her, James thought.

But, given the circumstances, what other choices did he have?

17

ERIC

Eric sat beside Lucian as they reported to the Commission. However, facing them this time was a very different experience.

I did it, Eric thought ecstatically, looking at the teleconference screen. *I found Liam Smith. I captured him—alive. And now you will all give me the respect I deserve.*

"Evening," Lucian said, commencing the meeting. "As you have heard, we currently have Liam Smith captive. He is here with us, locked in a cell at my estate."

"I must admit," one man said, "I didn't think it was going to happen. Christos—you have done the impossible. A job very well done; a job the Gods will bestow great reward upon you for. This is a day Sorin has visualized for many long years. It is a vision he will finally realize, thanks to you."

Eric bowed his head. "Thank you. It is an honor to serve the Gods, and to serve Sorin. It was a difficult task, but I always believed it was just a matter of time." *As you should have,* Eric thought, hating that anyone even doubted him, yet enjoying the pleasure disproving them gave him.

"Lucian, has Sorin given further instructions?" another Commission member asked.

"Yes. He is currently en route to Romania. And he is bringing Serena with him; she will soon be reunited with her son. The service will commence at nine o'clock, with his death scheduled for midnight. The service will be short, but I doubt—with what Sorin and I have planned—that he will be able to bear much more. At midnight he will be praying for death."

"And all members of the organization, Saratani and Escanta included, will be witness to the service?"

"Yes," Lucian responded. "It will be live streamed via our portal. For security reasons, it was decided to conduct the service privately at my estate. Liam is a man who should never be underestimated, and putting him in front of a big crowd is a risk we're not willing to take. Though I can't imagine how he could possibly escape, until his heart stops beating, extreme security measures will be taken."

Eric noted the chatter amongst the Commission delegates. They spoke quickly in higher-pitched whispers.

The Commission had not been invited to attend the service in person, but Eric had. *And rightly so*, Eric thought. He wondered how many of the delegates would be jealous of him, but he didn't care. *They can't stop me now*. Eric had been in Lucian's favor for some time, and now he was in Sorin's. *No one can stop me now*.

"Who will be attending the service?" another man asked, and Eric thought it a polite way of asking whether Eric had been invited.

"Myself, Christos, and Marianne," Lucian responded in a firm voice.

Eric doubted anyone was stupid enough to voice their disapproval, but he knew some were thinking it. He could see it in the narrowing of their eyes, the tightening of their jaws.

Get used to it, Eric thought. *Soon I'll be sitting beside you.*

"Can we see Liam now?" another member asked.

Lucian tilted his head, and then shrugged. "I don't see why not," he said and then opened the surveillance footage of the cells. He changed the screen options to display the surveillance to the Commission. Eric could only see the Commission members in a small screen now, which was disappointing. He wanted a wide-screen view of their faces when they looked at his accomplishment.

There was another round of excited chatter as they saw Liam, sitting in the cell, staring at the brick wall in front of him.

I wonder what's going through your mind, Eric thought, his eyes on him now too.

Was Liam imaging his death? Or was he thinking about Mak? Worrying about her? Wondering what her life would be like with Eric? Liam Smith truly loved her. He'd never, ever, have given himself up otherwise.

My wife was his greatest downfall, Eric thought, a smile as thin as a comma forming on his lips.

My wife—who I'll see again soon.

Without Liam to protect her, it wouldn't be long. Deacon Thomas had failed his girlfriend, and he would fail Mak, too.

Everything is as it should be, Eric thought. *Everything is falling into place.*

"Now," Lucian said, changing the screen display once more, showing their faces in full once more, "Christos and I must go and make the preparations for the service. We'll see you again this evening."

Eric looked to Lucian and saw a look of pure power, one that commanded respect. Lucian was able to show the world who he was without saying a word. And Eric had been fortunate enough to be his favorite student.

The screen went black and Lucian closed down the computer. He turned to Eric. "We have a lot of work to do today, my son. We'll prepare for the service and be ready to greet Sorin when he arrives, but let's talk to the Gods first."

Some men bonded over a glass of whisky, some smoked cigars together—but Lucian and Eric injected together.

"Let's call upon the Gods," Eric said with a smile so big it warmed his soul.

It was the perfect day, and soon Eric would meet the man who had held his fascination for so many years. A man so blessed by the Gods they had granted him the gift of life—eternal life.

One day, too, the world would meet Sorin, and Eric would be standing right by his side.

But first Eric would enjoy the glorious downfall of Liam Smith.

18

DEACON THOMAS

Deacon looked through the lens of his sniper rifle, feeding the surveillance back to Samuel.

"The building measurements match the blueprints," Samuel said via the earwig. *"They should be correct, given that they're relatively recent."*

Whoever owned this estate had recently undertaken some home renovations, including a total overhaul of the security system. They'd used a company from London, and Samuel had been able to hack their files. But the news wasn't good. It was the equivalent of trying to break into the Thomas Security headquarters.

It would be possible, though, if they could get Samuel access to the building's main board.

For the entire trip to Romania, and the few hours since they'd landed, they'd done nothing but strategize and re-strategize. It had been days since Deacon had slept, but he didn't feel tired. His mind and body were in battle mode.

We're coming, James. Hold on.

James' vital signs had been stable over the last few hours, so at least he wasn't being tortured—for the moment.

What are they waiting for? Deacon asked himself again.

Given what they'd gone through to capture James—hunting him for years—why wait?

When the Thomas brothers had a captive in their cells, they never waited. Get the information, and get it fast, because you never know what is around the corner. That was always their strategy.

But regardless of what Eric was waiting for, Deacon wasn't. He and Cami were taking the team in tonight. Deacon knew, though, that if they didn't get James out, it was almost certain everyone on his team would die tonight. Once they were in the estate, it wouldn't be an easy exit.

But I'd rather be dead than live with the fact I didn't try, Deacon thought. It wasn't even an option not to go in—and that brought him some peace.

"Fortunately, it's a similar system to the one that Eric had installed in the house in Jordan," Samuel said. *"Except there's two systems, and you and Cami are going to need to insert those wires at the same time. If not, the system will raise an alert and the building will go into lockdown. The only way you'll be getting out then is to kill everyone in the building."*

The words flowed easily from Samuel's voice, but Deacon knew he would be stressed about the wire changeover and taking control of the system. Deacon remembered when James had said that switching the wires and hacking the system sounded so easy, and Samuel had nearly thrown something at him. Now Samuel had to hack *two* systems in just as few seconds. The reality of the situation wasn't good, but that memory made Deacon smile. And if anyone could do it, Samuel could.

A noise disturbed his remembrance. "Do you hear that, Cami?" Deacon said, looking to the sky.

"Copy. It's coming from the south," she said, and Deacon knew from her position she'd be able to see the incoming plane.

He could see it a few seconds later and his eyes never left it until its wheels touched down on the private runway. There was a flurry of activity on the tarmac—security teams that had assembled to welcome the guests.

"Everyone, zoom your lenses in and I'll see what I can extrapolate," Samuel said.

Each member of the team that had accompanied Deacon and Cami were assembled at various geographical points surrounding the estate. With a compound of this size they needed an entire team to be on watch.

When the engines shut off the door of the jet opened and additional security teams departed. Deacon zoomed in on the man, his face unfamiliar. He spoke with the security teams on the floor, nodded, and then shook hands. The man's posture was stiff, rigid almost, like someone who had spent a lifetime in the military.

The security team on the ground parted and two figures walked toward the two men who had been talking.

Eric. A bolt of anger accompanied the realization.

And the man who had been in the photograph with Marianne.

Who are you?

Whoever he was, he had power. He gave the instructions, evident by his hand gestures and the nods of the men he was talking to.

The security team that had departed the jet reassembled on the stairs and two figures emerged from inside the cabin.

Deacon didn't recognize the woman who was taking tiny, shuffling steps forward. She appeared unstable on her feet and her back was hunched over like walking required tremendous energy. Perhaps for her it did.

Deacon adjusted his lens, getting a better view of her face—it didn't ignite a spark of recognition. But a spark flared when a man exited behind her.

"Samuel," Deacon said.

"Yeah, he's the unidentified man from Sarquis' drawings."

It wasn't *what* they had been waiting for, Deacon realized, but *who*.

They'd been waiting for their guests to arrive.

Deacon looked at his watch.

It was nearly noon.

At best, he thought, James had hours to live.

19

JAMES THOMAS

Time had ceased to exist without a reference point. He couldn't tell if he'd been alone in the cell for minutes or hours, though it felt like hours. And the only company he had was his mind—a tortured mind.

I failed her.

I failed Mak when she needed me most.

He felt his throat closing over as he thought of her.

He replayed the events of the night, looking at what he should've done differently. There were many things, but the one decision he regretted most hadn't been made that night.

I should've told her about Paris.

He closed his eyes, his stomach a ball of tight knots as he recalled the look on her face. She'd been devastated.

She will hate me now, but I still have to find her. I have to know if she's okay.

While he was locked in this cell he didn't stand a chance, but James knew Eric, and whatever grand plan they had ready for him, it wasn't going to be carried out in this cell. If it was done in true Saratani style, it would be a show of sorts, and that meant that they had to transport him. So far, they'd sedated him to do that. But James had a good feeling they'd want him awake for whatever they were going to do.

That will be your last chance, James thought.

Unless Marianne wasn't playing games.

But even that he had no control over at this point. She was making the moves, and he couldn't even respond because of the surveillance.

Sometime later—he couldn't tell how long it had been—the door opened, and Marianne entered with her husband. Eric had worn that same conceited smile on his lips since James had woken up, and James wanted nothing more than to smack it off his face.

"Tell me," Eric said, standing at the bars. "What's it like to be inside your mind right now? To know that everything has been ripped away from you, and that you're helpless to do anything about it. How does that feel, Liam?"

It feels like I want to kill you. "You do know I've been locked in a cell before, right?" James said, showing none of the emotion he felt inside. "But do you know what happened to those who locked me up? They met a very painful death."

Eric chuckled. "Always the optimist. Your luck has run out."

James raised one eyebrow. "Luck? Nothing about my life has been lucky."

"Perhaps you weren't lucky to be born into a family of traitors, but you've had some luck for sure. Otherwise we would've been in this position years ago," Eric said, the playfulness dropping from his voice.

"Call it want you want, Eric, but it was never luck," James said, trying to figure out the reason for Eric's visit—and also wondering if he wanted to know.

"Well, it doesn't matter now," Eric said. "Because for you, and your mother, luck *has* definitely run out. I came to give you this." Eric passed an envelope through the bars. "I'm sorry for your loss."

It was the most insincere condolence James had ever heard, and he knew Eric had meant it to be that way.

James focused on his breathing, on keeping his composure, as he opened the envelope and withdrew the images. They were from the night they'd gone in to rescue Maya, organized in time sequences.

Mak cuffed, Tom's slit throat, James on his knees.

James shuffled them through his hands. He didn't need a reminder; he remembered the events clearly, until he'd blacked out.

When James got to the last image, he paused.

Sister Francine.

Somehow, he refrained from closing his eyes, from heaving at the sight of the image. She had died that night, and she had died because of him. A good, innocent woman. One of the first people in his life that had shown him kindness.

Maybe it's not true, James thought, but he knew in his gut it was. James scanned the picture, hoping to see it was fabricated, that Eric was playing another game, but he saw nothing to indicate he was.

"The Russians weren't very happy when you put a bullet in Sokolov's head," Eric said. "How many innocent people have died because of you?"

"She died because of you, Eric, not me. But I don't think that worries you. I don't think you care who you hurt as long as you get what you want. You're addicted to power, to having people worship you, to bow at your feet. It's *pathetic*. And it will be your downfall."

The corner of Eric's lips turned up. "You're right," he said quietly. "I don't care that she's dead. It does not worry me at all. In fact, it gives me pleasure. Every time I hurt you, even if that's through someone else, it gives me pleasure. But your pain is just beginning, Liam Smith—you have no idea what awaits you tonight. And the best part of it all is that Mak will be present, watching it all."

I hope Marianne wasn't lying. "Why Mak, Eric? You walked away from her to join the organization. Why not leave her to live her life?" It was a question James had never been able to answer.

"You should know why...love."

James shook his head. "That's not the truth. You don't love her like I do, because I would never have been able to walk away from her in the first place."

Eric grinned. "Mak was chosen for me by Lucian. The mutual

friends Mak and I met through...all coordinated by Lucian. Mak was my first gift from the Gods...and do you think I would ever leave one of my gifts behind?"

James' mind raced.

Lucian?

How?

Why?

And how did Eric come to meet Lucian?

James was still missing so many pieces of the puzzle.

Eric flashed him an arrogant grin. "I'll leave you to have a think about that," he said, turning his back. He whispered in Marianne's ear, she nodded, and then he left her with James without another word.

James threw the envelope of images onto the bed. He didn't even want to touch them.

Grieve Sister Francine later.

Think about Lucian later.

Get out of here now.

Focus, James, focus.

"What do you want?" James asked.

"Nothing," Marianne replied, sitting down once more.

"Why does Eric want you to sit here and watch me?" James asked. "If I were to get out, you'd hardly be a match for me. And I know he's got men stationed outside that door." James nodded to the one Eric had just exited.

"I'm going to get your lunch," she said, with that same look in her eyes again—the message.

Alone again, James sat down on the bed. There was a brutal, relentless throbbing going on in both of his shoulders, but with his mind being so busy he was able to ignore the pain for the most part.

I have no idea where I am, what country I'm in, or what's happened to the people I love.

If only he could find a way to communicate with Samuel.

James looked over his surroundings again: hopeless.

Marianne entered carrying a silver tray and passed it to him through the slot in the cell bars. James took it, sat on his bed, and began eating, wondering if he'd find anything in this meal.

Marianne sat in the same chair, in the same position.

James saw her eyes fall to her watch and then return to him with her signature steady gaze.

"Keep eating, but listen to what I'm about to tell you," Marianne said, and James did as instructed.

"The sound on the cameras has been looped for thirty seconds. Listen but do not ask any questions—they can see your face, but not mine. At ten minutes before nine, I will come to prepare you for the service, along with a security team. There are two tunnels that I will lead everyone down. There is a blind spot in one of those tunnels as it turns a corner. My security team will be waiting there, with my daughter. We'll eliminate your security team and take another tunnel, one that leads to an exit. We'll have a window of approximately four minutes before Eric realizes what has happened. It's enough time—just. A car will be waiting.

"The newest members of Saratani, and even some of the older members, respect Eric. But there are many others that do not. He's hurt them, and their families, and they are ready to bring about his downfall. There are people willing to help us—to help me—because Eric will be punished for my betrayal.

"When we get out, you will protect me and my daughter. I will give you the information you need to settle with Biskup, and I will give you the information you need to come back in, with full resources, to eliminate this entire organization."

She paused, looking at him with a sudden ferocious intensity. "You're not the only one who is taking a risk, James. If I'm caught, I will be tortured and punished for the rest of my life—just like your mother. And just like your mother, my child will be killed before my very eyes. So, you ask: why I would do this? Because I don't want my daughter to suffer the fate I have. I do not want her married off to a man like Eric. Can you imagine what it's been like?"

He stared at her.

"Saratani has always been violent, but Eric has created a new breed of monsters. You've not yet seen what he's capable of, and my father, in his own way, is worse.

"There is no room for error tonight. And we have only one chance. But one chance is better than nothing. When I put a pistol in your hand—use it. And not on me," she said, with a hint of a smile.

"Eat, and get some rest," she said as the door swung open.

James' eyes flickered to Eric, standing in the hallway.

"Marianne, Lucian has requested your presence," Eric said, his voice calm, flat.

James' heart was pounding. Did he know what had just happened? Did he know what Marianne had just done? Or was it all part of a game?

James saw nothing malicious on Eric's face, but then he knew Eric could present whatever front he wanted to.

Marianne stood, not rushing, not appearing fazed by her husband's seemingly unexpected visit.

"Of course," she said as she followed her husband out.

20

MARIANNE

Her legs tingled beneath her, heavy and light all at once. Her blood flushed warm, her pulse loud in her ears.

Did they hear me? Was the sound not looped?

She wanted to put a hand on the wall for support, but she kept her back straight and put one foot in front of the other.

Christos said nothing as they walked, which wasn't unusual, but still the silence enhanced the panic blossoming in her chest.

Lucian requesting her presence also wasn't unusual.

It's nothing, she told herself. *It's probably in regard to the preparations for tonight.*

Tonight's service was to be one of the greatest events in the history of the organization. Sorin had his own reasons for doing it, but Marianne knew there was a secondary purpose. It was a lesson, to all members, of what happens if the leaders—and therefore the Gods —are disobeyed. Some leaders ruled out of respect, and others out of fear. Christos had the majority in the latter category. Her father, however, was a blend of both.

Marianne knew them well enough to fear them both.

Of the good things her marriage to Christos had given her, there were only three. Her daughter. The son she carried in her womb.

And the ability to conceal her true feelings.

The third she had learned quickly—thanks to Christos' brutal punishments. Punishments deemed suitable by the organization, but definitely not suitable to Marianne. She learned fast how to smile at him when she really wanted to stick a knife in his chest.

Christos held open the door for her.

She saw her father sitting at his oversized mahogany desk, and his gray eyes met hers. Eyes she'd once found comforting as an innocent child. The same way Makaela currently found her own father's eyes comforting. But Marianne knew her son would never have the chance to look at his father the same way.

When Marianne had fallen pregnant with Makaela, Christos had been manic; praying constantly to the Gods for a girl—he hadn't wanted a boy, even then. But now, six years later, when he'd insisted that they start trying again, he'd looked her in the eyes and said, "I will not have a boy. And I'll make sure of it." He'd changed over the years, and Marianne of all people didn't doubt what her husband was capable of.

"How is our captive?" Lucian asked, motioning for her to take a seat.

Marianne was grateful for the chair, unsure how much longer she could keep her legs from trembling.

Christos didn't sit, but instead remained standing, looming somewhere behind her, and that only made her more uneasy. She knew that, although he was capable of it, he wouldn't slit her throat from behind if he'd uncovered her plan. He wouldn't let her die that easily. Punishing Marianne would be his only hope of redemption. And the same for her father.

"The same. Introverted, quiet, but his mind is busy—I have no doubts. I've been encouraging him to eat so that he has energy for the service. And he is eating... However, I believe it's for different reasons."

Lucian raised one eyebrow. "He still thinks he has a chance to survive?"

"I think he's the kind of man that, until you stick a knife through his heart, will think that. Christos will agree, I'm sure," Marianne said, looking over her shoulder now.

Her husband stood an arm's reach from her chair.

"Yes, I agree. *Pathetically* optimistic," Christos said.

Marianne picked up the tone in his words. She didn't think Christos appreciated Liam calling him "pathetic" in the cell. She almost smiled.

"Optimism alone is never enough," Lucian said. "While it's good to believe, action is also required to make things happen. Liam's missing the latter ingredient." Her father sighed. "Anyway, enough about that. Sorin has made a formal request, one which you will obey."

Marianne almost fell forward with relief. This wasn't about Liam Smith—they hadn't overheard her. She shouldn't have been relieved, though, because whatever was coming next wasn't good. But her plan hadn't been uncovered, and she would do whatever Sorin wanted now to keep up her pretense.

Lucian folded his hands on the table. "Sorin has requested that you play a prominent part in the service this evening. You and Christos will, after all, be one of—if not *the*—most powerful couple in the organization. The members love you, as they love Christos. It's important for other women to be aspirational, to aspire to be the kind of wife that you are to Christos."

Aspirational? Marianne kept her expression steady.

"What does Sorin ask of me?"

"Sorin asks that you be the one to carve the *V* into Liam's chest, as Christos would do in a worship ceremony."

Marianne responded. "We've had this discussion before, and I prefer not to cut the sacrifices. Christos does it so well, and it is his role."

She didn't honestly care, because there would be no service this evening and she would be leaving forever. But, both her father and her husband knew she did not like this part of their ceremonies, and it would appear strange for her not to argue it.

Lucian's eyes darkened like storm clouds. "It does not matter what we've discussed before. Sorin has requested it, and you will do it."

Christos put a firm hand on her shoulder. "Of course she will," he said from behind her.

Marianne took a deep breath, and made a show of exhaling it. "If it must be done, then I will do it—for Sorin only. I would still prefer not to cut at future worship ceremonies."

Lucian looked thoughtful. "That is fine. In fact, I think if it is a rare occasion such as this that you do perform the cutting, it will make it all the more special." He smiled at his daughter. "I'm proud of the two of you for always doing what needs to be done. The Gods will reward you for this, Marianne."

She raised an eyebrow. "It is an honor to serve them," she said. "Is there anything else? I've barely seen Makaela today and I'd like to spend a few hours with her before the service this evening."

"No, that's it. Go to your daughter. But be ready to prepare Liam this evening," Lucian said with a glint in his eye.

"Of course. I'll be ready," Marianne said, waiting for Christos to lift his hand. It took him several seconds longer than she would've liked.

She walked herself out, feeling like she needed to take a shower. She always felt like that these days, yet no matter how often she showered, she couldn't wash away the disgust that hung from her skin.

She walked the tunnels that she'd run down as a child, laughing and playing, oblivious to the future she had been destined for. Now, she wanted to run toward the exit and keep running. Instead, she walked deeper into the building, because her daughter was there.

And she would do anything for her.

And for her unborn son.

Including betraying her family.

21

DEACON THOMAS

Deacon closed the zip of his kit. He was ready. They were ready—as ready as they were ever going to be.

He sat down on the stool and pulled out his phone. He dialed Samuel's number.

"I was just about to call you," Samuel said.

"With good news?" Deacon asked, making a light joke.

Cami walked toward him and he slid her a stool, putting the phone on speaker.

"Unfortunately not," Samuel said. "Maya's toxicology results are back. She was injected with heroin, and a combination of sedatives. She's exhibiting minor withdrawal symptoms, but the doc thinks it's best to transfer her back to New York and she wants to go home. In fact, her fiancé is demanding she be brought back so that he can care for her. I've instructed them that if we transfer Maya she will be—with medical support—like all of them, in complete lockdown until further notice."

Deacon looked to Cami, who shrugged. "Might as well."

"What's Mak had to say about this?" Deacon said.

"Mak has been...a little difficult. I informed her that it would be best for her to go back to New York as well, but to come to Thomas

Security with me so that she can remain included in what's going on. She absolutely refused. Haruto took some initiative and informed her that if she didn't agree, he would force her."

Deacon grinned as he noted the change in Samuel's voice.

"Well, after that she said she was going to pack her bag," Samuel continued. "Haruto thought she was taking too long so he went to check on her. She wasn't in the room, and she wasn't packed. He found her in the garage, standing at the trunk of the car. When he walked up to her she pointed a pistol at him, loaded and cocked, and told him in no uncertain terms that she'd been taught to shoot, that she was a good shot, and that she was not leaving."

Cami pressed her lips together, clearly trying not to laugh.

"And Haruto's response?" Deacon asked, wishing he'd seen that scene play out. And if they all got out of this tonight, they probably would replay the surveillance footage.

Samuel chuckled. "Apparently he held his hands up and backed away. He told me, 'She is definitely James' girl.'"

Deacon smiled, but his chest felt heavy, too. If they got James out tonight, his brother was going to have to deal with the repercussions of what had been said, and shown to Mak. Deacon didn't know if the damage to that relationship could be repaired. He'd never thought the relationship was a good idea, but he still worried about what the end of it would do to James. And James surely had to be thinking that now. His head must be filled with questions and no answers.

"One other thing," Samuel said. "This morning, Mak sent an email to her boss asking for a one-month leave of absence for personal reasons. She informed him that she would continue the case review for the gangland murder but would not be attending to any other work-related matters. It was approved."

"She's done with decisions being made for her," Cami said. "And she's angry and hurt. We're not going to be able to hide things from her anymore, or give her excuses of why we can't disclose details. She's not going to have any of it."

"What do you want me to do about the screens tonight? Do you want me to shut them off?" Samuel said.

Deacon shook his head. "Leave them on. James already has a mess to deal with there and if she feels like we're shutting her out and hiding more from her, it's only going to make the situation worse."

"All right," Samuel said. "Now, the pilots are on standby and the planes are ready. Is there anything else to do?"

Deacon looked past Cami to the men sprawled out in sleeping bags. Deacon struggled to see an unoccupied square of the gray carpet. New recruits had been sent in from Biskup and although Deacon didn't like the guy—at all—he was damn resourceful, and Deacon was grateful for the support.

However, because the new recruits hadn't been trained, they would serve as pure ammunition power. Deacon and Cami's team would eliminate the majority of the border security on their way in. The new recruits were to stand on the boundary walls, armed and ready to eliminate anyone that threatened the exit plan.

"No. We'll rouse the teams soon, suit up, and then test communication devices," Deacon said.

The time was near.

We're coming, James, Deacon thought. *We're coming for you.*

22

MARIANNE

Marianne held her daughter's soft, silken hair in one hand as she ran a comb through it.

"Mommy, I want a plait," Makaela said as she played with the doll in her arms.

"Mommy, can I *please* have a plait," Marianne said, correcting her daughter.

Makaela tilted her head back, her big eyes shining, a cheeky grin on her soft pink lips. "Mommy, can I please have a plait?"

Marianne kissed her forehead. "Yes, you may, Kaela." Marianne used the nickname she'd given her child so that she didn't have to call her by the name of Eric's first wife.

Marianne inhaled the sweet scent of her daughter, of her innocent daughter who should never have been born into this world. Her sweet daughter whose life Marianne was risking.

As Marianne's lips rested on Kaela's forehead, her chest squeezed her heart.

Her hands began to tremble and she closed her eyes.

You need to do this. For both of your children. Give them the life they deserve.

"Mommy?"

Marianne opened her eyes, smiling at her daughter. "Yes?"

"What are you wearing tonight? Daddy said he's taking you somewhere special to celebrate," she said excitedly.

He would say that.

"I'm wearing a gold dress and the red, sparkly crown," Marianne said, and her daughter's eyes lit up.

"Ooh, so pretty, Mommy. What are you celebrating?"

Death.

"Some very special guests have come to visit Papa," Marianne said. "Nina is going to stay with you tonight. I want you to go to sleep when she tells you to. She'll read you two stories, and then lights out."

Makaela scrunched up her nose, eliminating the doubt in Marianne's mind. Her daughter was willful, and stubborn, and Marianne planned to negate that tonight by giving her a sedative. Marianne felt terrible about it, and it ate at her conscience like a leech, but she couldn't have Makaela awake while they ran through the tunnels. Makaela would cry, she'd ask questions, she'd be terrified. Marianne didn't want her to have to go through that and it was better that she was asleep. Better for all involved.

Marianne wove one strand of hair over another, forming the plait, and then tied it with an elastic band.

Nina walked in, smiling as she saw Makaela. "A very pretty little angel," she said and Marianne smiled.

Her daughter was many things, but a little angel she was not. Although it meant she was sometimes a difficult child to correct, Marianne liked that her daughter was strong, bossy, and boisterous. It would help her survive in this world.

"Thank you, Nina," Makaela said.

"Okay, Kaela, please go and clean up your toys now before dinner," Marianne said. Her daughter gave a sigh as she pushed her hands against Marianne's knees, standing up.

When Marianne was sure her daughter was out of hearing range, she motioned Nina toward the kitchen.

"Is everything in place?" Marianne said as she turned on the tap, the running water helping to obstruct her barely audible voice. She set about washing the few dishes in the sink, taking her time.

"Yes. We're ready. How are you feeling?" Nina said.

"Terrified. And nauseous...the morning sickness is getting worse, not better. I've been fighting to hold anything down all day."

"Hang in there," Nina said. "Your nightmare is nearly over."

Marianne hoped—prayed—that Nina was right. But Marianne prayed to a different God than her husband did.

Marianne turned off the tap and wiped her hands dry with the dishcloth.

"While you start Kaela's dinner I'll go and do my makeup," Marianne said.

In the bathroom, Marianne closed the door, holding her hand against it, letting it support her. It was one of the few rooms without a camera. She was almost always being watched.

What am I doing? she asked herself again. She was risking her children's lives. *Maybe they're better off staying here,* she thought, and then dismissed it immediately. It was not the best life for them. Marianne knew Kaela would come to hate the life that would eventually be imposed on her.

And her son would never live to see his first birthday.

She took a calming breath, pulled back her shoulders and sat down at the makeup vanity. She picked up the bottle of makeup remover with fumbling hands, only to drop it.

Get it together. Be strong for your children.

She picked up the bottle again, wiping her makeup away, cleansing her face.

You'll never get a better chance, Marianne.

She knew this building like the back of her hand. She had staff willing to help her—to die to help her.

And she had a man who was desperate to get out, at any cost. A man even her husband secretly feared.

Once Liam Smith's hands were free, she'd put a weapon in them.

We'll make it.

We have to.

23

JAMES THOMAS

Darkness settled around him as the sunlight faded.

How much longer? James thought, rubbing his hands over his face as he sat on the edge of the bed.

He'd analyzed Marianne's actions over and over again in his mind. He had no reason to trust her—not a single one—but she was his only chance of escape. He didn't understand her motives, but James thought being married to a maniac like Eric was motive enough.

He thought about Eric again now, and how infrequent his visits had been.

He's busy, James concluded. *Probably busy preparing things to torture me with.*

The door swung open and the lights were flicked on. James squinted, giving his eyes a moment to adjust to the change. Men, dressed in suits, entered through the door—ten of them, James counted. And Marianne came in behind. They parted for her, like she was royalty. James supposed that in the world of Saratani that she was.

She looked at him, as composed as he'd ever seen her, and he questioned her motives again. Jewels glittered on her hair, and her gown flowed with each step. She looked as striking as she had at the worship ceremony.

"Walk toward the bars, turn around, and then put your hands through the food slot," she commanded.

James stood, but didn't immediately move toward the bars. Instead he took note of the security team in front of them. Watching their body language, concluding who was in charge, and who were the weak links—all evident by the sideways glances and fidgeting when James didn't obey and they thought they might have trouble.

"You're wasting time. Don't make this more difficult than it needs to be," Marianne said with a neutral voice, but her eyes turned cold.

He stepped forward, coming to a stop at the bars. Slowly, he turned around, sliding his hands through the slot. Cold metal hit his wrists, binding them together.

The angle made his shoulders throb, but if he didn't get out of these cuffs soon, his shoulder wounds would be the least of his problems.

"Take a step forward," Marianne commanded.

James obeyed, and he heard the click of the lock. He didn't expect what came next.

A jolting electrical shock knocked him to his knees, stealing his breath and sending crippling bolts of pain through his body. James fought for air, and to remain conscious. He heard the man behind him laugh, and say, "Not so tough now, are you?"

James knew that if he got his hands free, the man was going to regret that.

James was panting, still recovering, when Marianne commanded, "Stand him up. We need to go."

Two sets of arms hauled him upright, his feet just touching the floor. Marianne turned on her heels without giving him a second glance. James wouldn't be able to see her face now, and that worried him.

Three men walked behind Marianne, but in front of James. There were two men on each side of him, and another three at the rear. James had faced worse odds.

He looked at the men a step ahead of him, identifying where they kept their weapons. If he could get his hands free, he could get his hands on one of their pistols and put a few of the men down before they even realized.

But his hands were cuffed—and so James continued to walk.

He did a full assessment of their surroundings. It looked like a castle, a very old one. Marianne opened a door, one that led into a tunnel-like structure.

"The second tunnel has a blind spot," Marianne had told him.

The tunnel had a series of steps, and of course they were going down.

This sick organization loves the underground, James thought.

Marianne increased her pace, moving the team faster.

James lost his footing once, but rough hands kept him upright, sending another burst of pain through his body.

Focus, James, focus.

They came to another door and Marianne entered a code, unlocking it.

They stepped into the second tunnel.

This is it, James thought.

He focused on his breath, on keeping his mind calm, on preparing himself for anything.

Or for nothing.

He peered between the men; glad he was tall enough to see over Marianne's shoulder. If he saw another door approaching, he would know Marianne had been playing games. And then he was going to play his own game with what little time he had left.

The men continued to march him forward, and full-blown doubt grew in James' mind.

And then he saw a corner ahead, followed by the straightening of Marianne's shoulders. It was slight, so slight, but he'd seen it. She was preparing herself.

This is it, James thought, hope replacing doubt.

To Marianne's credit, her pace remained the same despite what she must've been feeling inside. She was a brave woman to defy Eric —a man she likely knew better than anyone.

As the walls began to round, James' focused on his breath.

Stay calm, use every opportunity that comes.

The tunnel seemed to turn one-hundred-and-eighty-degrees, sloping down, and when James thought they surely must be through the corner Marianne dropped to the ground and guns began to fire. The three men dropped in front of him and James reacted—fast. He kicked the man behind him and head-butted the man to his left, loosening his grip. It all happened in the blur of a second. The man on his right appeared startled and it didn't take James more than a second to get free of his grip. James moved to the side, getting out of the line of fire.

The security team reacted, reaching for their weapons, but whoever was firing at them was faster. The gunfire was so loud his ears rang as the men around him fell to the ground. When the gunfire ceased, James looked over his body, amazed a bullet hadn't hit him.

Marianne ran toward him with a key in her hands. He turned, his breathing fast, and the second the lock popped he ripped his wrists apart. A pistol landed in his hand, thanks to one of Marianne's aids.

"Run!" Marianne screamed to the entourage lining the walls.

Nine men, James counted as his body reacted, were following them. It was then that he noticed, a tall, strong-looking man, carrying a child huddled in a blanket. A child that, incredibly, seemed to be sleeping.

James continued to sprint forward with no idea of where he was going. But his wrists were free, his hand loaded with a weapon, and he had a great deal of hate and resentment to fuel his body.

James didn't know if he had the upper hand or if Eric still had it, but he had re-entered the game.

And this time he would not lose.

Game time.

24

DEACON THOMAS

"Hold!" Samuel's voice came through his earwig strong and fast and Deacon's hand froze mid-air, his fingers holding the wire.

"James is moving!" Samuel explained. *"Fast. Vital sign analysis shows he's running—sprinting."*

Is he making an escape? Where is he going?

Deacon dropped his hand, pressing his back against the wall. He was in a compromising position and the sooner he moved the better. He had no idea what his brother's plan was, but someone inside that building surely had one. And if Samuel accessed their security system it could blow the entire operation.

"Can you match his location to the blueprints?" Deacon said, looking over his shoulder again. Cautious, alert.

"Not perfectly. I think he's in some kind of passageway or one of the connecting tunnels. It's twisting and turning." Samuel's voice was vague, as if he were concentrating on multiple things at once.

"Hang on..." Samuel said, and Deacon pushed aside his impatience. He could only stay in this position for so long. It was too bright, and he risked being caught by a camera.

Samuel continued. *"I think I know where he's going. There's an exit that one of the tunnels leads to. If I'm reading the blueprints correctly, and if no structural changes have been made, that should be where he's going. I'm loading the GPS data onto your phones."*

Deacon drew his phone, opening the app. A surveillance image of the estate flashed up and a blue plus sign was moving across the screen.

"Plan B. Cami, forget the wire," Deacon said. "Bring your team and meet us at the exit point. If James can get to it, we'll help him get out."

Deacon prayed he was making the right call.

Trust your instincts, go with your first thought. That was the advice James had always given him.

Deacon crouched down, keeping his shoulders against the wall as he ran back toward the shadows where his team was waiting.

Once he reached them, his eyes darted from point to point. He hadn't been seen—at least he didn't think he had. Deacon used his hand to gesture them forward. The estate was enormous, and that presented multiple challenges on its own.

With every step Deacon surveyed his environment vigilantly.

They moved fast, working around the building, dodging the security lights and keeping low beneath the cameras.

If James was making a break for it, Deacon knew he would have minutes at best before someone realized.

But what if he wasn't? What if they were transporting him?

But then why would they be sprinting?

You've made the decision now, Deacon told himself. *Focus.*

He checked his cell phone as he ran, making sure they were still heading in the right direction. They were, and they were close.

Deacon came to a skidding stop, pressing up against the wall when he heard voices.

"Hold!" Deacon whispered.

"Copy."

Deacon's ears strained, listening to thick accents. The men weren't speaking in English. He couldn't understand what they were saying, but if Deacon could get close enough Samuel might be able to enhance the audio and translate it.

"Two voices. I'm going closer. Translate it if you can, Samuel," Deacon said, motioning for his team to hold back.

"Copy."

With a pulse thumping in his chest, Deacon crouched lower, assessing the overhead security. He could get to the corner at least without being seen.

He took one silent step after another.

When he got the edge of the wall, he asked Samuel, "Can you hear them?"

"Yes... They're talking about a service... A service tonight... They're annoyed that they can't watch it because they have to work..."

Before Samuel said the next words, Deacon knew something had happened by the change in their voices.

"They know he's making an escape!" Samuel said. *"Security reported they didn't arrive at the hall on time. They're alerting Eric!"*

Deacon reacted, trusting his instincts, and firing a bullet into the chest of each man.

Two perfect shots.

Two less men to sabotage James' escape.

25

ERIC

Eric bowed to the Dumnezeu: Sorin.

"It has been an honor to serve you, and to serve the Gods," Eric said with a hand on his chest. He was facing the man he'd only ever seen photographs and paintings of.

"When Lucian first brought you into the organization, he told me you were going to do great things," Sorin responded. "But perhaps even he underestimated you. You have done better than great; you have done the impossible. You are the future of our organization."

Eric inhaled, his chest expanding as he absorbed the energy that surrounded Sorin like an aura.

This is it, Eric thought. *This is the end goal. I will be Sorin's successor, and one day I will be the Dumnezeu. I will be the most powerful man in the world.*

I'm going to give you the show of your life, Eric thought, suppressing his smile.

"Excuse me... I apologize for the interruption," a timid voice said behind him, and Eric spun on his heels, giving a deathly glare to the man who had dared to enter the service room.

The man gulped upon seeing Eric's face. "Your wife has requested your presence for a moment," he said.

Eric froze. Why would Marianne do that? She knew the plan, and this was not part of it. She knew how important this night was.

Steam was billowing from Eric's ears as he turned back to Sorin, bowing once more.

"Our guest has arrived," Eric said confidently. "Excuse me while I conduct the final preparations."

Eric kept his eyes forward but he saw Lucian's eyes narrow. He too knew this was not part of the plan.

"You may be excused," Sorin said and Eric backed away as fast as he could without raising suspicion.

As Eric closed the door, he opened his mouth to speak, but the man beat him to it.

"He's gone," he whispered, panicked. "Liam's gone, and so is your wife. They're in the tunnels."

It took Eric a moment to process it before a wild storm swept through his mind. "Lock it down! Lock the fucking building *down!*" Eric sprinted toward the elevator.

This can't happen.

This can't happen!

He banged the buttons while dialing the surveillance team.

"What the *fuck* is going on?" Eric demanded.

The voice on the other line was just as frantic.

"We don't know, but someone hacked our system. They looped the footage. He's running for it, making an escape. He's going to exit out of the Nishka tunnel. We've got footage back on them now."

"Where's Marianne? How did he do this?" Eric asked as the lift descended four flights.

"Christos...she's leading him. She has Makaela." The voice was full of trepidation—a messenger who feared of getting shot.

Eric's blood froze over like a lake.

You stupid fucking bitch!

26

JAMES THOMAS

James heard the sound of striding boots before the first shot was fired.

They had company, and a lot of it.

James could see a door ahead, but judging the increasing intensity of the footsteps, they weren't going to make it.

Marianne heard it too, and she looked over her shoulder. The color drained from her cheeks and he wondered if this was the first time he'd seen her so unguarded.

James assessed the situation. There wasn't another corner to use to their advantage. There was nothing but a straight section of tunnel ahead. They had no option but to aim and shoot and hope for the best. The fact that the people James were with hadn't shot him by mistake a few minutes ago gave him some hope they were a decent shot—hopefully he hadn't just gotten lucky.

"Stop!" James commanded. "But you, keep going," he said to the man carrying Makaela. Marianne might have started this mission, but James was going to call the shots now. "Line the walls, keep your back against them, and fire at anything that comes toward us. Make your shots count!" James just hoped he could make his own count. He took a long, deep, steadying breath, knowing he'd have to push through the immense pain that would come when he raised his weapon—and kept it raised.

The thudding of footsteps loudened and James knew they only had seconds to spare before the men rounded the corner.

Marianne's eyes were torn between her daughter and her entourage. James wondered if she even knew how to shoot a gun. She didn't have one in her hands.

"Marianne. Get behind him. Stay low," James said. He was not going to tell her to go for the exit—not without him.

James saw the shadows on the wall first.

"On my count," James said, taking a deep breath. "Three, two, one!"

James fired relentlessly. Men were falling, but James wasn't entirely sure it was his doing.

A wailing scream came from one of Marianne's team—a woman—and James knew she'd been shot, but he didn't dare take his eyes off of the approaching men. James counted his shots, calculating how many he had left—provided the magazine had been full.

He heard another scream, and then another. He still didn't take his eyes off of the targets, but as he continued to fire, all hope faded. The men were getting closer, and there were too many of them. Even if they managed to hold them off, they were going to run out of ammunition.

Think, James! Think!

He took his eyes away only for a second. He saw three of their team down—three out of seven. "Marianne! Kick me their weapons!" he hissed.

James didn't know if she heard him, but when his eyes landed on the pistols she knew what he wanted.

"Stay low, use her as a shield," James said.

Using a dead body as a shield was unpleasant, but it was better than getting shot yourself.

James bent down to get the weapon, recoiling when a fire burned fiercely in his arm.

He gritted through clenched teeth, gulping in air, not even bothering to look at his shoulder that now had two bullet wounds.

Focus, James. Block it out.

If he didn't get out of this tunnel, he was going to be in much more pain than a bullet could cause.

He forced his body down again, scrapping up one of the weapons. The second was too far out of reach. James held it in his left hand and fired once more.

But the men were still closing in.

Marianne's high-pitched scream echoed through the tunnel, drawing James' eyes away from Eric's men.

Men, more men, coming from the exit door.

James swung his arm around, his finger on the trigger.

"James! Hold!"

Even with the rioting noise in the tunnel, James recognized his brother's voice and he wanted to cry with relief. Deacon moved men in front, men with bigger guns and plenty of ammunition—Biskup's men. The noise was earsplitting.

Deacon passed him a new weapon—James' own pistol—and immediately James felt better—more hopeful. Few things felt more comforting to James than the weight of his own gun in his hand.

There was a pause in the gunfire and James looked forward at the mass of bloody bodies. It had taken Biskup's men with their automatic weapons only a few seconds to win this round, but there would be another. James knew Eric would be sending every breathing man their way.

"Get these guys out!" James said, looking at the only two of Marianne's entourage still standing. "And she's with us!"

Deacon did a double take, his eyes widening as they set upon Marianne.

His eyes questioned James, but they both knew now was not the time.

"Where is she, Deacon? Where is Mak?" James asked. He had to know that she was okay.

"She's safe," Deacon said. "We've got her."

James said a silent prayer, grateful Marianne hadn't lied to James about that either.

James scooped Marianne up from underneath the small pile of dead bodies and held her arm as they ran toward the exit.

The break in gunfire didn't last long, but this time James didn't stop. He ran faster, his eyes on the door.

"Let him out!" James said where one of Biskup's men had the man carrying Makaela held hostage. "They're with us!"

The man looked like he was going to fall over in relief.

"Come on!" James yelled when the man appeared too terrified to move. "Cover her with your body," he instructed, without adding, *so that you'll get shot instead of her.*

The door opened and the fresh air hit James in the face, giving his body a renewed burst of energy. He tugged Marianne with him.

The first face he saw outside was Cami's. She stood like a solider with her weapon ready and a team behind her.

"This way!" she commanded and they ran after her.

But when gunshots began to hit the ground around them, they had no choice but to stop and fire back. James pushed Marianne behind him, shielding her. So far she'd delivered on everything she'd promised. And if she had the code, she was even more valuable.

James fired at the men on the balconies. He lost count of how many there were. And every time they knocked one down, another seemed to pop up. Eric was utilizing every resource he had.

But where is Eric himself?

James had no concept of time, he hadn't for days, but Marianne had said they'd only have four minutes. Where had Eric been when he'd found out?

Focus, James, focus.

It was getting harder to, though—his head was becoming increasingly light, and James wondered how much blood he'd lost. He still hadn't looked at his new bullet wound. It was a flesh wound, but he already knew it was deeper than the one above it.

The gunfire took a moment to breathe and the group moved

again. James had no idea where he was going, but he trusted his team.

"Exit 42," Cami called as James saw another group running toward them. Given that they weren't firing, James knew they were Biskup's guys.

James turned and ran with Deacon and Marianne by his side, but he kept his eyes up, looking at the building that loomed above them like something out of a horror movie.

And at the top, a single light was on and a silhouette stood at the window, watching.

The hairs on his spine stood up and an icy shiver ran through him.

27

MARIANNE

James' grip on her arm loosened and she looked to him, but his eyes were diverted. She followed his gaze to the tower, seeing what had captured his attention.

Marianne stumbled.

Sorin.

She knew her father and her husband would be on the ground, shutting down the estate. They would be doing everything they could to salvage the situation, because they knew what the consequences of her betrayal would be—they would be punished for her actions.

It was Sorin in the window, and Marianne could feel the power of his gaze even with the distance between them. And she thought James felt it, too, because he seemed to have to consciously tear his gaze away.

It was a momentary pause and then they were sprinting again, surrounded by men. Tens of men. Marianne wondered how she ever thought she could do it alone.

We should've had enough time, she thought. *What went wrong? And where is the car?*

There should've been two cars: one for her, James, and Makaela, and one for the people that had helped them escape.

She looked ahead now, keeping track of the man that had her daughter. Her beautiful, sleeping daughter, and Marianne felt no regret for sedating her now. Tonight's events were not something she wanted her daughter to have to witness.

James gripped loosened on her arm again, but this time it was due to the warm liquid pooling underneath his hand—liquid that was trickling over her forearm now. She wondered how James was even standing right now, but she didn't have the emotional room to care. He was her ticket out and they'd come this far.

We have to make it, she thought.

If not, her punishment was going to be as great as his, likely worse.

She focused on staying upright as she struggled to keep up with James. The morning sickness had been particularly bad today, sucking the energy from her, but her legs continued to move regardless. Adrenaline kept her going, along with fear. Fear was always a powerful motivator.

She couldn't see where they were headed, but when she heard the sound of idling vehicles, she ran faster. They were so close.

Please, God, Marianne prayed, *help us.*

She wondered if Christos was also praying to his own Gods.

Marianne looked to the security walls that encased the estate. Why was no one shooting at them? Marianne's eye darted along, she could see men standing on the wall, their weapons ready, but the triggers weren't being pulled.

They're not my father's men, Marianne realized with a rush of relief.

Marianne's lungs burned now and she wanted to stop running, to keel over and vomit. How much farther?

Bullets were still being fired in the distance and Marianne wondered who was shooting, and how many men and woman had died tonight.

They ran though a gate, reaching the outside of the estate. Vehicles were waiting—a lot of them.

Marianne was shuffled into the back of a van, along with the

Thomas brothers. She searched desperately for her daughter, but she couldn't see her.

"It's better if she's not with you," James said, resting his head back against the metal panel of the van.

"Where is she?" Marianne demanded.

The man she knew now as Deacon Thomas kneeled in front James, pulling his lips to the side as he looked at his wounds.

"Get the medic kit out," Deacon commanded and a flurry of activity happened behind them. "And scan her for a tracking device."

"Where is my daughter?" Marianne asked forcefully as two men pulled her up into a standing position, sweeping over her with two large, flat, rectangular devices with a small handle. When the black devices didn't make a sound, or appear to light up, she was told she could sit again.

Deacon turned to her, his gaze sharp. "Look, I don't know what happened tonight and I have no idea why you're here, but I'm not sure I like it. Your daughter is in another car, because if your husband saw James and yourself get into this car, he'll target it. It's safer for everyone involved if she's separated from you until we get far away from here. Now, please be quiet, because I need to stop his bleeding," Deacon said, and then looked over his shoulder.

One of the men passed him the kit and he began pulling out items.

"I can help you," Marianne said, even though she was tired to the bone.

"Just rest," Deacon said, without looking at her.

Marianne sat playing nervously with her fingers. There were no windows to see out of and as the van drove, turning at fast speeds, the nausea crept up to her throat.

What if our car is attacked? What if I don't get to my daughter? Who will take care of her?

Marianne felt a panic attack coming on, so she focused on Deacon, trying to draw her mind away from the dark reality of the night.

She watched him inject the anesthetic, dig out the bullet and stitch it up, all while swaying in the vehicle.

"Where are we at?" Deacon asked, to no one in particular.

Marianne figured he was using a communication device when he responded with, "Copy."

Deacon looked over his brother, exhaling a small sigh, then moved toward the front of the van. He looked side to side, up and down, and then said something to the driver.

He came back to kneel in front of James, but he looked to her. "When we're safe, and on the plane, you've got some explaining to do."

Marianne nodded. "I'll tell you everything...when my daughter is back in my arms."

He raised one eyebrow but said nothing. Nor did he look at her again until they reached their destination.

The van slowed and before it had even stopped the men were up and moving.

"Airport is secure, let's go!" Deacon said as three men moved in, helping to lift James' unconscious body.

Deacon held out the palm of his hand, keeping her from moving, and for a moment she feared he wasn't going to take her with them.

"Let's go," he finally said, taking her arm. She didn't think it was a thoughtful, helping gesture, but rather a move to make sure she did exactly what he wanted her to.

The engines were already purring, ready to take off.

Marianne pulled back. "I'm not getting on until my daughter's here."

"She's already on the plane," Deacon said.

When he stopped at the stairs, motioning for her to go first, she hesitated. If her daughter wasn't on, how would she get off with Deacon behind her?

Deacon swore, moving ahead of her, taking the stairs two at a time.

Marianne followed him, pausing at the entrance—until she saw Makaela.

Marianne rushed toward her daughter, taking her from the arms of the woman Marianne recognized from Christos' surveillance shots: Cami.

"Sit here," Cami said, her voice as reserved as Deacon's.

Marianne sat, holding her bundled daughter to her chest, ferociously holding back the tears that threatened to overwhelm her. She buried her face against the sweet, soft, skin of her daughter and rocked her back and forth.

She'd risked so much, and in the tunnel, when it seemed impossible that they were going to make it, she'd been filled with loathing regret.

In that moment she'd hated herself for the choice she'd made.

But now there was glimmer of hope for their future.

For all three of them.

28

DEACON THOMAS

She was huddled over her daughter, her clothes stained with blood. The red crown was crooked on her head and tangled in hair that had come loose and knotted.

What happened inside that house?

Deacon didn't like that she was with them, let alone the child, but he knew James' wouldn't have taken her without a reason to. She must've helped him, and perhaps James was planning to use her for more information.

Deacon really wished his brother was awake to explain this.

But he was also grateful James was alive. It had been a close call in the tunnel. Another thirty seconds and it would've been a very different story.

Deacon checked over the group's other injuries, patching up and stitching what he could. It was an hour before he took a seat opposite Marianne, her eyes glistening when she looked at him.

"Start from the beginning," he said, watching her carefully.

She took a deep breath and cleared her throat.

"From London, James was sedated and transferred to the compound in Romania," she said, and Deacon thought it was interesting she used the name James.

"And who sedated him?" Deacon asked.

She paused, and then answered. "I did, initially. And then Christos delivered the subsequent doses."

Their eyes met, and Deacon nodded for her to continue.

"The estate belongs to my father, Lucian. James was taken there because of the security measures it provided. I spent most of my childhood in that house, so I know it well. I began to formulate an escape plan. While the majority of the organization worships Christos, there is a percentage that despise him. Those people were ready to see his downfall, and were therefore willing to help me—even at their own peril."

"He is your husband, and from what I've seen, you have no problems with who he is and what he does," Deacon said.

She glared at him. "And what do you think it's like to be married to him? What choice do you think I had?"

Deacon heard the bitterness in her words.

"I did what I had to do to survive," Marianne said. "I do not agree with his practices, nor do I pray to his *gods*."

Her words were short, staccato, and Deacon, despite not wanting to, believed her.

She cast her eyes down at her daughter and her features softened. She looked back to him. "By helping James escape, I risked punishment at least equal to what they had planned for him. And they would've killed my child, right in front of my very eyes, as part of that punishment. It wasn't an easy choice."

"So why did you do it? You risked your child's life," Deacon said.

"I was born into that world. Children begin to learn about the Gods and the ritual practices when they are five years old. From there, they begin classes, but the horrific practices—such as sacrifices —are not learned about until they are teenagers. It's a very slow, but usually effective, form of brainwashing." She cleared her throat, and Deacon wondered how it was that she'd managed not to be brainwashed. Or maybe she had been, but had broken through it at some point.

"At nineteen I met Christos, and a few months later I was told he would be my husband. There was no choice, and I began to resent my father at that stage. It was not the life I wanted, but I was warned that if I disobeyed I would be punished. I already knew enough to know what such *punishments* entailed."

She seemed to recall memories of them, and then shook her head.

"The first three years of our marriage were unbearable. Eric's kindness didn't last long... I wanted to die, to kill myself. I seriously considered it, even began planning it, until I learned I was pregnant. At that point I knew I had to find a way out. I did not want that future for my daughter, and the older Kaela got, the more I knew she was like me and would hate her life in the organization."

Her eyes flickered to James.

"When I learned that it was him, and probably you," she said, looking back to Deacon, "that had found us at our house in Amman, my hope was that you'd find us again and kill Christos. That would've at least made it easier to escape the organization. When I overheard a conversation between Christos and my father, advising that 'Liam' had a clear shot but didn't take it, aiming for Christos' hand instead, I wondered why. What did Christos have that he needed?

"I'd been secretly collecting information about my husband for years and I knew all about the deal with Biskup. When Christos realized that Liam Smith and James Thomas were the same person, I realized that James needed the code—to secure Makaela's safety."

Interesting, and now Deacon knew why his brother wanted her. "Do you have the code?"

She looked him square in the eyes. "Yes."

If she was telling the truth, once they gave the code to Biskup, they could deliver a fatal shot to Eric. If they'd had that option from the beginning, Eric would've been dead a long time ago.

"What is the code for, Marianne?" Deacon asked.

"It's for a delivery system," she said in a quiet voice, looking around her, perhaps to see who was listening.

"Biskup commissioned Christos to design a unique trigger activation system for a nuclear system. Christos did that, but he never intended to use it for nuclear weapons... He intended to use it to spray airborne particles—droplet nuclei—over an entire country with one release. It was part of his and my father's master-plan for world domination."

Deacon lowered his voice. "Airborne particles contaminated with an infectious disease?"

Marianne nodded. "The vaccine has already been developed and Christos began mixing it with our alchemized blood about a year ago. Christos planned to vaccinate all members of the organization before he hit the first few countries on his list—the countries with the highest number of organization members. He wanted the world to watch on in horror as the disease seized the populations, leaving only the organization to survive. And then he would begin recruiting— showing the world that the Gods had protected them. He was conveniently going to leave out the fact that our blood had been treated with the vaccine and our survival was not a product of the *Gods* at all."

He's more insane than we realized, Deacon thought.

"Why partner with Biskup, then? Why not do it on his own?" Deacon asked.

"Biskup had technicians and other resources that the organization didn't. Anything Christos asked for, Biskup somehow managed to get."

Deacon sighed. Resources in the wrong hands.

"Going back to the code, how do you know it's the correct code for Biskup's system?" Deacon asked. "If James confirms your story when he wakes up, we're going to take you to Biskup and you're going to give him the code. If it's incorrect—you might find yourself wishing you'd stayed with Christos."

"I have the correct code. I know it, because Christos was foolish enough to write it down in a safe he thought only he knew about," Marianne said, raising one eyebrow.

James was right, Deacon thought with a smirking grin—Eric had met his perfect match.

29

MAK ASHWOOD

Mak grabbed her ringing phone from the couch seat beside her. It was Samuel.

"Hello," she answered, looking away from the screen for the first time in hours.

"Good news. They're on their way back to London. They'll touch down in a few hours. James is stable, but he has multiple wounds that need treatment."

He's alive. Mak closed her eyes in relief.

Samuel, likely misunderstanding her silence, continued. "Let's focus on the positive—he's alive and he'll make a fine recovery in time."

"Thank you, Samuel," she said.

"Mak...there's a few *unexpected* guests returning with them. And they're going to be taken to the townhouse until we can figure out what to do from there."

Mak's eyebrows creased together.

"Eric's wife, Marianne, and her daughter are with them," Samuel said, cautiously.

"*What?*"

"I know, I know, but it looks like our first impressions of her were incorrect," Samuel said.

Aiding Eric to hold captive and drug my sister was an incorrect assumption?

Mak opened her mouth to speak, but Samuel got in first. "Marianne has very useful information, information that is going to resolve your case, and then she's agreed to help us find Eric again so that we can end this once and for all."

"She injected my sister with *heroin*, Samuel," she said through clenched teeth.

"And she also helped James escape. Look, I'm not excusing what she did—at all—and none of us are particularly thrilled about having her with us. But, James promised her protection in trade for helping him escape, and until he's awake and can tell his side of the story, she's with us."

Mak blew out an exasperated breath.

"Okay," she said, lost for words. James had a lot of talking to do, on many fronts.

"One more thing you should know..." Samuel said. "Her daughter's name is Makaela."

Mak stilled—Samuel's words took a moment to settle in. *Eric named his daughter after me?* It was a sickening thought.

"It's disturbing on many levels," Samuel said.

Mak shouldn't have been surprised by anything Eric did anymore, but that had caught her by surprise. She couldn't even formulate a response to Samuel.

"Try and get some rest, Mak. It'll be a few hours before they land yet," Samuel said.

Samuel had been the only one she'd communicated with since Deacon and Cami had left and she was grateful he hadn't turned off the screens—because she knew he could've and there wouldn't have been anything she could've done about it.

"I will," Mak said, eventually, her mind still reeling. She pushed aside Samuel's new information. She didn't want to think about Eric anymore. She just wanted to see James. Every time his heart rate had spiked, she'd feared she would never see him again.

"Does it get any easier, Samuel? Knowing that they're going on a mission and might not come out alive?" Mak asked.

"No, it doesn't. Every day we spend together we grow closer, and so every time they risk their lives it gets harder. But I also know it's who they are. They fight for each other—and for the people they care about—and I love that about them," he said. "I'll message you when they land and are on their way."

"Thank you, Samuel," Mak said, meaning every word of it.

She hung up the phone and looked to Haruto, who looked as bored as anyone possibly could.

"They're on their way back," she said.

"Of course they are. I told you not to worry… James has more lives than a cat," he said, chuckling at his own joke.

Mak stood, taking her phone and her new pistol with it. "I'm going to have a shower and rest."

Haruto smirked, looking at her. "Still don't trust me?"

Mak scoffed. "No, I don't," she said.

Mak went to the bathroom, put her pistol on the vanity, and turned on the hot water. She undressed and stepped under it, let it run over her tense muscles.

James was out, and he was alive, and she wanted to cry with relief. But with his return came a reality that she didn't want to face but knew she had to. He was not the man she'd fallen in love with—not entirely. And she didn't trust him to tell her the truth about who he was. So where did that leave them?

Mak lathered the shampoo and massaged her scalp as she continued to search for a resolution that didn't exist. She conditioned her hair, washed her body, and when she was done she conceded that there wasn't a clear answer.

Eventually, she turned off the water and stepped out. She dressed, dried her hair, and then lay down on the bed with her pistol and phone beside her. But her eyes didn't close, they couldn't, and her stomach knotted itself into a tight ball.

Part of her didn't want to know the truth, it was easier not knowing, but never again would she turn away from the truth, no matter how much she wanted to. She'd made that promise after she'd found out about Eric's lies, and she would keep it now.

Mak continued to stare at the ceiling, her thoughts jumbled in her mind, until she received a message from Samuel.

En route. ETA forty-five minutes.

Mak went back to the lounge room where two more of the Tohmatsu boys were sprawled out on the couches, joking amongst themselves.

"Mak, we ordered a ton of pizzas—enough for everyone. They'll be here in a few minutes," Haruto said.

"Good idea, thanks," Mak said, though she was unsure if she'd be able to stomach much of it.

One part of the ordeal was over, but another was just beginning.

30

JAMES THOMAS

Cami had James' position in the front passenger seat, and Deacon drove. As they pulled into the townhouse a cold sweat broke out over James' skin. He so badly wanted to see Mak, to hold her, to kiss her, but he also didn't know what to expect. She knew the worst about him, and given all of the stress she'd endured in the past week, James didn't know how she was going to handle it.

I should've told her about Paris, James thought again, shaking his head. That was the worst possible way for her to find out.

Deacon turned off the ignition and their eyes met in the rear-view mirror.

On the jet, James had asked Deacon if Mak would speak to him upon their return. He simply said, "She'll speak to you." James hadn't needed him to say anything more.

He took a moment to brace himself, and then he slowly slid across the backseat. His vision blurred with the movement, but Deacon provided a steady support as he helped James to his feet.

They took the stairs slowly and James could hear the television playing. He could also smell pizza.

Marianne, carrying little Makaela—whom they'd all agreed on the plane would best be called "Kaela" from now on to avoid any confusion—came in behind them, backed up by the rest of the security teams.

Haruto was the first person James saw. Haruto grinned, and said, "Thomas, brother. Looking good!"

James gave a faint smile. "Good to see you, too," he said, lifting his eyes.

He found her immediately, standing across the room. Their eyes locked and James, struggling to keep upright, felt his composure cracking. Her chest tightened as she looked him over, her lips pressing together. She moved toward him.

"All right," Deacon said. "The party is over. James, you're going to bed."

James was grateful for the exit—he wanted to get away from everyone and be alone with Mak.

Marianne stood behind them with a now awake Kaela.

James heard Cami say to her, "You can use the bedroom and bathroom on the third floor, I'll show you."

James and Deacon waited for them to pass, knowing they would move much faster. And then Deacon helped James to hobble up one flight of stairs.

James sat on the bed as Mak walked into the room.

"Just give me a few minutes to set everything up," Deacon said, helping James to sit back against the pillows.

Deacon then disappeared out of the room and James looked to Mak once more. Their eyes met again, that same electric connection there—it always had been right from the start.

Deacon returned and James let out the breath he'd been holding.

His brother set up an IV system, administered some drugs, and then cleaned the wounds again. James saw Mak watching Deacon, doing her own assessment of the wounds. James didn't want to hide them from her—he didn't want to hide anything anymore. Her pupils dilated when she saw his chest.

When Deacon finished applying the bandages he excused himself, closing the door behind him.

Slowly, she walked toward him and sat on the edge of the bed.

Her eyes looked him over again. He guessed that there had been many times over the past few days that she didn't think she'd get this moment. He'd had many of the same thoughts.

Chemistry and tension crackled between them in even amounts.

"I don't know where to start," James said.

"No, neither do I." Her voice was soft, but not weak—and not angry, either.

He looked at the bandages on her neck, fighting the urge to remove them and inspect the wounds himself to make sure they were healing. He would get Deacon to do that later. Right now he had to explain himself.

"Some of the things Eric said were true, and some were exaggerated. Others were complete lies," James said, wanting to start by clearing up the simple things first, easing into the conversation, trying to get the words stuck in his throat to flow.

"My name is Joshua Hart—or at least that's the name the first orphanage gave me. I don't know my birth name—the one my parents gave me. None of that was a lie. And I was an agent for the CIA," James said. "That was also correct, but I didn't decide to leave on my own—I was forced to, as such. I was selected to lead a mission with a team of agents, and a team of Rangers. I selected the teams, ultimately choosing Deacon's team, although we'd never worked together. That's how we met."

Mak nodded, and he continued. "That mission was a bloodbath. To this day, both of us believe that we were set up. They wanted certain people eliminated, me in particular, because I'd uncovered something they didn't want me to know. So, they created a false mission and sent us in to die. They used innocent Rangers and agents as collateral so that it wouldn't look like a set up. Deacon and I were the only two people that walked out alive.

"From there we went into hiding and set about discovering who had set us up. Did we make them pay?" James paused. "Yes," he said, meeting her gaze. "We did. Me more so than Deacon." James couldn't pretend he was something he wasn't.

James blew out a breath. "The video he showed you...that boy, the one that looked so young, was in fact a few months shy of eighteen. But he was also the head recruiter of boy soldiers for a criminal organization. The video was taken from CIA footage—I was interrogating him for hostage information."

Mak tilted her head back slightly and James knew she was trying to process it.

"What about the man's face you apparently took off in New York?" she said with hard eyes. "Did you do that and then come to me afterward?"

He sighed—that's exactly what he'd done. "I did it because I wanted to scare Eric. I didn't know what his plans for you were and I wanted him to think twice before doing anything that would put you in danger. I did kill him before I took off his face, so it wasn't a form of torture...if that makes it any better."

"Oh, God," he heard her whisper as she drew in a tight breath, hiding her face behind her hands. "Keep going," she said, finally looking back to him.

"That man was one of Eric's spotters, Mak. What Eric didn't tell you was that he's in the business of preying on young, innocent woman. He abducts them, hooks them on heroin and then sells them. Human trafficking. Don't feel sorry for the man that died that night—the world is a better place without him."

James looked deep into her sea-blue eyes. "I do not kill innocent people, Mak. I don't go looking for trouble. But, if it comes my way, or the people I love are threatened, then I do what needs to be done. You've always known that."

She gave a tight small nod, and then she cut to the chase. "Do you want to tell me about Paris?"

James closed his eyes, unable to look at her.

"James," she said gently.

He felt like a plastic bag had been pulled over his head once more.

"I'm sorry, Mak, you should never have found out that way," he said finally. "It's not entirely how Eric played it out."

James exhaled a shuddered breath. "I didn't know...I didn't know she was pregnant. The phone call Eric mentioned did happen, but she never told me she was pregnant—I only found out...after." James swallowed. "And she wasn't a girlfriend. I've never lied to you about that—the 'no girlfriends' rule. She was an acquaintance, someone I knew from the agency. She knew who I was, she didn't ask questions, and I thought she was a safe way of satisfying certain...needs. With her I didn't have to worry about either of us getting attached."

He took another deep breath. "The phone call came a week before it all happened. She called and told me that she needed to talk to me about something. I was already suspicious that she was informing on me by that point and Samuel was digging for proof, trying to find some evidence. He found it. I arrived a day earlier than expected. She never got the chance to tell me."

Mak was the one who looked away now.

"I did what I did to her because informing on me threatens my life, and the lives of Deacon, Cami, and Samuel. I used her to set an example—so that anyone would think twice about striking a deal to inform on me in the future. I left no evidence behind—or at least I didn't think I had—but I knew that people would come to the conclusion that I was the one who had killed her.

"After, I was searching through her house, looking for information. I found an ultrasound..." His voice trembled and he looked away.

Tell her, James. You need to tell her.

"I tried to save her, but it was too late. I took a sample of amniotic fluid to a laboratory...the results came back positive. The baby was mine."

His body trembled as he looked at her.

"That's why you're so cautious," she said, a tear running down her cheek. "Why didn't you tell me?"

"I couldn't," James said, hot tears stinging his own eyes.

"You could've, and you should've. What security risk did it present? Why didn't you tell me?"

"Because I was too *ashamed*!" James barked, his voice breaking.

She recoiled, her eyes wide. He didn't know what answer she'd been expecting, but judging by her reaction, he didn't think it was that.

He spoke more softly again. "I didn't know if you could love me if you knew, and I was terrified of losing you. I *am* terrified of losing you."

"You were never going to tell me, were you?" she said with a thick voice.

He knew what answer she wanted to hear, but she already knew the truth.

"No," James said quietly. "I wasn't." He looked down at his hands.

He'd killed his child, someone he should've loved and protected, and so maybe this was his punishment—to lose the woman he loved.

She was silent for a long time.

"What happened to them? What did you do with her body?" she asked quietly.

It kept getting worse.

"I buried them...separately," James said.

She looked thoughtful, and then it looked as if she might vomit.

"I don't know why," James continued. "I wanted to bury him—it was a boy—in his own grave. Somewhere nice, somewhere peaceful. Somewhere no one would ever find him... Maybe I should've buried him with his mother, I don't know..." James wiped away the tear that fell from his eyes. He realized it was the first time he'd ever shed a tear over the incident, and it was the first time he'd had to force himself to deal with it—to talk about it aloud.

"So many times I've thought about what I did and wished I could go back in time. I would never have hurt her if I'd known, and I think that's why she did it. She had an intrauterine device, or at least she had one and had it removed at some point. I was careful regardless, but one night I didn't have protection and so I took the risk. One time is all it takes... I believe she knew I was going to find out that she'd been informing on me, but thought that if she was pregnant with my child, I wouldn't hurt her. I'll never know for sure, but I think that was her motive."

James wiped his wet cheek, looking away from her. She surprised him when she took his hand.

"You should've told me. And I think there's probably more that you should still tell me," she said, her own cheeks wet.

"That's the worst of it, I promise," James said. "There is no secret worse than that."

She gave him a sad smile. "I can't imagine one."

He took her other hand, threading his fingers through, stalling.

"Are you always going to tell me what you want me to know and nothing more?" She eyeballed him and although he didn't like the question, he liked that she'd used the word "always"—there was hope for them yet.

"No, Mak. I don't repeat my mistakes. I know I should've told you about Paris. I just... How do you tell the person you love that you did something like that?"

"I don't know," she admitted, silent for a moment. "You saved my sister. And you saved my life. I can't love you enough for doing what you've done for me—right from the beginning. I'm indebted to you in so many ways, and I don't just mean financially, although that's another story. But I don't know how to move forward, either. It's too much... it's too—"

"I know it's a lot," James said, cutting off her rambling, which he knew was stress-related. "Your sister was kidnapped, Tom was murdered in front of you, and Eric tortured you emotionally and physically. I know the toll that takes on someone, and it's going to take you some time to process everything. And that's okay—more than okay."

He wiped his thumb over her wet cheek.

James continued. "My first thought when I woke up and realized what had happened was of you. My only thoughts from there were how to get out so that I could find you and make sure you were okay. You never left my mind."

He looked at the dark circles under her eyes, guessing that she hadn't slept more than a few hours since this ordeal had started.

"I didn't know if I'd ever see you again," Mak said with a gravelly voice. "And yet here you are, and I want to hold you, and care for you, and tell you everything is fine between us, but I can't."

A tear fell from her chin and James cupped her cheek, looking deep into her eyes. "I know it's not okay—I didn't expect it to be," he said softly.

31

MAK ASHWOOD

It was a gutting stab of fate that in these past few minutes she felt closer to the man she loved than she ever had—and yet there was an invisible divide between them, one that held her back from falling into his arms and staying there.

His chest rose and fell and his skin burned against hers. It was hard to see this side of him, to see him hurting and vulnerable.

"I'm sorry, Mak," James said, clearing his throat. "I'm sorry I didn't tell you, and I'm sorry that you found out the way you did. That should never have happened."

He brushed his thumb over her cheek, wiping away her tears once more. Tears she desperately wished would stop flowing.

For several minutes neither of them moved.

"What do we do now?" Mak finally asked.

The security situation wasn't over—even if Marianne had the code. Eric was still on the loose, and Mak didn't need to be told that he would be furious, humiliated, and very dangerous right now. More dangerous than he'd ever been.

James took a deep breath. "Biskup is on his way to London, and once he arrives we'll take Marianne to meet him so that she can give him the code. Provided that all goes well, Biskup will no longer be a threat to you."

He gave her a small smile.

"But," James continued, "we still need to deal with Eric and the organization. That's not over yet, but it will be soon... Take some time, Mak, as much as you need. You need to sleep, you need to eat, and you need to work through everything in your mind before we have a chance at moving forward. I know you need that."

His eyes were clear again, his voice calm once more. She wished she could be so composed.

She looked down at their hands—somehow their fingers had interlaced, wrapping over each other. Mak wondered at what point of their conversation that had happened, and if either of them had even realized it was happening. Their relationship had always been like that—magnetic—emotionally and physically.

She nodded and he cupped one hand around her cheek, pressing his lips against hers.

His kiss stole the oxygen from her lungs and made her head spin.

And then he stopped, pulling back.

He gave her a smile that didn't reach his eyes—eyes that now naturally looked lighter, more open. It was like they changed with his vulnerability.

"I love you, Mak," he whispered.

Mak kissed his forehead, letting her lips linger. "I love you, too," she said, before standing. "Do you need anything?"

He shook his head. "No, it's okay. I just need to sleep and rest now."

She resisted every urge to crawl into bed beside him.

"Get some sleep," she said softly before she moved toward the door, closing it behind her. She darted for the bedroom she'd been given and almost ran straight into Marianne.

"Sorry, excuse me," Mak mumbled as she hid her face, not stopping. But it was too late—she knew Marianne had seen her red-rimmed eyes.

And Marianne was the last person Mak wanted to see right now.

32

LUCIAN

The candlelight flickered, casting shadows across the room. Sorin sat at the window, his eyes diverted toward the red streaks that lit up the sky like fire. Lucian had seen the spectacular sunrise many times before, the breathtaking array of red that gave view to the rolling hills and Norway spruce pines in the distance. However, Lucian didn't think for a second that Sorin was admiring the sunrise. Nor was he distracted by it.

"I saw him," Sorin finally said. "I stood at this very window, watching your men fail to capture him. And he saw me—he looked straight up to the window. As did your Marianne."

Sorin turned, facing Lucian. There was fire behind his eyes.

"Marianne betrayed us all," Lucian said, humiliation and anger seeping into his soul. His daughter had committed the gravest of sins. She had betrayed her husband, her family, and her Gods.

"And you shall pay the price for her sins, Lucian. As will her husband." Sorin raised one eyebrow. "I ordered for him to be locked up. I don't trust him."

"I'm aware. He wasn't involved in this, Sorin. I promise you that Christos didn't know—"

"Promise me? You didn't know about Marianne's plans, so how

can you promise me he didn't know or isn't involved somehow? You can't. Be very careful of what you say, Lucian."

Lucian nodded, giving Sorin a moment to settle his temper. He then put his hand to his chest, bowing. "We plead for leniency, Sorin. I have served you and the Gods for all my life. I have never failed you before. Let Christos out of the cell and I will work with him—I won't let him out of my sight. We will find Marianne and bring her back to us to face her punishment. We will not fail you."

Sorin stood, viciously swinging a back hand into the tall candelabra, sending it hurtling across the room, the metal clanging as it landed on the tiled floor. The candles landed on the cold surface and fizzled out.

Lucian didn't jump, he didn't falter. He understood Sorin's rage. Lucian's own blood had been simmering since he'd learned of the news.

"You *failed* me last night!" Sorin roared. "And you humiliated me! The service, which should've been broadcast to our entire world, was *cancelled*. How do you think that looks to our people?"

"How many years have I been by your side, Sorin? I understand the consequences, but I also understand how to right the wrongs," Lucian said, his voice strong and confident.

With a voice that sliced the air, Sorin asked, "And how will you do that?"

"When a family member betrays the organization, as you know, we punish them—according to the Gods—by sacrificing their family. They must watch, and then they must die. But perhaps we should ask the Gods for a new punishment, as clearly the current one was not enough to dissuade Marianne."

Sorin's eyes narrowed and Lucian knew he had his attention. He was willing to hear him out, as self-serving as his argument was.

"What do you propose?" Sorin asked.

"Is it greater punishment to watch the sacrifice of your family, or to perform the sacrifice yourself, and then have eternity to have to live with what you've done?"

Sorin tilted his head. "Do you truly believe that you are capable of killing Marianne?"

Lucian didn't hesitate. "Yes. And Christos is capable of the same."

"And what about the child? Makaela shares the same blood." Sorin's eyes twinkled.

"She will be sacrificed as well," Lucian said. "We will do whatever is required of us." Lucian loved the little girl...but he loved the Gods more. Lucian didn't know if Christos could do it.

Lucian would need to make sure he did.

Sorin tapped two fingers on his chin, thoughtfully. And then he sat, much more gracefully than he'd stood, on the window ledge once more. "I'm prepared to ask the Gods for the punishment system you suggest...but there is one problem, isn't there?"

"Yes," Lucian said, clasping his hands in front of him. "We do not know where they are, but we will find them."

"And how will you do that?"

"By using the one piece of bait we haven't thrown at Liam: his family. He must be intrigued, don't you think, to know why we've been hunting him? To know why the Gods want to punish him?"

Lucian joined Sorin at the window.

"Liam Smith is a natural born killer, but there's a softer side to him as well. He's loyal to his core, and although he doesn't know his family, for how long do you think he can watch them suffer and not try to help them? He'll come for them, but this time he won't escape. And without Liam Smith to protect Marianne, we'll find her and her daughter. This way, everyone wins." The corner of Lucian's lips turned up. "Christos and I will perform the sacrifice, Sorin. It will be the most powerful message we can send," Lucian said.

Sorin's eyes locked on Lucian's. Hypnotic power swirled within them.

"I will consult with the Gods. Leave it with me," Sorin said, exhaling, dismissing him.

It was a start.

Lucian bowed and backed away, retreating from the room.

It was time to visit his son-in-law.

33

ERIC

Eric ran his fingers through his hair, tugging at the ends.

I'm locked in a fucking cell! Who ordered this?

He'd been in the security room, talking to the new surveillance expert after he'd beheaded the one who had enabled his wife to betray him, when a team of men had come in. They'd cuffed him and handled him like a sacrifice.

I will not be sacrificed, Eric thought viciously. *I will get out of here and I will find a way to fix this!*

A door opened and Lucian entered.

Eric stood, bowing his head.

"I'm sorry you're in here... Sorin ordered it, Christos, but I have another meeting with him in a few hours. I'll get you out. In the meantime, I brought you these," Lucian said, passing a box through the food slot.

It was a syringe and two vials. A gift from the Gods.

"Thank you, Lucian," Eric said, closing the lid on the box. It took everything he had not to load one now and inject. But he didn't. He needed to show composure, to show he could think straight—that he could formulate a plan that would save them both.

"So you met with Sorin this morning...how was he?" Eric asked the question, but he had a fairly good idea of exactly how Sorin was feeling.

Lucian shook his head gently. "Furious," he said, sitting in the chair Eric had seen Marianne sitting in when Liam was in the cell. He'd trusted his wife—he'd never seen her betrayal coming.

"Sorin's plan is to sacrifice us. However, I'm working on an alternate plan to rectify that. I'm going to get you out of this cell, Christos. And then we'll do this together, because both of our lives are at stake."

"Thank you, Lucian. I didn't see it," Eric admitted. "I didn't see a single sign that she would do this. I can't understand why she would've. Everything was perfect—the service would've secured our future within the organization." He bared his teeth, a sudden ferocity overtaking him. "She took that away, and she took my daughter with her."

Lucian crossed his legs, pulling his lips to the side. "Christos, even if I manage to strike a deal with Sorin for our lives, Marianne's will not be saved. She will be sacrificed. And your daughter—"

"My daughter is innocent!" Eric said loudly, thinking of her cherubic cheeks and sparkling eyes.

"But she isn't, is she? Not in our world. I know that you love her, as do I, but her mother's betrayal unfortunately seals her fate, just as Liam Smith's was sealed."

Eric couldn't speak, he couldn't agree, even though he knew Lucian was right. The Gods would ask for Makaela to be sacrificed regardless of any plan they concocted.

"Let's focus on finding Marianne first," Lucian continued, "and then perhaps we can try and plead for Makaela."

Christos didn't need to search Lucian's eyes, he'd heard it in the man's voice—there was no hope for his daughter, and he knew it.

"We will have to do something spectacular, Christos, to pull this off. The Gods have only once forgiven a member whose family has betrayed them. But we are unique, we hold positions of high power, and we have served the Gods well. There is a chance, however small, that we can redeem our souls."

"What are you suggesting?" Eric said, wrapping his fingers around the bars.

"I do not know yet—I haven't had long enough to think about it. I'm trying to placate Sorin for the moment and buy us some time. While you are, unfortunately, stuck in here—think about it," he said, standing. "I'll come back this evening. We'll brainstorm together then."

"Lucian," Eric said, looking into the steel-gray eyes of the man that should have been his father. "Thank you."

Lucian gave a small nod and then exited.

The door slammed shut, the bolt locked, and Eric sank back onto the bed.

The box lay beside him and he opened it, sticking the needle into the vial and drawing a dose. He did his best thinking when he was connected to the Gods.

Use the power of the Gods—they will guide you. That's what Eric had always been taught.

He pushed the needle into his vein, and tilted his head back in relief as he pushed the plunger with his thumb. He felt the energy immediately.

With his face toward the Gods, he pleaded for mercy, and for a chance at redemption.

And then he got to work. He walked the length of the cell and back again, thinking, strategizing. Strategizing how he would take vengeance on his wife, and on the man that had caused him so much humiliation: Liam Smith.

Back and forth Eric went, never stopping. When Lucian came back, he would have a plan. Eric would save them, they'd be redeemed, and then he'd earn back his position to become an Elder.

Crossing me was the biggest mistake of your life, Marianne.

34

JAMES THOMAS

James opened his eyes, startled. He looked around him, settling back on the pillow, when he realized he was in the townhouse. He'd woken up in too many unfamiliar places lately.

It didn't take his thoughts long to settle where they always did: on Mak.

His body longed for her—craved her. She was so close, in this building, possibly in the bedroom next door, and yet she was so far away. All he wanted was to have her tucked up against him, her touch soothing his soul.

James closed his eyes again, wanting to escape to the realms of sleep once more—sleep that had only been possible due the sedatives Deacon had given him. His brother had come in not long after Mak had left. He'd taken one look at James' face and had known things hadn't been fully smoothed over. There had been no smugness on Deacon's face, no pleasure he took in seeing a relationship he'd never thought was a good idea, being put on hold. Instead, when James had told him he wanted to sleep, he'd knocked him out for... almost eight hours, James realized, rolling his head to look at the clock.

James sighed. His chest ached—an ache that had nothing to do with Eric's carvings.

Remembering the pain Eric had inflicted upon him reinvigorated James. *I'm coming back for you, Eric.*

That had to be James' focus now and the sooner James came back for him the better. And the sooner they gave Biskup the code the better, as well, because that meant he didn't have to get Eric alive.

James *wanted* him alive, he wanted to punish him, to make him suffer. But if James could only get a fatal shot, he would still be satisfied.

Get up, James told himself, and he pushed his hands against the mattress, slowly swinging his feet onto the floor. The walls tilted, but quickly returned to normal.

He knew he was in no shape to be going anywhere tonight, but he was hoping that the meeting with Biskup would be a celebration, not a battle.

God I hope you have the correct code, Marianne.

If she didn't, James didn't know what was going to happen.

He found a fresh set of clothes on the chair in the corner. His arms throbbed violently as he slid the T-shirt over his head but somehow he managed to dress himself. He checked his bandages, noting his wounds were weeping. Deacon would need to change the dressings before they left.

James paused at the door, listening to the voices coming from the floor below them. He couldn't hear Mak's voice.

James took a calming breath and then walked out, using the walls for support as he descended the stairs.

The Tohmatsu boys were still sprawled out over the lounges. James knew they must be getting cabin fever but they didn't show it. Instead, they were making inappropriate jokes and entertaining the rest of the house. There were too many people in the townhouse and James wondered where they were all going to sleep tonight.

James didn't even need to look for Mak—their eyes found each other. James gave her a small smile.

"Sleeping beauty is awake," Haruto said, giving him a smart-assed grin.

"Yeah, yeah," James said, grateful for the distraction. "Can you get your feet off my couch?"

Haruto chuckled, swinging his legs down. "Here, sit," he said, patting the now free couch cushion. "Want some food? I'll get you something."

"I'll get it," Deacon called from the kitchen.

James lowered himself onto the cushion, concealing how much pain he was in.

Deacon came to kneel in front of him. He passed him a plate of food and a bottle of juice. He lifted James' sleeve, assessing the wounds. James knew he didn't like the amount of weeping he saw.

"Where's Biskup at?" James asked, spooning a forkful of pasta into his mouth.

"He's here. He'll meet us when we're ready," Deacon said. "When you're ready."

James wasn't ready physically, but he was ready emotionally.

"Organize the meeting for ten o'clock," James said. That would give him enough time to eat, for Deacon to re-dress his wounds, and for them to get to the building. They planned to use the same one they'd used for their initial meeting.

Deacon looked like he might argue, but he didn't. "I'll let Marianne know."

James looked over the guests. "Where is she?"

"Bathing Kaela. Speaking of... Mak," Deacon said, looking at her. She looked up.

"We've got a job for you. Someone needs to look after Kaela tonight," Deacon said.

"Me?" She looked genuinely surprised.

Deacon shrugged. "Do you think Haruto would do a better job?"

The Tohmatsu boys chuckled and James even managed a grin.

"Uh, okay," Mak said slowly.

Cami sat beside Mak, smiling. "You have five siblings. Surely you know how to entertain a kid for a few hours."

"It's been a while, Cami," Mak said bitingly.

"You'll be fine. We bought her some toys and coloring books today, she can play with those," Cami said.

James couldn't believe how drastically things had changed in the past twelve months. They'd gone from a tight circle of four, rarely letting anyone into their world. Now James had a girlfriend—hopefully still had a girlfriend—they had the Tohmatsu boys hanging out with them, and in addition they had another woman and a child with them for the immediate future.

James looked to Deacon, almost positive he was thinking the same thing. He made a face that almost made James laugh.

And the reality of their situation was sealed when a giggling voice came bounding down the staircase and into the lounge room. She ran straight toward Deacon, who was still kneeling by the couch.

"Hello," she said, smiling.

James watched the interaction, amused.

"Hello, Kaela," Deacon said and James was glad she was speaking to his brother and not him. He would've had no idea what to do.

"Are you hungry?" Deacon asked.

"Yes," she said, but then Marianne spoke from behind her.

"Thank you, but she's not—she's already had dinner."

Marianne gave her daughter a warning look, and Kaela smiled toothily back at her.

She's going to be a handful, James thought.

"Ten thirty," Deacon said to Marianne.

She gave the slightest of nods. "Is..." Marianne looked toward Mak, and then back to Deacon.

James saw Mak watching and he figured she hadn't been downstairs long either. He wondered what she'd done all day.

"Thank you," she said to Mak, who nodded in response. Marianne looked back to her daughter. "Kaela, this lady is going to look after you tonight while I go to a meeting."

James wondered if Marianne hadn't used Mak's name on purpose. It was an awkward situation.

"You?" Kaela asked, looking at Mak.

Mak have her a big smile and nodded. "Yes, me."

Kaela ran around the couch before Marianne could grab her. She put her hands on Mak's knees. "Hi, my name's Makaela."

"It's nice to meet you, Makaela. My name's Mak."

James and Deacon looked at each other and then looked away quickly.

James once again wondered what Marianne had thought when Eric had told her he wanted to name their daughter Makaela. He wondered if she'd had a say in it. *Surely not,* James thought.

"Kaela, please let Mak eat her dinner. Come and sit with me," Marianne said, holding out her hand.

James saw Mak exhale a long breath.

Deacon dimmed the car lights and then looked to James, and then to Marianne.

James looked over his shoulder. If Marianne was nervous, she wasn't showing it.

"Let's do it," James said.

The front door of the house was unlocked—Biskup had once again been gracious enough to leave their house unlocked for them.

"Evening," James called out.

As with their last meeting, Biskup had taken comfort in the upstairs lounge room. That meant James had to take the stairs. He was panting by the time he was half-way up. Even Marianne cast him a worried look.

James kept going but took a moment to get his breath back when they reached the top. Biskup would've assumed he'd been injured after being taken and held hostage, but James preferred Biskup not to know quite how bad the injuries were—just in case.

James led the way in, acting surprised when he saw Maksym sitting on one of the couches even though Samuel had already warned them.

"Biskup. Maksym...good to see you again," James said, taking a seat opposite them.

Maksym grinned. "And you. Close call, I hear."

James shrugged. "Part of the business. This," James said, holding his hand out, "is Marianne. Eric's wife."

Maksym winked at her and James saw a flash of recognition in her eyes. She likely remembered him from the worship ceremony.

Marianne nodded hello and sat in the single armchair beside James.

Biskup's eyes landed on her like she was prey. "This new development came as a total surprise. I wonder what he did to you to make you join our team."

James raised his eyebrow at *team*. He thought of them as a means to an end.

Marianne wore her frosty composure. "You know him, and therefore I'm sure you can imagine."

"So," James interrupted, wanting this over with as quickly as possible. "As it turns out, there is someone else with access to the code."

"And if she gives you that code," Deacon said. "You no longer need Makaela Ashwood. And you'll stop pursuing her. Are we on the same page?"

"We're writing with the same ink," Biskup said, smiling, wiggling his eyebrows.

Biskup then nodded to Maksym, who leaned over, producing a gold metal box. He opened the lid, revealing a laptop.

James was aware they were giving Biskup a code for a potentially lethal device, one that could cause mass fatalities. Maksym's fingers fluttered over the keyboard and then he turned it toward Marianne.

"Before we do this," James said, "tell me the purpose of this nuclear system."

Biskup tapped his fingers on his knee, one after the other. "For safekeeping," he said, smugly. "I don't intend to actually use it—not when it would damage my own land and interests—however, it's serves as a very useful threat, don't you think?"

The answer gave James some peace. He nodded to Marianne.

The room seemed to collectively hold their breath.

"The code is a sequence," she said. "It has six parts."

She typed on the keyboard and then sat back, watching the screen.

She typed the next sequence. And then the next. No one spoke—you could've heard a pin drop in the room.

James prayed again that she knew the correct code.

She typed the last sequence and closed her eyes. James wondered if she was praying to her god.

The computer chimed and she opened her eyes. When her lips spread into a thin, arrogant smile, James knew she'd unlocked it. She turned the computer back to Biskup.

"Well, well, well..." Biskup basically licked his lips. He looked between the brothers. "I didn't actually think you could pull this off, but I figured I didn't have anything to lose by making the deal. Admittedly, I didn't see it turning out this way." His eyes stole to Marianne. "Nonetheless, the end goal was achieved. But..." he said.

James had never liked the word *but*.

"But," Biskup continued, "I still want him. Now you've put a thirst for his blood in my mouth I'm not satisfied."

"I can taste his blood, too, and I'm not satisfied either. Rest assured, I'm going back in for him," James said.

Maksym nodded, and James could see the hunger in his eyes, too. "How many of our men do you want?"

"All of them," Deacon said.

"When do you want them?" Biskup asked.

James responded. "Tomorrow. Get them on a plane tonight. How many are you sending?"

"Another eighty at least," Biskup said.

How many men did Biskup have at his disposal? That was an impressive number, particularly given the number they'd lost since they'd joined forces and the additional teams that were already in London.

"Plus me," Maksym said. "And don't bother arguing about my state of health. It can't be any worse than yours. You look like shit."

Biskup chuckled. "Apologies. He has no tact."

That's not his worst quality, James thought.

"We'll be devising strategies over the next week or so, with Marianne's inside knowledge of the organization. We'll make a plan from there. Is there a deadline on this deal?" Deacon asked, getting back to business. He obviously wanted to get out of here as soon as possible. James was sure they all did.

"Two weeks," Biskup said cunningly. "You boys seem to work well under pressure."

James stood. "We'll secure a new training facility big enough to accommodate the group. We'll send you the details, and we'll see your boys tomorrow."

35

MAK ASHWOOD

The sound of the television was obscured by Haruto's snoring, but Mak didn't care—she wasn't watching it anyway. She looked to her wrist again. They'd been gone three hours and counting.

Mak looked down at the little girl asleep in her lap. Her eyelids didn't twitch, her dreams weren't haunted by nightmares. She slept peacefully. And she probably should've been in her bed, but Mak hadn't wanted to move her and risk waking her. It had taken a long time for her little mouth to quiet down.

Mak didn't hear the car come in, and she didn't realize they were home until Marianne walked in, pausing when she saw Mak and her daughter.

"I'm sorry. She fell asleep like this and I didn't want to wake her," Mak said, trying to guess what Marianne was thinking.

Marianne shook her head. "It's fine. Thank you, Mak," she said, putting her hands underneath her daughter, lifting her. Makaela grumbled and then wrapped her arms around her mother's neck.

Marianne looked over the Tohmatsu boys, perhaps to see if they were sleeping, and then spoke quietly. "For what it's worth, Mak. I'm sorry for what we did to your sister—for what I did. And I'm sorry for what Eric's done to you."

Mak's opinion of Marianne was another a tug-of-war in her mind. She still wasn't okay with what she'd done to Maya, but Mak knew sometimes people did what they had to in order to survive. She thought Marianne was one of them. "I know what you did for James. So, thank you."

Marianne looked as if she might say something more, but then didn't.

"Good night," she said, passing Deacon as he walked in.

He sat on the edge of the coffee table, facing Mak.

"How did it go?" Mak thought the answer was likely to be good since Marianne was back in one piece.

"Biskup has the code. He's no longer a threat to you. That part is resolved," he said.

Mak felt a small surge of relief. "Thank you," she said. Like his brother, she could never thank him enough.

"You know that this isn't over until Eric is captured or killed, whatever comes first, and until the organization is dismantled. Biskup is sending in additional recruits and we're going to stay in London and train them."

Deacon sighed. "Eric was mad before, furious, and he's going to be even more so now. We want you to go to Tokyo with the Tohmatsu boys. They'll take care of you until we finish this."

"No," Mak said with a firm shake of her head.

Deacon looked at her, his eyes serious. "We don't know how long this could go on for. You won't be able to leave this townhouse—you won't even be able to go out to the balcony for fresh air. We're trying to do what's best for you."

"I'll decide what's best for me," Mak said.

"You'll have to live with Marianne," Deacon said, as if that might sway her decision.

It wasn't an appealing option, but Mak knew that if she went to Tokyo she'd be shut out of this case again. If she lived with Marianne, she'd have a much better idea of what was going on. "I'll deal with it," Mak said.

"Okay," Deacon said reluctantly. His expression softened. "Do you want something to help you sleep tonight?"

Mak knew that question had a double meaning. No, she was not really okay. But, no, she did not want to drug herself to sleep. "I'm fine, but thank you."

Mak hadn't seen James since they'd returned. Had he gone straight back to bed?

"How is he?" she asked.

Deacon gave her what seemed to be an honest answer. "Managing. Right now, what James needs to focus on, though, is healing. He should be taking some considerable time off, but he's not going to do that, and I can't force him to. But we can't make another move until he's at least healthy enough to stand on his feet and run."

Deacon's eyes locked on hers. "We're going back in one last time, Mak. This time we'll get it right. And this time we'll finish it."

Desperation spread through her chest like a fog. She wanted this over before more people died. Before something even worse happened to James.

"Go to bed, Mak. Get some sleep. In situations like this, anything is possible, so the best thing you can do is rest and eat while you can. You never know when you might need your energy."

Mak nodded. She would rest, but she doubted sleep would come. Every time she closed her eyes, images haunted her: Maya's cut chest, Tom's lifeless eyes, James gunning down his pregnant girlfriend, Eric's taunting smile. For as long as she'd lain in bed today, staring at the ceiling, sleep had evaded her. It was even harder knowing James was in the room next to her.

36

JAMES THOMAS

James opened his eyes and rolled onto his side. A pair of eyes looked back at him and James recoiled in response.

Deacon laughed. "Where did you think I was sleeping? We're a bit short on beds, if you hadn't already worked that out."

It took a moment for James to recover from the shock. It wasn't the first time they'd had to share a bed, though. In fact, during their very early days in hiding, they'd stayed at a bunch of rundown motel rooms—the type that took cash and didn't have surveillance—and they'd booked one room only for security purposes. Sometimes they were lucky to get twin beds, sometimes they drew the short straw and got only one bed.

"Ha. I didn't think about it," James said, lifting his arm to wipe the crusty sleep from his eyes before he thought about it. He grimaced as pain from his arm shot to his toes, and he lowered it gingerly.

"Marianne and Kaela have one room," Deacon said. "Cami's in with Mak. The Tohmatsu boys are on the couches and everyone else is in sleeping bags wherever they can find a spot on the floor." Deacon sat up. "I spoke to Mak last night. She's refusing to go to Tokyo."

James wasn't surprised. "Then we'll move them to the other safe house."

Mak wasn't going to like that, either. But James wasn't sure how long he could keep the Tohmatsu boys in London, and he wasn't letting Mak stay in this townhouse. It was secure, but the other safe house they had was like a vault. It was windowless, steel framed, and hidden in the center of an apartment complex. Unless you knew the codes, you weren't getting in, or out.

"I was thinking the same thing. Marianne and Kaela are going to have to go there, too."

Slowly, James sat up, propping himself up with cushions. He assessed his bandages—they were soaked with weeping fluid. Eric had done a real number gouging the holes in his arms.

"I want to start working with Marianne," James said. "I want to know everything in that head of hers—people, buildings, security systems. Her knowledge is a huge advantage that we should fully exploit."

Right on cue, James heard a giggling voice in the hallway.

"That kid has more energy than any of us," James said.

Deacon shook his head. "God help Marianne if she takes after her father."

God help the world, James thought. "Well, if they're up, let's get to work."

Deacon threw back the covers. "Sit on the edge of the bed. I'll change your dressings first."

~

The mug of coffee cradled in James' hands warmed his body and he did his best not to think about the woman at the end of the table. He focused on Marianne instead.

"Who's this?" James said, sliding one of Sarquis' drawings toward her, the unidentified portrait.

She only needed to take a flickering look at it. Her forehead creased. "That's Sorin. He's the Lord of the organization—no one has more power than Sorin," she said. "Where did you get that?"

"A man named Sarquis," James said.

"Ah, that explains it. We wondered what happened to—" She stopped abruptly, her eyes lifting to James.

James didn't even bother to look at Mak, although Sarquis was one person James hadn't actually killed—he hadn't had a chance before the man had swallowed the cyanide tablet.

"I didn't kill him—he committed suicide when he realized we were closing in," James said, leaving it at that. "I found these in his house, along with drawings of you, Kaela, Eric, my father, and him—Sorin."

"I don't believe he's ever met Sorin. Few people have. He's virtually a recluse. I've met him a few times only, and most of those were in my younger years when he was less of a recluse." Her head angled as she took a closer look at the portrait. "I think he drew this from a photograph that's in one of the textbooks."

"Textbooks?" James asked.

"The organization has a curriculum with courses and workbooks for each student, or recruit, as they're sometimes referred to," Marianne said. "I'm almost positive it is. The angles look right."

"Why did you think Sarquis would've created these portraits?" Deacon asked.

Marianne looked thoughtful. "Did he see you before he committed suicide?"

Her eyes were on James, so he answered. "Yes."

"I don't think he was planning to give them to you, then," she said. "I would assume that he was keeping them up his sleeve in the event he ever had to bribe someone within the organization."

James considered this before he slid her a printed photograph. "Who is this?"

She hesitated. "That's Serena... She's your mother, James."

James felt all eyes on him.

Marianne continued. "She's Sorin's wife, although he's not your father."

Now James knew why Eric had called James a "bastard."

"Any other family I need to know about?" James asked.

"Yes, you have a half sister. Sorin and Serena's daughter." Marianne waved her hand dismissively. "She'll be no help to you, though. She takes after her father."

Interesting. He'd always wondered if he'd had any siblings.

"Our intelligence expert," James said, keeping Samuel's name out of it at this stage, "has been monitoring your father's estate. He said no planes have come in and it looks like no one has left. But lots of activity has been coming in on the ground—cars. We think it's additional security."

"Then they're planning something. And they'll do it there," she said confidently. "That building is a maze of tunnels and secret rooms. If you don't know it, it would be very easy to get trapped inside. It works to their advantage."

"Except that you know the building," Cami said.

Marianne shrugged. "I know it, but that doesn't mean that it makes it easier to move around it. If you're thinking of making an attack, you'll have to wipe out their entire surveillance system. It will be impossible otherwise. And you would have to draw them into certain areas of the home. Otherwise it would take too long to work through the house and find the people you want to eliminate. The chance of getting caught would be extremely high."

James rolled out the blueprints of Lucian's estate and passed Marianne a red marker. "Firstly, look over these closely and tell us if any of it is incorrect—if any renovations have been made. And then draw a circle around the main areas of the house, labeling them."

James took a sip of his coffee, watching her.

There was no conflict in her eyes, nor any hesitation in her hands. She had been ready to betray her family a long time ago.

Her eyes scanned each one, rotating through the three floor plans. "I'm not an expert on reading these things, but it all looks correct," she said tentatively.

James didn't like her lack of conviction. He did admit, though, that as far as floor plans went, these particular ones were difficult to read due to the multiple tunnels and connecting structures that made up the main house.

"These are the cells where you were kept." She drew a large red circle, followed by a squiggly line. "And these are the tunnels we went through."

She shuffled the papers again, drawing one circle after another. "Master suite. My suite. Kitchen. Security."

On the third paper she drew a circle around a tower-like structure. James knew it was the one he'd looked up at on the night of their escape.

"This is the guest wing. That's where Sorin is staying," she said, meeting his gaze. She'd seen him in the window, too, then, James thought.

"Where are the rest of the security rooms? There can't only be one for an estate that size," Deacon said.

Marianne looked down again, leaning in as she scanned the floor plans. She drew five more circles on the single sheet alone.

James looked to Deacon and they both shook their heads, silently agreeing.

They couldn't go back in while security would be expecting them.

"We can't use that house," James said. "It's not going to work."

He looked into his empty coffee mug.

We need to draw them out, he thought. *We need to take back control of the situation.*

They'd been playing Eric's game thus far. He'd chosen the worship site. And they'd taken James to Lucian's estate.

That's why they've stayed, James realized. *They're hoping we come back for them. They're laying traps, anticipating our arrival.*

"We're not going to hit any of their buildings—at least not initially. We're going to make them come to us," James said, looking at Deacon.

His brother looked thoughtful and then James saw the spark in his eyes.

Marianne looked between them. "How are you going to do that?"

They both looked to her at the same time.

She sat back, her head rapidly turning from side to side. "No. That wasn't part of the deal."

"As you'll remember," James said. "I never made a deal. I couldn't talk. You told me what was going to happen and I followed along. We'll continue to protect you in this, but you absolutely have to play a part."

She was still shaking her head.

"If what you say about your God's punishment system is correct, they're going to want you," Deacon said. "They're going to want to punish your entire family. And we all know Eric—he's going to try and do something to salvage his life. I have no doubts your father is also busy scheming along with him. But whatever plans they have, we can be sure it involves one thing—getting you back."

"I'm not doing it," she said.

James raised an eyebrow. "Do you want this to end? Your life, and your daughter's life, is not safe until they're all dead. If you want us to succeed, you damn well better help."

She looked to the ceiling, and then sighed heavily. "What do you want me to do?"

James' lips curled up. "Let's send Eric a video." He looked to Cami and Deacon. "Let's send him one just like the one he sent us of Maya. We'll tell him that we'll trade you, Marianne, for him. We won't, of course," he said quickly, to ease her fears. James didn't believe Eric had ever truly intended to trade Maya, either. "He'll come, with an army of supports, for us both. As the cherry on top, we'll tell Eric to bring someone with him."

Lucian.

37

ERIC

Lucian didn't return last night. And he still hadn't returned today. Eric wrapped his fingers around the bar, gripping it in frustration. And fear.

Where is Lucian?

And why am I still stuck in here?

I am their leader, Eric thought. *I am not done yet.*

His teeth sawed against one another.

This is all Marianne's fault.

She took my status, my power, and my daughter.

And I'll kill her for that.

Although it gave him no comfort, Eric knew he wouldn't die until Marianne had been found. Therefore, he had time. Time to formulate a plan. Time to win back respect. Time to plead his case to the Gods.

But first, he needed to get out of the damn cell.

And then he'd set about finding Marianne. She'd be with Liam—she would've negotiated protection as part of the escape deal. It could be a good thing—kill two birds with one stone.

My darling wife, I'm coming for you.

Eric heard voices outside and he sat down on the edge of his bed. Lucian walked in.

"I'm sorry, Christos. I was held up in meetings with the Commission all night. They want to enforce the traditional punishment system. The sooner we have a plan, the better." He handed Eric another box.

But another box meant another day in this cell.

"Take it," Lucian said. "I'm getting you out of here, but it's taking time. I need to convince Sorin that you're more valuable on the outside."

"Thank you," Eric said, pleased despite the circumstances to have another few doses. He needed to call upon the power and wisdom of the Gods now more than ever.

"I can't believe she did this to us..." Lucian said, and the lines on his face seemed to have deepened over the past few days. "She'd always served the Gods so faithfully, or so it seemed."

"I thought so, too," Eric said.

"The funeral for Pavel Sokolov was held today. The Russians are angry, Christos—livid. We need to find Marianne and Liam before they do. We can't let the Russians find them first—they'll kill them. And if we don't have them to sacrifice to the Gods, we will be the sacrifices."

"Get me out of this cell," Eric growled. "I can work with the Russians. I can fix this! Just get me out."

Lucian nodded, standing. "Give me one more day and I'll get you out." The door closed behind him.

One day is too long, Eric thought. *I need to get out today.*

38

LUCIAN

The Russians were incensed that the Ranger had taken out their man. It had poured gasoline on an already flammable relationship. Lucian wouldn't have cared except that his salvation depended on finding his daughter, his granddaughter, and Liam Smith.

We have to find them first.

But how? He had to get Christos out of the cell—he was better at this than Lucian was.

Lucian had had men looking for them on the ground and via surveillance. They hadn't even had a hit on any of Makaela Ashwood's family. Liam Smith had everyone bunkered down somewhere—likely in multiple locations.

Lucian knew they'd have to draw him out now. And they'd have to use Serena to do it.

A mother's love knows no boundaries—at least when it came to Serena it didn't. For thirty-nine years she'd suffered at Sorin's hand for her betrayal. And yet, day after day, year after year, she'd refused to speak a word about her son. She'd never told them how she smuggled him out, or to which orphanage she'd first taken him. She'd never said a single word—no matter how excruciating the pain had been. Serena planned to take her secrets to the grave, and not once had Lucian seen any recognition of regret in her eyes.

But you'll regret it when we find him, Lucian thought with a smile.

Lucian's cell phone rang. "Yes?" he answered.

"You're going to want to see this. Meet me in S3," Sergei—his new surveillance analyst—said.

Lucian hung up and rushed toward the control room. Staff raised their eyes to look at him, but no one said anything about his striding pace.

The control room was quiet when Lucian walked in but the image projected on the screen brought him to a halt.

"Your wife was stupid enough to think that she could trust me," Liam Smith said, smiling at the camera.

Lucian saw his daughter to the left of Liam, bound to a chair, her head flopped down toward her chest, her bruised and bloodied face visible to see.

"I used Marianne to escape, and now I'm going to use her to get what I want." Liam paused. "I want you, Eric. Or should I call you Christos? We all have multiple names, don't we?"

Liam gave a crooked smile.

"I'm going to make you a deal," Liam said, and Lucian realized he was repeating the words Christos had said to him in his video. "I'll swap Marianne and Makaela—your beautiful little daughter—for you. A clean trade. After all, I no longer have use for either of them."

Liam's eyes were like a magnet, drawing Lucian in.

"Your men can take your treacherous wife and give her to the Gods—hopefully that'll be enough to save your daughter from becoming a sacrifice. But the longer you wait," Liam continued, "the more inclined I am to simply kill your wife and be done with it. She won't be much good to you dead, will she? I'll give you her location details, and all you have to do is come and get her."

Liam smiled again.

"Oh, and one more thing: I'd like you to bring Lucian with you. We have some unfinished business. I'll see you both soon."

The image focused on Marianne. Her lip was split, her eye purple and swollen, her hair looked wet. Blood trickled from her forehead and down her cheek. Lucian couldn't tell if her hair was wet from water or from blood.

The camera changed and an image of a smiling Makaela flashed up.

"Say hello," a voice said—Liam's voice.

"Hello!" Makaela said, giggling.

And then the screen went blank.

Lucian's limbs tingled and he felt like he was swallowing shards of glass.

"Send that to my phone," Lucian said as he turned on his heels.

He headed for the door.

39

JAMES THOMAS

James saw Marianne scrubbing at her skin, but the makeup wasn't coming off easily, and if she kept rubbing her skin it would become raw.

The garage had been turned into a studio, a special-effects makeup artist had been hired, and Deacon was recruited as the cameraman. It had taken seven hours to prepare a twenty-second video and now James was exhausted.

He'd hidden his injuries underneath his sweater, despite Eric knowing they were there. And the makeup artist had even applied makeup to his face, hiding the dark circles under his eyes. When James looked at the footage he was impressed at how healthy his face looked. He definitely didn't feel that way.

He took the stairs slowly, climbing up to his bedroom. His eyes were refusing to stay open. He was almost at the top step when Mak walked out of her bedroom, stopping when she saw him.

The only words they'd said to each other in the past few days were polite hellos. James hated it.

He looked at the bottle in her hands. He didn't recognize it, but it looked like a cosmetic product of some sort. He wondered if it was for

Marianne. They were being very amicable, despite the situation. All in all, it was an awkward house to be in right now.

"How are you going to do this, James? You can't stand on your feet for more than a few hours. How are you going to fight against Eric and his men when they come?"

James was selfishly pleased to see the worry on her face.

"It'll be okay, Mak," James said. "We're not giving them the address for a few more days. And I'll be on the back line. Deacon and Cami will be at the front and will lead the teams. They'll call the shots."

"A few more days isn't enough, and you know it." Her voice was choked, laced with emotion.

James climbed up the last step. He was so close to her now, and it would be so easy to wrap her up in his arms.

"We need to capitalize on this situation while we can. My injuries aren't going to be fully healed for months, and we can't wait that long. I want this over, Mak. For all of us." *But mostly for you.*

"I don't want you to do this," she said quietly.

"And miss capturing Eric? I don't think so," he said with the slightest of smiles. "This time will be different, Mak. I won't fail you this time."

Three times Eric had gotten away from him—slipped through his fingers—but James knew this time was different. He didn't have to preserve Eric's life now that Biskup had the code, and that meant he could pursue him at all costs.

"I'm going to get some sleep," James said. He told himself to move, to leave her, but he stood like his feet were glued to the carpet.

She didn't move either.

It wasn't uncomfortable, it wasn't even awkward. He gazed into her eyes, losing himself in them.

A door at the bottom of the stairs opened and closed, breaking the spell James had slipped into. He placed a soft kiss on her forehead and then forced his legs into motion, retreating to the bedroom.

40

MAK ASHWOOD

His kiss lingered on her forehead long after he moved away. She hadn't expected him to do that—to kiss her—and it left her stunned and wanting more.

Deacon walked up the stairs. "What's that?"

She didn't respond for a moment, but then shook herself as Deacon got closer. "It's a different makeup remover," Mak said, holding up the bottle. "It might be better than the other one."

"We probably should've kept the makeup artist around to clean her up, but given the content of the video that would've been a bit weird," he said, smiling. "Did you see James come up here?"

"Yes. He's gone to bed," Mak said. "He's not well enough to do this, Deacon. He's going to get hurt. He's going to get killed."

Deacon looked to the bedroom door and back again. He lowered his voice. "You and I both know that he's going to do what he wants to do. He's not going to sit this out, no matter what any of us say. I'm going to do everything I can to cover and protect him."

Everything might not be enough. Mak didn't doubt Deacon, but he couldn't control everything that happened.

"Give that to Marianne before she takes another layer of skin off. I'll clean his wounds and give him something to sleep. I'll get him as healthy as possible in the time we have," Deacon said, and with a nod he too disappeared into the bedroom.

Mak looked at the bottle in her hands and then took one step away from James, and then another. As she approached the lower level she heard Kaela laughing at Marianne, telling her she looked like a clown. When Mak walked into the lounge room Marianne looked better than she had a few minutes ago. Still, there were traces of red, white, and purple on her skin.

"Try this," Mak said. "I don't normally use stage makeup, but it works well."

Marianne shot her a thankful look.

Mak made a coffee and then joined Cami and the team at the dining table. They were drawing up strategic plans for the building they were intending to use.

How many properties did Thomas Security own?

Mak watched on keenly even though she thought there was little she could do to help.

When Mak's eyes flickered to Marianne she saw that the makeup had finally come off. She also noticed how pale Marianne looked. Her skin was tinged green, too, and that wasn't because of the makeup.

Marianne sat down on the couch, pulling Kaela into her lap. She turned on some cartoons and from where Mak sat she could see Marianne close her eyes. He put her fingertips across her forehead like she had a headache, or was unwell. Her breaths were long, deliberate.

No one else seemed to notice—they were either absorbed in the operations meeting or still downstairs in the garage.

Maybe it's just stress, Mak thought. Stress-related headaches and nausea were both common, and Marianne had good reason to be stressed.

They all did.

Mak picked up the pile of portrait drawings sitting on the corner of the table.

Sorin.

Mak studied his face, noting the sharp angles and hollow cheeks. She wondered how old he was. Despite the lines in his face, there was also a vibrancy captured in the portrait.

She shuffled to the next one. *Makaela.*

And then the next. *Marianne.* In the portrait she wore a crown and oversized teardrop earrings. She looked regal and elegant—Mak couldn't deny her that.

Mak shuffled the papers, looking down at Eric—Christos—now. Hate began to flow in her veins.

She shuffled to the next paper, surprised to see it was a photograph. It looked like it had been taken in a shopping center. It was an image of Marianne with an older man.

A man Mak recognized.

Mak stole a look at Marianne. Her head rested on the cushion and she looked as if she were asleep.

"Cami?" Mak interrupted. "Who is this?"

"That's Marianne's father, Lucian," she said, briefly lifting her eyes from the strategic plan. She did a double-take when she saw Mak's expression, and her eyes narrowed. "Why?"

"I know him," Mak said. "He was my lecturer. My first year at university."

The room went quiet and all eyes looked to her—excluding Marianne's.

"He was your lecturer?" Cami asked with wide eyes.

"Professor Lutz," Mak said. "How long have you had this photograph?"

"A little while."

"I thought so," Mak said. "I could've given you that nugget of information earlier, if I'd been shown this."

Mak put the image down. "Do you know who Carl Junez is? Or are you still trying to figure that out?"

"We don't know."

"I would bet my life that this is him," Mak said, putting the image down. "And do you know how Eric met this man?"

"No, we don't."

Mak stole another sideways peek at Marianne. "Professor Lutz was—maybe is—Eric's Aunt Silvia's boyfriend."

41

JAMES THOMAS

There was a knock at the door before it swung open. Deacon was applying a fresh bandage to James' chest. A chest now carved with the chants of the Gods. James wanted to take a knife and carve something else just to remove the words from his skin. If he'd had more healing time he might've seriously considered it—with anesthetic this time, of course.

Cami barged through the door. "You're not going to believe this. Mak knows Lucian. He was one of her lecturers her first year of university."

James' jaw dropped into his lap. "What?"

"She was looking over Sarquis' portraits and amongst them was the surveillance image of Lucian and Marianne. Mak recognized him. I've got Samuel on it already," she said.

Lucian picked her out for me, Eric had said.

"Now it makes sense," James said, thoughtfully. Deacon and Cami looked at him expectantly.

"While I was captive I asked Eric why he'd chosen Mak. Why he couldn't let her go even though he'd walked out of her life. He told me that Lucian had picked him out for her, and that she was his first gift from the Gods. Apparently, Eric never abandons a gift from the

Gods—that would be disrespectful." The words tasted like acid in his mouth. "I asked Marianne how Lucian would've known Mak. She said she had no idea. In fact, she said she hadn't known anything about Lucian choosing Mak for Eric until he'd told me and she was in the room. Although, she had said it was common that wives were chosen for the male leaders, so it was highly possible it occurred that way. Eric wasn't a leader, but I have a good feeling Lucian led him to believe he would be, and that having a wife chosen for him was one of the first steps."

"So, that answers Eric's obsession with Mak," Deacon said. "Albeit in a very deluded way, although this entire organization is deluded, so that doesn't have any significance. But why did Lucian choose her?"

James couldn't think of a single reason why.

"Mak also likely answered how Eric was recruited into the Escanta," Cami said. "It appears Lucian was at the time Eric's Aunt Silvia's boyfriend. Samuel's working on this, too."

"We looked into every single family member and their partners. We didn't find him," James said. It had been the most extensive search Samuel had ever done on one family.

"Because he didn't want to be found," Deacon said, his eyes narrowing. "I'll bet even Aunt Silvia has few photographs of him."

"What name was he using?" James asked.

"Professor Morgan Lutz."

Cami's phone rang and she answered it, putting it on speaker.

"We've opened the box now and I've got a team working on this," Samuel said. James thought he sounded like a kid about to go to Disneyland.

"Go ahead," James said, indicating they were alone and together.

"Interestingly, I can't find any photographs of the man. But, I have confirmed that there was a Professor Lutz at Mak's university and I've confirmed he was one of her lecturers. Originally it looked like the trail stopped there, except that in his file there was an address for a rental property. The lease was in his name—nothing unusual. I went back to Aunt Silvia's file, and at one point she had a mail redirection to the same address—at the time he was renting it."

James chewed his cheek absentmindedly, trying to piece it all together.

"It doesn't stop there. Professor Morgan Lutz is not his real name, of course. Five years prior to this, Aunt Silvia had another boyfriend, Lutz Morgan. Still not his real name, we don't think, but we found something very interesting about Lutz Morgan... Open the photograph I just sent to your phone. Tell me who you think it looks like."

They all leaned forward, their heads almost brushing together. James took one look before he took the phone, holding it upright in front of his eyes. "Oh my God," James whispered.

"Exactly," Samuel said. "That was his wife. She died in a tragic car accident on the same day Mak was born."

James couldn't tear his eyes away from the photograph. The same sea-blue eyes, the delicate nose and high cheek bones, the white-blond hair. The similarities were striking. It could've been Mak.

"His heart must've skipped a beat when Mak walked into his lecture hall," James said. *The obsession was never about Mak, it was about Lucian's own wife,* James realized. A wife he couldn't let go of despite her death.

Deacon whistled. "Wow. Are we assuming that he thinks this is his wife reincarnated—given the date—or that he just thinks this is some kind of gift from the Gods, some kind of sign, maybe?"

"A gift, or some kind of sign," James said quickly. "If he thought it was his wife reincarnated, I think he would've taken Mak as his own wife, not set her up with Eric. I'm sure age gap isn't relevant to these people." James tried to mentally calculate how large the age gap would've been, but he wasn't sure. It was very difficult to tell how old Lucian was.

"Well done, Samuel," James said. "Well done."

"We're digging. We'll find out who he is... Mak didn't recognize Sorin by any chance, did she?" Samuel joked.

"No," Cami said, smiling. "We didn't get that lucky."

"Damn," Samuel said. "Signing out."

James hung up the call and passed the cell phone back to Cami.

"Mak also thinks Lucian is Carl Junez—the name on the wedding card that she couldn't place a face to," Cami said.

"Very likely," James concluded. "What reason do you think Lucian gave Aunt Silvia for his name change?"

Deacon shrugged. "He could've said anything...a deranged student stalking him, a business deal gone bad. If she still verbally called him Morgan, it's likely the family never knew about the name change. We need to look into her further, though, just to make sure she's not involved."

"Where is Mak now?" James asked.

"She was sitting at the dining table when I came up," Cami said. "Do you want me to get her?"

"Yeah, I'll speak to her," James said, looking around for his T-shirt.

Deacon saw it first and grabbed it, helping James to slip it over his head while lifting his arms as little as possible.

"Do you want me to speak to her?" Deacon asked, but James shook his head. "No. I'll do it."

His bedroom door was open and Mak stopped at the threshold of the room.

"I'm going to the camp to check on the training, which Maksym is currently in charge of," Deacon said. "And then Cami and I will organize the supplies we'll need."

"Thanks," James said, waiting for Deacon to leave before he continued. "So, you know Lucian, huh?" For once James knew exactly what thoughts were inside Mak's head: *You should've kept me informed.*

"Take a seat," James said, nodding toward the bed. He drew his cell phone from his pocket and opened the Thomas Security program, pulling up the image of Lucian's deceased wife.

He passed it to Mak, noting her reaction.

"What... For a second I thought that was me!" She looked to James.

"I looked twice, too. I would at least swear she was your mother, but she's not," James said quickly, so as not to spawn any confusion there. "As it turns out, this woman was Lucian's wife. She died in a car accident on the day you were born. Don't even ask me about the coincidence of that, and your uncanny resemblance, because I don't have an answer."

Her attention returned to the photograph.

James didn't want to tell her that she was chosen as a "gift" for Eric, and that's why he'd married her, but Mak had made it very clear she wanted to know the truth and he was, reluctantly, going to give it to her.

James told her about the questions he'd asked Eric and his response.

"I was a gift? Some kind of prize? That's why he married me?"

"I don't know if that was the only reason, Mak. Only Eric can answer that. But it seems that's at least how your relationship came to be. Your meeting wasn't accidental—it was set up."

"I don't know why I'm surprised," she said, bitterly. "That marriage should never have happened. It will forever be the biggest regret of my life."

In the hours since he'd returned from Lucian's estate, James had asked himself more than once if she regretted their relationship. If she did, at least he wouldn't be the biggest regret of her life—James was happy to give that title to Eric.

"What does this change?" Mak asked, seeming to brush off the bad news fairly easily.

"At this stage, it answers some questions but doesn't necessarily change anything. The more we can find out about Lucian, though, the more we hope we can find out about Sorin. Lucian seems to be the one closest to him, and perhaps they have a similar relationship to what Lucian and Eric have.

"Intelligence is often like this. It comes in the form of little pieces of scattered information of seemingly little significance. But, when it all comes together, that's when you see the relevance."

"Like pieces of a puzzle," Mak said and James nodded.

"Are you upset by this?" James asked, unable to read her now.

Mak scoffed. "I probably should be...but honestly, I just don't care. I never loved him—although I didn't realize that at the time.

And now I can only hate him." She put the phone in her lap, playing with her fingers. "I want him to die, and I don't know what that says about me—it goes against everything that I believe in."

It's not our decision to take a life. She'd said that to James once. He'd disagreed then and he disagreed now. Some lives needed to be taken to save the lives of others—of other innocent people.

"All it says is that you've seen the ugly side of life, and you better understand the consequences of it," James said, sitting back when he realized he'd been subconsciously leaning in.

James focused his mind, getting back on task.

"Tomorrow we're going to move you and Marianne to another safe house and the Tohmatsu boys are going back to Tokyo."

"Where are you going?" she asked.

"To the camp. I need to train these men. We're going to send the address to Eric in"—he checked his wrist—"twenty-four hours."

She rolled her lips over one another. "And how long do you think it will take them to respond?"

James shrugged. "Twenty-four to forty-eight hours, probably... about the same amount of time it took us to respond to Eric. Deacon will be in charge and call the shots once Eric and his men arrive."

Her lips puckered together.

"How long was Deacon a Ranger for? Or can you not tell me?" Mak asked.

"Deacon was a high-ranking Ranger and he had been for many years when we met. He was one of the best, that's why I selected him. But unfortunately I unknowingly brought him into a massacre... His life would've been very different if I'd selected another team," James said. Deacon's life had taken multiple, life-changing routes.

Mak's eyes flickered to the door, and her voice lowered. "What was said by the Russian about his girlfriend... I assume that was Nicole?"

James nodded.

"Is that what happened to her?"

James sighed, frowning. "Unfortunately, yes, amongst other things they did to her. Deacon couldn't get to her—his legs and arms were bound, but even if they hadn't been, he'd been beaten so badly that he couldn't walk. I had to carry him out. Nicole had already passed by the time I got there." James didn't want to give any more details than that. "Do you now see why I enforced the security provisions I did?"

"Yes," she said, meeting his gaze. "How do you get past something like that?"

The past few weeks had given him a new understanding of Deacon's pain. James had come to close to the same fate and he'd realized in those moments that he would never recover if that happened to Mak. He didn't know how Deacon went on with life.

"You don't," James said.

42

LUCIAN

Serena lay on the bed, her arm full of intravenous lines. Some were filled with fluids and medication. One, however, was filled with blood —alchemized blood.

Her eyes fluttered open and Lucian wondered whether Serena felt him watching her or if she'd heard the door slam behind him.

Sorin joined him at his side. Serena looked between them, her eyes calm. Serena either had a fascinating ability to hide her emotions, or she just no longer cared what they did to her. She was dying, after all, and Lucian knew she was praying for the day to come soon.

Sorin, however, was praying that that day did not come too soon —and he was doing everything he could to keep her alive.

"Your son sent us a video," Sorin said, and Lucian saw no reaction on her face. Absolutely nothing. Her forehead didn't wrinkle, her pupils didn't dilate, she didn't even blink. Her reaction, remarkably, was the same when they'd told her that her son had escaped.

Lucian wasn't a fool, though. Serena cared. But a lifetime under Sorin's hand had trained her well.

"He's an arrogant bastard, much like his father was," Sorin continued. He leaned in until the tip of his nose brushed hers. "And he's going to end up just like his father. Butchered to death."

Serena's chest rose up and down evenly. Lucian thought it inflamed Sorin's soul that he could no longer get any form of reaction from his adulterous wife.

Serena's plan might've worked, all those years ago. She might've succeeded had it not been for one thing: her son's black eyes.

For three months that beautiful little baby boy looked upon them with clear blue eyes. A healthy, baby boy. A royal boy. A son who would've gone on to replace Sorin. For three months she fooled him, but slowly the eyes began to turn, and there was nothing Serena could do to hide it.

"Leave her," Sorin said with a dismissive wave. "Let's talk," he said as he led Lucian into a separate dining room. A butler poured them tea. They waited until he left the room.

"What is our response to this video?" Sorin asked.

"Security teams are on standby. Transportation is on standby. It has become a waiting game until we receive the address," Lucian responded. "Christos is waiting in his cell, Sorin. I'm asking you again to release him. Remember why you put him in charge of finding Liam in the first place."

Sorin sneered. "He failed me."

"Give him another opportunity. He's never had more motivation to succeed."

Sorin smiled lightly—he knew full well why Christos had such *motivation*. "What is Liam waiting for?"

"I don't know," Lucian answered, honestly. "His injuries aren't going to be healed for a long time, so he can't be waiting for that. Perhaps he's waiting on men?"

"Do we know if he's still in cohorts with Biskup?"

Lucian cringed internally. He'd been hoping to delay informing Sorin until he had Liam Smith, his daughter, and his granddaughter in captivity; but currently he had none of them, and now he had to deliver another blow.

"Yes, it seems he is," Lucian said slowly. "Security received an alert to a tracking device Eric created for the nuclear system he designed. It has been activated."

Lucian held his breath.

"Marianne?" Sorin's voice could've chilled the cup of tea in his hands.

"I can see no other way. I now believe she had been planning her escape from the Saratani for a long time. Perhaps she didn't know exactly how it would happen, not until Liam Smith was in her care, but it's become apparent she had been watching Christos carefully for some time."

Sorin was silent for a moment, turning the teacup by its rim. "I've consulted with the Gods, Lucian, and I've deliberated on the punishment system you presented.

"I will show mercy on you, as mercy was bestowed upon me after Serena's betrayal. But no mercy will be shown to your daughter or to her daughter. As soon as we have extracted all useful information from her—including every single person who helped her escape— you and Christos will carry out the sacrifice ceremony and perform all of its rituals," Sorin said, his eyes as cold as the Antarctic. "There is one more thing, though... I want to set a very strong example, and you will need to pay an additional price for your salvation. I will sacrifice one of your wives."

Lucian cleared his voice, maintaining his calm. "Which one?"

Lines creased around Sorin's eyes as he gave a calculated smile. "You get to choose."

Lucian said nothing as he sat there. He had three wives, all alive and well. He wondered why Sorin was giving him a choice; did he think it would torment him? Did he want to see which ones he favored?

"When would you like the decision?" Lucian asked.

"When you have Liam Smith, your daughter, and your grand-daughter captive. This is your only chance to redeem your soul, Lucian. Think very wisely about your next move."

Lucian bowed his head.

The heels of his dress shoes echoed through the tunnel as he walked. The very same tunnel that his daughter had betrayed him in.

Christos was still behind bars, and from the reports Lucian had been receiving, he was growing increasingly agitated. At last count, Christos had been pacing for seven hours straight.

Lucian stopped at the double doors that led to the cells.

The man bowed and then unlocked the door.

"How are you holding up?" Lucian said as he entered.

"I need to get out of here," Christos said. "There are things I can do, plans that I can put into action."

Lucian nodded. "I know, son. But first I need to speak to you about two things. First, it seems your code has been entered into Biskup's nuclear system."

Lucian paused, watching Christos carefully. There was surprise—and then a small grin. It wasn't the reaction Lucian was expecting.

"Would you care to explain why you're smiling?" Lucian asked.

"Because the code has two stages. The first stage is the sequence. It will activate the initial stage. A second sequence must be entered within seventy-two hours, otherwise the system will shut down. I stored the second sequence separately—in my mind. No one but me has it. Alexandr Biskup will realize soon enough, and I imagine the call to Liam Smith won't be friendly."

"Why did you write down the first sequence?" Lucian asked.

"It was a test for those closest to me—to see if I could trust them. However, I never thought my wife would be the one to steal it," Christos said with a clenched jaw.

"And what if Biskup used the device before it shut down?" Lucian asked.

Eric grinned. "He can't. It looks active—and it is, partially, but there's a secondary process that enables the detonator. That secondary process requires the second sequence. If Biskup wanted to use the system, he'd need to enter both sequences first. They can be entered one after the other...if you know where to enter it. I didn't design prompts to pop up, obviously."

Clever man, Lucian thought.

"Very well then," Lucian continued. " Second, Liam Smith has made contact. He made a video that is remarkably similar to the one you sent him. He's beaten Marianne to a bloody pulp and he wants you to come and get her... He obviously thinks that she's of no value to him now that he has the code—or thinks he does—and that she helped him escape. But we need her, as a sacrifice, to save ourselves, and Liam would know that—he knows she's of great value to us. And he's right. We're going to get her back, and that's why I have permission to do this." Lucian held up a key and saw relief transform Christos' face.

Lucian put the key into the lock, turning it until it opened.

"One shot, Christos. Command your men and devise a plan. Without Marianne, Sorin will soon be carving your chest."

43

MAK ASHWOOD

The bleak, white, windowless walls made her throat tickle. The safe house was a glorified prison cell.

"It will keep you safe," James said, accurately reading her thoughts. "The team has brought in enough food to feed the three of you for a week, just in case there's any delay—which we're not anticipating." James said.

Mak didn't see any doubt in his eyes, but how many times had the tables turned in this fight?

Cami patted Mak's shoulder. "Let's hope Marianne can cook," she joked, and Mak rolled her eyes. While Mak had been obedient in the weapons and physical training requirement, the cooking courses hadn't gone so well.

"They purchased mostly pre-prepared meals," James said. "All you need to do is put them in the microwave."

Mak nodded. A sense of foreboding stirred in her stomach and it had nothing to do with her new living quarters.

They were moving them into the new safe house because they were going to send the message. The bait would be laid for Eric and his men, and that meant once again that James, Deacon, Cami and all of their men would be going into battle. So many lives had been lost in the last one, and Mak had a strong feeling many lives would be lost in the forthcoming one. What were the chances that the three of them would come out of this alive?

The handover for the house was brief. They had a television to watch, but that was it. Once James and Cami left they would be locked inside until someone let them out. Mak was glad Samuel had downloaded all of her case notes onto her laptop. At least she could work on the gangland murder review case—it would keep her mind busy.

"I'm going to put her down," Marianne said, carrying a sleeping Kaela in her arms. She headed off in the direction of the bedroom. There was only one. Mak was sleeping on the couch.

James came to stand in front of her, and spoke quietly. "You can still go to Tokyo. You'll be safe there. I can get you on a plane in an hour."

"I'm not going to Tokyo," Mak said. There was no hesitation in her mind and none in her words, either.

James pressed his lips together, looked away and then back to her. He sighed, a clear indication that he wished she would go.

"They're ready," Cami said from behind Mak, and James looked away for a fleeting moment and nodded.

"Be careful, please," Mak said.

He looked at her for a long moment, and then, swiftly, he cupped her face with one hand and whispered in her ear, "I love you. You'll always have my heart." He kissed her cheek and walked away.

He's saying goodbye, Mak realized, but the realization came a moment too late. She turned on her heels as the door closed. She heard it lock and then a gaping silence filled the apartment.

Mak didn't know how long she stood still, staring at the white-painted door. It could've been minutes, or hours, and an eerie sense of loneliness filled her.

It was the sound coming from the bathroom that finally pulled her from her thoughts. A sound she'd heard this morning, and the day before. A sound that would explain Marianne's greenish pallor that Mak had caught on more than one occasion.

Mak went to the kitchen and poured a glass of water, taking it toward the retching sound. She knocked on the door.

No answer.

The sound of Marianne heaving up breakfast finally stopped, so Mak knocked again.

The door opened and Mak stared at a white-faced Marianne. Mak held out the glass.

"Thank you," Marianne said, sitting on the edge of the bath.

Mak noted Marianne's shaking hand as she brought the glass to her lips, taking a tiny sip. Mak thought she might be worried it would come up again.

"When are you due?" Mak asked.

Marianne looked like she was going to deny it, but then changed her mind. Mak thought perhaps she just didn't have enough energy to keep pretending.

"Four months," Marianne said.

Mak was surprised it was that soon. She couldn't even see a bump on Marianne's stomach, although she was wearing an oversized sweater.

The thought made Mak's mind recoil. James had said the same thing about his child—it had been five months old, and he hadn't seen the bump before he'd killed her.

"Why are you keeping it a secret?" Mak asked.

"I didn't know if it would change our arrangement. I didn't know if being a pregnant woman would be another liability for them." Her eyes met Mak's. "I don't know these people, and yet I entrusted my life, and my daughter's life, to them because I was so desperate. I didn't know if an unborn child could be used to their advantage in any way, so I hid it. I've hidden it from almost everyone."

"From Eric? Why?" Mak asked.

"Because it's a boy," Marianne said. "And Eric made it very clear he would not have a son. He only wanted little girls."

Suddenly, it all made sense—why she'd taken such grave risks. Mak didn't doubt that she wanted to take her daughter away from such an organization, but she was even more certain that the decision to leave had been made concrete in Marianne's mind when she found out her unborn child was a boy.

"They won't hurt you, Marianne. That's not who they are," Mak said. There were a lot of things Mak didn't know about James, but she knew deep within her soul that Paris had been an accident. She knew it.

"I kept it hidden from everyone because I trust no one," Marianne said, and then suddenly looked around her. "Are there cameras in here?" she whispered.

Mak sighed. "I don't know," she said, thinking it very likely there were.

Marianne spoke in a hushed voice, "I don't want them to know. Please don't say anything. Please."

"You're going to have to tell them at some point—obviously," Mak said. She wondered if they already knew, or were at least guessing at it, but hadn't said anything.

"I just want this to be over, and then I'll go with Kaela, and I'll look after us on my own. I just want a quiet life with my children, Mak. That's all I want. I'll go and live in some remote country away from it all. Please, just let me tell them when this is over."

Marianne's eyes pleaded.

"Okay," Mak said.

Marianne gave a tired smile. She took another sip of her water, inhaling shakily. She then looked back to Mak, her eyes deadly serious. "You don't know how lucky you are that Eric disappeared and left you when he did."

44

ERIC

"Show me the video," Eric said, stepping through the open cell before it could close on him again. He felt the power shift within his body.

He was free.

He was angry.

And he was ready to act.

Lucian handed him a different cell phone, one Eric recognized as his own. The one he'd been stripped of before he'd been locked up.

Marianne will pay for all the insults I've endured, Eric thought. *She will die an excruciating death.*

Eric located the video file and pressed play.

The sight of his beaten wife didn't stir any feelings of sympathy. Eric was glad she was suffering. He squinted, looking at her injuries.

You are a despicable man, Liam Smith, but on this occasion I thank you.

But Eric wouldn't let Liam kill her. No, Marianne was his wife— and *he* was going to kill her.

The video ended and Eric looked up. "No, Lucian, you can't go. You're too important to this organization. We can't risk your life."

Lucian stared at him impassively. "I must. Marianne is my daughter, and therefore I share in her betrayal. We must work together, Christos, like we have always done. We must succeed now. We must."

Lucian's gray eyes swirled. Determination. Ambition. Power.

The Gods are with us, Eric thought.

"Have you received the location?" Eric asked.

"No, not as yet. So use this time wisely. I've already instructed all Saratani recruits to be on standby. Sorin's security team is also going to work with you to devise the plan; however, they will remain with Sorin until our return."

"That's wise," Eric said, moving toward the door. He needed to shower, to wash away the grime and sins bestowed upon him by his unfaithful wife. And then he would concoct the plan of his life.

A plan that would show them all exactly who he was.

If Liam Smith thought if they'd been at war, he was wrong.

The war was just beginning.

45

JAMES THOMAS

"This time we definitely over-packed," James said to Deacon. The brothers were standing on the tarmac watching the men load the black boxes onto the commercial-sized private jet. James didn't know how much this trip was costing—nor did he care.

"Always better to be over-packed than under-packed," Cami said, coming to stand beside James. "By the way, I was right. Marianne is pregnant. Five months. She admitted it to Mak a few hours ago. Eric doesn't know."

"And she's hiding it because?" James asked, his eyes still on the boxes.

"She doesn't trust us. And apparently Eric said or did something to make her believe he'd kill the child. Apparently he only wants her to bear daughters."

"Add it to the list of things that are very fucking wrong with him," Deacon said.

"Her pregnancy doesn't change anything other than the sooner we finish this the better," James said.

They all agreed.

The last black box made its way up the conveyor belt.

"Let's go," James said.

He followed Cami up the stairs and they took their seats as they waited for their final few guests to board.

James looked over the plane. There was barely an empty seat.

Maksym came to sit beside them.

"Fellas...and lady," he said, smiling at Cami. She didn't return the gesture.

"I like you," Maksym said with a wink.

"The feeling isn't mutual," Cami said, deadpan, and James hid his smile. Cami could handle herself on and off the field.

"You might change your mind once you get to know me," Maksym continued.

"Not a fucking chance," Cami said.

"All right," Deacon said with a small grin. "Let's talk business." He rolled out new blueprints, and then continued. "This is our newly acquired property. Once we're on the ground and set up, we're going to send Eric the address. We'll set up triggers surrounding the building so that we know when they're approaching—whether that be via the ground or above it."

James nodded. "Once a trigger has been activated, the men will only have a few minutes to get into position. They'll need to be ready at any moment, and they'll need to move quickly."

Deacon drew circles all over the blueprints. "These are the vent locations. It's going to be tight, but it's an effective strategy."

Maksym wet his lips. "I like it. I like it a lot."

"The second team," James said, rolling out the blueprints of Lucian's estate, "will start hitting here, here, and here." James picked up another pen, drawing three circles. "We're going to hit both at the same time. The men are to take out security one by one—silently. They need to keep the estate locked down until we get there."

James' gaze was penetrating. These men wanted Eric, and Eric only. But it didn't end with Eric—not for James, and not for Mari-anne. It ended with Sorin.

"We're following your orders," Maksym responded.

"Remember that," James warned. "And don't stop to gloat this time. Shoot."

"I don't repeat my mistakes," Maksym said.

~

James' head moved in an arc, looking over their new building. They'd added another property to their portfolio, but James knew that this one was about to fiercely depreciate. Tomorrow, after they blew up what was left of it, destroying all evidence of their battle, the residual land would be its only value.

"Start working on these vents and the bullet proof lining," James said to Cami. "Deacon and I will set the triggers."

James unzipped his kit, filling it with additional items from one of the black boxes. With every movement pain riddled his body, but he refused to take any medication other than ibuprofen. He couldn't be drowsy. He needed to be alert—his mind and body sharp.

Just get through tonight—maybe the next few days, James told himself, unsure when Eric was going to respond.

It was going to end one of three ways, and all would allow for plenty of sleep. Either they'd win, and this nightmare would be over, and James would go back to New York where he could sleep and heal, or he'd die in battle—giving him eternity to sleep. Or perhaps Eric would recapture him, which would ultimately lead to the same.

Just keep going.

James packed the final items he needed and then lifted his eyes, searching for Deacon. He spotted him across the room, pointing at the ceiling, instructing Maksym and a group of gathered men. They were nodding their heads.

James worried about having so many men on the ground. While it provided ammunition power, keeping control of them could be difficult. If just one failed to follow their orders, the plan could go to hell. They'd emphasized that over and over again in training, but these were blood-hungry men whose brains could go haywire during battle. The groups he was most worried about were the ones going to Lucian's estate.

Worry about what you can control.

James focused his mind and, as he continued to watch the men, that familiar tingling in his spine started, and then intensified. The adrenaline, the rush of being on the field. The entrance of Liam Smith.

James Thomas was a wounded man, one too emotionally invested in this fight. One who wanted to kill Eric for what he'd said to Mak. James couldn't blame Eric for the problems James and Mak were experiencing now—James had done that himself when he'd killed his child and hadn't told her about it. But Eric had exploited it, and he'd tormented Mak—physically and emotionally—and that made James' blood boil.

But this couldn't be personal. He couldn't allow his emotions to get in the way. He had to be the cold, hard, man that Eric had described him as.

James Thomas was not that man.

But Liam Smith was.

Deacon jogged over to him. "Ready?"

"Let's lay some traps," James said with a grin.

46

ERIC

Their thick Russian accents enhanced their violent words.

"We want the Ranger, too. We want both of them. We want to cut off their fingers and toes, one by one, while they scream for mercy."

Eric nodded. "My friends, I will honor the arrangement I had with Pavel. You can have them for three days. After that, I get Liam. The deal is the same, but you can keep the Ranger."

One rubbed his hands together. "Pavel is going to smile down from the heavens while he watches."

Eric resisted rolling his eyes. The Russians were fools—they had no idea that they prayed to a God that didn't exist—but right now, Eric needed them.

"He will," Eric said, grinning. "And what a show we'll give him."

"When are we going in?"

"Tonight," Eric said. "We don't want to give them any more time to prepare than *we* need to prepare."

The location had surprised Eric. Romania. He'd expected them to choose somewhere in their territory—London, maybe. At first he'd thought that it was a ploy, that maybe they weren't going to be at that building at all, but would instead hit Lucian's estate again. But that would give Eric the advantage, and he knew Liam wouldn't do that.

Plus, when Eric had ordered a check on the building he'd seen that the title had been transferred—to a foreign company that was obviously a cover for Thomas Security—and when he'd sent his men to scope the address from nearby buildings, they'd seen activity. They were there.

But who was to say Marianne and his daughter were there, too? Eric couldn't verify it, and he was only going to get what information Liam wanted him to. It was the same game Eric had played with Liam. The game Eric had won—until his wife had betrayed him.

Eric's chest seared with anger. It did every time he thought of that deceitful bitch.

Ultimately, though, it didn't matter whether Marianne was there or not. The first step was to capture Liam Smith and the Ranger. Once that was done, there was no chance of them protecting Marianne—if that's what they were still doing—and then Eric would find her. And then he'd find Mak. There was nowhere they could hide from him. Even Liam Smith hadn't been able to hide forever.

There's always a way to draw them out, Eric thought, the corner of his lips turning up.

Always.

"Get your men ready," Eric instructed. "Meet in the Grand Hall in two hours."

The Russians had been on a plane the moment Eric had called them. He hadn't had to say a convincing word. Killing Pavel Sokolov was like writing your death date in stone. Fury was seeping from the pores of Sokolov's descendants.

Eric grinned. They were going to torture the Ranger even worse than they would torture Liam Smith. But it would not be worse than what Eric had planned for Liam himself.

That would be a new kind of hell.

∿

Eric looked into the eyes of Sergeant Kosti—Sorin's head of security. Eric had just finished detailing their plan, as per Lucian's request.

Lucian wanted another perspective on it, which infuriated Eric, but he kept his mouth shut.

"He's going to know you're coming," Kosti said. "He'll have trip-wires planted everywhere. You're not going to have the element of surprise, so you need to compensate with brute force—ammunition."

Kosti looked over the Grand Hall, and then grinned. "Which you have. Always ask yourself this: What is their objective?"

"Their objective is to kill us both," Eric said through gritted teeth, looking at Lucian.

"Because he believes he has the code and so he can kill you now?" Kosti asked. "Sure, he may take the fatal shot if he thinks that's all he's going to get. But for you in particular"—Kosti looked to Eric—"if he doesn't have to immediately kill you, he won't. He's going to want to punish you.

"For you..." Kosti looked to Lucian. "He probably does just want to kill you."

$\sim$

Eric stood in the safety of his security team one block away from the target building. His frontline men were approaching and Eric listened keenly. An explosion in his earpiece made him wince and then he heard the echoes of similar explosions—unified like a chorus. Eric smiled.

With no element of surprise they'd had to get creative. They were blowing up each entrance, forcing back whomever was guarding the doors and providing an opportunity for his men to get inside.

See you soon, Liam Smith.

A voice came through his earwig. *"Entering now."*

Eric held his breath, excitement flapping in his chest like a butter-fly's wings.

"What the..."

The tone of his soldier's voice made Eric pause.

"It's empty... the floor is empty. I can't see anyone."

Empty?

No it's not, Eric thought. He didn't buy it—not for a second.

He checked in with the men working their way across the rooftops.

"Confirm, we can see snipers positioned around the building."

Eric shook his head. "He's there. Find him. Move the next team in. Search the levels," Eric commanded.

"Team Two, move in..."

Eric's feet were itching to move, but he couldn't, not until his men had scoped the building.

"First floor... There's no one here... Team Three, move in... Second floor..."

The smile fell from his lips.

What is going on?

Where are they?

After a pause, the commands resumed. *"Empty... Third floor... Team Four, move in..."*

Eric quickly calculated the number of men comprising his teams. He had over ninety men in the building now. He had one more team to send in before he went in himself.

"Fourth and final floor... Team Five, move in."

Eric held his breath.

"Clear... Clear... Clear..." The calls started coming in, and Eric's pulse quickened.

"Christos, there's no sign of life in here... It's silent."

"Check it again!" Eric said. "Check the ceilings, check the air vents. I want to know where they are!"

"Copy."

If Liam Smith wasn't there, where was he?

Eric dialed security at Lucian's estate, pacing as he waited for the call to be answered. Eric didn't give them a chance to finish their greeting.

"Is anything happening there? Is the property secure?" The words came out so fast that the man on the other end seemed to take a moment to decipher his sentences.

"We're secure," he confirmed, and Eric hung up.

Where are you, Liam Smith?

Eric breathed in through clenched teeth.

"Hang on!" a voice said again, and then whispered, *"They're here... I heard a little girl's cry."*

A grim smile grew on Eric's lips. *Good girl, Makaela,* he thought. *Cry for Daddy.*

Eric motioned for his security team to move in the direction of the building.

"It's silent again. We've checked the ceilings and air vents. We can't see them. The building isn't rigged—" He stopped mid-sentence. *"That's her again. Where the fuck are they? No one move."*

Makaela would respond to Eric's voice, he knew she would. He was going in.

"Lucian," Eric said stridently. "We're going in. Makaela needs to hear my voice."

"I'll follow in behind you." Lucian's voice came through loud and clear.

The hairs on Eric's arms stood up as he laid his eyes on the red-brick tower that had once been a shipping office.

Where are you, Liam Smith?

47

JAMES THOMAS

"Hold," James heard Deacon's command, firm and confident.

Come on, Eric. Come inside. Come and find us.

Despite being squeezed into a space much too small, James' body wasn't cramping. His body hummed, his mind alert and focused. Eric wanted Liam Smith, and tonight that's who he was going to face.

"Hold," Deacon instructed, his warning more severe.

James wondered if any of the men were claustrophobic—he hoped not. There was room for a body and a gun only. It wasn't a pleasant location to wait, but James had been in worse—a lot worse.

"Target identified. Entering in three, two, one..."

James adjusted his body, twisting his spine, one eye looking through the crack in the adjoining walls.

Hello, hello, James thought as he set his eyes upon Eric. His breathing remained steady, but his pulse hitched a notch.

The whispers of Eric's men hushed as he made his entrance. He was shrouded in security—a ring of protective brawny men.

"And so we meet again, Liam Smith!" Eric called out, his voice echoing through the empty rooms.

James tried to decide if Eric sounded bitter or overly confident. Neither would serve him well.

"I know you're here, Liam," Eric said. "I would like to see my wife, and my beautiful daughter, Makaela." Eric's voice grew louder and James knew what he was trying to achieve—he wanted Makaela to hear his voice and react. Eric was doing exactly what they'd hoped he would.

"Target two identified. Approaching west entrance..."

Welcome, Lucian, James thought. His finger was steady on the trigger. It was almost time.

"Hold," Deacon instructed again, and James knew it was the last time he'd issue that command.

Lucian's stepped into James' field of view and he saw those beady gray eyes sweep over the building. It was a view afforded only by James' position, because Lucian too was shielded by security.

A little girl's sob—as faint as summer breeze—caused heads to snap.

Eric used his hand to issue men up the metal stairs. Lucian took a step forward. And then another.

One more step, James whispered to himself.

Lucian turned on his heels, as if he heard something. He looked right to where Cami was stationed. James watched Lucian's hands, which were tucked in his coat pocket.

Did he hear something? Or are his nerves getting to him?

James thought the latter. Of the things he knew about Lucian, most of which James had learned through Marianne, Lucian was not experienced in the field. Yes, he could cut a sacrifice to pieces, and he could punish those who disobeyed the Gods. But he was not a tactician outside of his domain, nor was he experienced in commanding men. This operation was out of his league, and there was an edge to him tonight that James hadn't seen in his estate. His shoulders sat higher, his jaw locked a little tighter.

Lucian turned away and took another step toward Eric. That was his biggest mistake.

"Three," Deacon began, and James lined up his pistol to the circle hole cut in the metal sheet.

"*Two, one!*"

The sound that followed was ear-piercing.

Blood sprayed from the men as their bullets made contact. They dropped in a perfectly synchronized display of carnage.

"They're in the walls! They're in the walls!" one man screamed.

Eric's men had finally found them, but they were far too slow to react. The men still standing began to fire back and even though James knew he was behind a wall of bulletproof sheeting, instinctively he still pushed back against the wall behind him.

Eric's security team bunkered around him while Lucian's tried to move him out. Unfortunately, they were right in the center of the building.

James took his finger off of the trigger only to load a new magazine. He watched with delight as the body count rose, piling one upon the other. But some men were starting to separate, using the metal stairs as shielding. It was a smart move.

James could see Eric screaming, but his voice was drowned out by the earsplitting, thunderous cracks of gunfire. It sounded like they were in a wild storm.

"*James... Eric...code...shoot ... *" Samuel's voice came through James' earwig, but he couldn't hear it for all the noise.

"Repeat!" James screamed, hoping Samuel could hear him.

Samuel's voice came through like static. It was impossible to hear.

Deacon was also trying to issue commands at the same time. James couldn't understand any of it, and that meant their men couldn't either. But when Deacon busted through the drywall, exposing himself, all of Biskup's men followed.

The color faded from Eric's face as men exploded through the walls like a scene from a horror movie. These weren't demons or zombies, though, but they were men ready to kill. Hungry for it.

Eric ducked down, hiding behind his security team. James looked to his brother, who had his eyes focused on Lucian. Cami was watching Eric. James was supposed to stay in the wall, to let them fight, but he couldn't.

Cami's shot hit one of Eric's security men, taking him down. But Eric, being the smart bastard he was, used it to his advantage. He used the dying body as a shield.

James kicked the wall, cursing when it didn't fall forward.

What? James thought as he looked at the wall. And then he saw the additional bolts. *Deacon.* His brother had known James was going to do this, and so he'd tried to lock him in the wall, or at least make it a challenge for James to get out.

James' eyes flickered back to Eric. They were getting closer to the door and bullets were being pelted at Cami. She had to retreat slightly, shielding her body with the drywall frame.

No! James thought, gritting his teeth. *Not this time, Eric. You're not getting away this time.*

James fired at the bolts, taking care to hit the right angle. He did not want the bullet coming back at him. He fired twice more, kicking the door as adrenaline rushed him like a force.

James looked down. Eric was only a few feet from the door.

No!

James looked above him. The vent. He grimaced as he hauled his body up, crawling into the vent and then through it and into the ceiling. He sprinted toward the hatch in the roof, grunting as he pushed it open, pushing through the pain in his body. He climbed the rungs, jumping onto the rooftop. He looked for the men they'd stationed on the rooftops, spotting clusters of them already engaged with Eric's men. They had their backs turned, their attention diverted.

James sprinted toward the east end of the building, scooping up a sniper rifle from the weapons they'd left there earlier.

As he neared the edge he saw them: Eric had two security men still alive, and they were running. James looked through the lens, calming his mind, calming his hand. He pulled the trigger, bracing for the gun's kick back.

The target fell to the floor, but Eric didn't stop—he didn't even look back.

James aimed at the second man, who was already wounded but

still capable of moving fast. James braced again, taking a steadying breath. He pulled the trigger.

As the man tripped and fell, Eric stumbled, too. His head snapped up and down, left and right. He looked panicked—which was exactly how James wanted him to be.

And then Eric looked to the rooftop. He paused, and that was all that James needed. He aimed through the lens, pulled the trigger and heard Eric's cry.

James dropped the weapon, assessing his next move.

Eric was clutching his shoulder, blood dripping onto the concrete underneath his feet. He looked back up to James and then he turned and ran.

James ran across the rooftop, jumping on to the next. His head was woozy, his legs were like columns of concrete that he couldn't move fast enough. But he was moving. And he wouldn't let Eric go. Not now. Not ever.

James took his eyes off Eric only to jump across to the next building. Two more buildings. Two more buildings until he hit a street and he had to get down to the ground. He came to a halt, peering over the edge. Eric was still running, but he was slowing down—he was losing blood.

James looked for a fire escape—he couldn't see one. But he saw a ledge below. And then another. One skirting the window of each level. If he could hang onto the ledge, he could drop down to the one below.

This is going to hurt, James thought, but he was already scaling the wall before reason stopped him. He had one focus only—Eric.

James swung his legs over as an agonizing jolt stole his breath.

Focus. Breathe.

He took three seconds only to steel himself as he kept his eyes on the ledge below. His fingertips clung to the rooftop wall, and then he let go.

He fell down one floor, scraping the skin from his hands as his feet landed on the thin edge and he grappled for the window frame.

He wobbled but managed to steady himself before he toppled backward.

James looked down, spotting Eric. He was across the road, and he was gaining too much distance.

Focus.

James scrunched up his face, preparing for the agonizing fire that burned through his arms as he lowered his hands onto the ledge and let his feet dangle once more.

Move, quick, James thought. *But don't fall.*

Falling from there wouldn't kill him, but it could leave him seriously injured—and unable to capture his prey.

"James?" Deacon's voice shouted through the earwig.

James let out a grunt as he fell one more floor, grabbing the wall as he saw the sparkling stars above come into view as he lost his balance. He gulped in a deep breath, pulling himself back against the wall. That was closer than he would've liked.

"I'm outside. I've got Eric. Get Lucian!" James said through short breaths. His body was exhausted and queasiness rolled though him like a rough sea. His body wanted to sit down and close his eyes—rest for a minute—but his mind told him to keep going. One more floor.

"Argh!" James grunted, swinging his legs once more. He'd placed only his toes on the ledge before he swung down again, landing on the ground like a sack of weights rather than a nimble cat. He rested his hands on his knees, bent over, gulping in air, but his eyes were on the road ahead.

Move.

James focused on Eric, and never had he been more motivated by a target. Blood droplets on the concrete ground acted as a trail, but James didn't need it. He could see the man ahead.

James' breath was labored, his body screaming with every step he took. His vision blurred, and he saw two images of Eric.

James pushed through, his eyes never leaving the bleeding, running man. With each step, he gained a little. He didn't know if Eric heard him, or if he was just checking behind him, but when Eric looked over his shoulder and saw James behind him, his eyes doubled in size.

He turned and ran with a renewed energy.

James pushed harder. It was tempting to fire another shot, but he didn't want to kill him. Eric didn't get to die that easily. James wanted him to hurt—he wanted every remaining second of Eric's life be an excruciating experience.

A car drove past them and seemed to slow down, but it didn't stop. They weren't in the best of neighborhoods, and with one man bleeding out and being chased by another, James didn't blame them for accelerating away.

Eric split in two again and James knew he had to catch him before his own body gave up. He couldn't shoot now, because he couldn't even focus his eyes well enough.

Keep going, James told himself. *Push through.*

Eric stumbled, tripping on an uneven block of concrete, and it provided James the opportunity he needed.

He sprinted forward, defying every protest his body made.

Eric was just getting up as James skidded to a stop, flattening his shoe against Eric's back.

"Don't. Fucking. Move!" James said as he pushed him to the ground.

Eric's face smashed onto the concrete and James put a knee in his back, using all of his weight to hold down the struggling man.

He drew his pistol from his back pocket and held it to Eric's temple while he delivered a blunt kick to Eric's groin. Eric screamed and then his body went limp.

"And this is for Tom!" James yelled hoarsely, before delivering a second, brutal blow.

James dropped his pistol, heaving, resting on all fours. Blood flowed down his arms, from which wounds he had no idea. His hands were gashed and bleeding and although he couldn't see it, James was sure his chest wounds had opened from the exertion of scaling the building.

His skin was slick with blood.

Focus.

James pulled a small coil of rope from his pocket, binding Eric's hands and feet. His eyes were like slits, seeing double, sometimes triple.

Stay awake! James told himself.

That's the last thing he remembered.

48

DEACON THOMAS

"James?" Deacon shouted as his eyes remained on a retreating Lucian. He was backing toward an exit, his security team using the dead bodies as shields.

But it wasn't Lucian's men that were firing back at Deacon, blocking him from ascending to the lower level—it was the angry Russians.

If Lucian or Eric were issuing any commands, they seemed to be completely disregarding them. The Russians were working their own plan, and Deacon was their target.

"James?" Deacon called again.

No answer. His brother either couldn't hear him, or he wasn't capable of answering. Deacon prayed it wasn't the latter.

A bullet hit the drywall above his head and Deacon cursed, pressing his back flat against the steel shielding.

"Cami?" Deacon asked.

"Copy."

"Confirm location," Deacon said, watching the scene below.

Bodies were piling up, limbs protruding at unnatural angles, flesh torn apart.

One of the smarter Russians had grabbed a board of metal-lined drywall and was using it to shield their men at the front. And they were inching toward Deacon.

This isn't good, Deacon thought. There was nowhere to go—he had to push back, and some help would be good right now.

"Your three o'clock. I'm trying to move to get you some cover, but I'm in a bit of a pinch," she said.

That makes two of us.

"Maksym, confirm location," Deacon said.

"Six o'clock. I'm trying to hit the Russians from behind," Maksym said, followed by a whistle. Deacon assumed he narrowly escaped a bullet. *"Where is Eric, Deacon? I can't fucking see him!"*

Why wasn't James answering? Deacon ignored the tightening of his chest and refused to let his mind run wild with the possible answers to that question.

"Maksym, can you get to the front exit?" Deacon asked. Maksym's help taking down the Russians would be very useful right now, but he needed to find James.

"Possibly," Maksym said, his voice laced with doubt.

"Eric is out there with James—somewhere. Go and find them! And watch your back!" Deacon commanded, weighing up his own options.

Lucian was still retreating, and he was getting closer to the back exit than Deacon liked.

You're running out of time, Deacon.

The Russians continued to advance. If Deacon was going to use the device in his pocket, he had to do it now.

"Code 33! Clear out from the Russians. Retreat!" Deacon shouted, fiercely hoping all of his men could hear him.

Deacon pulled a flashbang from his pocket, his eyes darting, searching for his men.

"Code 33! Retreat! Shield your eyes!" Deacon commanded—screaming—as he spotted a few lone men still trying to break the Russian's front line.

This time they heard the command, but their retreat caught the attention of one of the Russians. He stopped shooting and looked around, his eyes wild.

"Three, two, one!" Deacon activated the device and threw it into the center of the building. He covered his eyes, counting the seconds until he opened them again.

Men were stumbling around, clutching their eyes, blinded by the flashbang. Deacon's men reacted, taking full advantage and gunning the men down.

Deacon had a window of opportunity and he took it.

He ran toward the stairs, shooting as he moved. Cami was right behind him. Deacon took the stairs three at a time, his feet so light he didn't even feel the metal underneath him. He jumped down to the concrete floor and fired a shot into the forehead of an approaching Russian.

Deacon searched for Lucian—he was almost at the back entrance. The flashbang hadn't impacted them—they'd had their backs to it.

No you don't, Deacon thought. *You're not going anywhere.*

"Maksym? Check in!" Deacon shouted.

"I'm outside. I've found two of Eric's security men and a lot of blood," Maksym replied.

Oh, fuck, Deacon thought. "Keep looking! Follow the blood!"

Did Eric have more men outside? James should never have left the building, but James had never wanted the blood of someone as badly as he wanted Eric's. And that was not a thought Deacon made lightly.

Focus, Deacon.

He skirted around the metal columns that held up the staircase landing. The metal pinged as bullets hit it, but Deacon ran faster. A bullet shot past his ear making a whirling sound. Deacon didn't slow down—his eyes were on the target.

One of Lucian's security men saw him first and Deacon fired a running shot, hitting his chest. The man was down temporarily, but Deacon knew he'd have a bulletproof vest on. He fired a second shot, landing it in the man's forehead—now he was down for good.

Deacon ducked behind the cylinders they'd strategically placed around the building for cover. He peered around. *Four men to go.* And Lucian.

Bullets penetrated the cylinder, but it held up under the assault. Deacon looked to the next cylinder—that was his target.

He checked over his surroundings. While he didn't like how close Lucian had gotten to the back door, it was an advantage for Deacon now. Most of the battle was taking place in the center of the room and that reduced the chance of a bullet accidentally taking Deacon out.

He squatted in position, preparing his body to launch up and fire as he darted to the next cylinder. His eyes locked on the man to Lucian's left, and then propelled himself forward.

Bullets bounced off the metal all around him, but Deacon made it to the next cylinder unharmed. He rested his back against it, giving his body a few moments to recover from the explosive burst of momentum he'd just put it through.

Deacon pulled a mirror from his pocket.

Three men to go.

There were two more cylinders between Deacon and Lucian. It wasn't enough. Deacon needed to take down another man before he moved again.

Deacon crouched, curling his back to stay hidden behind the cylinder. He peered around but jolted back. Lucian's men were aiming straight at them.

Deacon pulled another flashbang from his pocket before again shouting, "Code 33! Code 33!"

He gave his team a few seconds to shield their eyes.

Deacon launched the flashbang toward Lucian's men and waited until he heard the snapping crack followed by the explosion. Deacon jumped up, firing at the stunned men as he ran forward. He shot two down before the third recovered from the shock.

Lucian was screaming, clutching his eyes, and Deacon knew he hadn't escaped the flashbang a second time. Lucian's gray eyes would never see daylight again. Deacon ignored the man for now, letting him stumble around in a wild, panicked rage.

As the security man brought up his weapon, Deacon knocked it from his arms, sending the pistol flying through the air. Deacon lunged at him, taking him to the ground and delivering a fist to his cheek. Blood and spit ejected from his mouth like a rain shower.

The man grunted, growled, and then swung his arm, hitting Deacon's shoulder. Deacon's grip loosened and the man took full advantage, rolling him and delivering a breath-stealing blow to Deacon's stomach.

Deacon gasped for air, ducking as the man went for his head next. Deacon brought his knee up, reciprocating the man's friendly gesture.

Metal clanged behind them and Deacon saw Lucian flat on his back, still clutching his eyes, screaming for help.

The distraction allowed the man to get in another blow, this time hitting Deacon's jaw. It was followed by a sharp burst of pain.

Deacon gritted through it, braced himself, and then pulled a pistol from the man's holster and held it to the man's chest.

The man looked at him with alarmed eyes. Deacon fired it twice and then pushed the limp man off of him. He didn't know if the bullets had penetrated the vest, and he wasn't taking any chances. He fired another two bullets into the man's forehead.

Deacon stood, swaying, wheezing for air. He laid his eyes upon Lucian—a man writhing on the floor.

Deacon knelt down beside him. "You should've closed your eyes... And you should never have come after us," Deacon growled before he rendered an incapacitating blow to Lucian's head.

The man went soft, the slight rise and fall of his chest the only sign that he was still alive.

Deacon sat back on his heels, allowing his body one minute to recover.

Cami was still fighting the remaining Russians.

There were clusters of Biskup's and Eric's men warring it out, but the groups were getting smaller and smaller.

Deacon looked over the carnage. He'd seen less blood on an army battlefield.

"Maksym?" Deacon said, hauling his body up onto his feet.

"Copy. I've got them. I thought James was dead when I first got here. Eric, too. If you want Eric to live, you better get your ass here—he needs treatment, now!"

Deacon ran back to a cylinder, one they'd filled with medical supplies. He grabbed a kit.

"Where are you?" Deacon asked.

"Six blocks north, sprawled out on the fucking pavement!"

Damn it, Deacon thought.

They needed to blow this building and get out of there before enforcements turned up. Deacon couldn't believe they hadn't already —Samuel must be doing a good job of blocking the lines.

"I'm coming! Drag them out of sight and keep pressure on Eric's wounds until I get there."

Deacon checked to make sure Cami had cover. Three of Biskup's men had moved in, backing her up. He called over the closest of Biskup's men and ordered two of them to stay beside Lucian. Deacon wasn't worried Lucian was going anywhere, but he didn't want to take the risk that one of Eric's men might drag him out. And until Deacon knew for sure that they didn't need Lucian, he wanted him alive.

Deacon slipped out the back entrance.

49

JAMES THOMAS

James' eyes sprung open and he jolted upright.

"Easy, easy," Deacon said with a hand against his abdomen.

"Welcome back," Maksym said jovially, patting his back.

James looked around, trying to piece the night together. He was in a van.

"Eric! Where is he?" James said suddenly, recalling an image of Eric on the concrete.

Deacon tilted his head and James looked in that direction. Eric was flat on his back with intravenous lines protruding from his arms.

James' jaw clenched.

"You nearly killed him," Deacon said, matter-of-factly. "And your-self." His tone changed, and James knew Deacon was fuming.

"He was not getting away this time. I couldn't let that happen," James said.

James did an assessment of his own body. His T-Shirt was off and fresh white bandages had been applied to his chest and arm.

"I had to pump you with adrenaline and replacement fluids."

James didn't care. It was worth it. His eyes settled back on Eric. "Did you sedate him?"

"Yes. He'll be taking a nice, long sleep," Deacon said.

"No one wakes him but me. I'm going give him the same wakeup call he gave me." James' voice was low, deep, tight.

I can't wait to hear you scream, James thought.

Deacon nodded. "While you were out, we took down Eric's men. And Lucian. He's in the other van. Got him with a flashbang—the fucker can't see a thing."

"Karma is a bitch," James said, grinning. "Well done."

"Thank you."

James paused, his eyebrows creasing. "Where are we? Where's Cami?"

"We're a few miles from Lucian's estate. The men are refueling, and Cami's in the van with Lucian—she's fine. The perimeter has been taken down. We need to move soon if we're going to do this tonight," Deacon said.

The brothers stared at each other. James knew what Deacon wasn't willing to say aloud. That in his physical shape, James was a liability. It was true, but James couldn't sit this one out. This was his fight. Sorin wanted *him*, not Deacon. James had to find out why, and then he had to end it—once and for all. That wasn't a job he could give to anyone else.

"We're doing this tonight." James didn't even question it. "Pass me the medical kit."

Deacon looked like he wasn't going to, but then he did.

James dug through it, finding the drugs he wanted. His head was throbbing in unison with the entire body—his pain had a heartbeat all of its own. He felt dizzy, and he was sure he would feel even worse when he was on his feet. But if there was one thing James was good at, it was pushing through the pain.

He stabbed the needle into a vial, noting several of the men in the car were watching him with interest. He mentally calculated the dosage again, making sure he didn't accidentally overdose himself. Deacon's eyes were watching him like a hawk, though, so he needn't have worried.

James inserted the syringe into the intravenous line Deacon had left in his hand, and pushed the plunger until it stopped.

He also drew a small dose of pain relief—enough to keep him upright, but not enough to give him serious side effects. He didn't want to take it at all, but he knew he had to.

Deacon passed him three energy bars and James consumed them while Deacon detailed the plan once more to the men.

James looked over the men. Alexandr Biskup would be proud— they hadn't even bothered to wipe the splattered blood off of their marred faces.

"This is a different mission," Deacon said. "We need to be as silent as ghosts. Take down the security man by man, team by team. Do not rush—do not use your weapons unless you absolutely have to. This is to be hand-to-hand combat until instructed otherwise. Understood?"

The men nodded, their heads moving up and down, fast. They were still excited. One round of bloodshed was apparently not satisfying enough.

"Good. Relax for a few more minutes," Deacon said before turning back to James. "When Eric wakes up, make sure you leave him well enough to talk."

James frowned.

"We've got a problem with that code," Deacon said, pulling his lips to the side. "The system shut down. Biskup doesn't know why, but he's pissed and he wants Eric alive and talking. It's very lucky you didn't kill him."

James rubbed his forehead, trying to rub away the hammer banging against his skull. "Very lucky," he said. The damn fucking code just kept rearing its ugly head, but this time James had a solution, and he was looking right at him.

"I'll make sure he can talk. In fact, I want him to. I want to listen while Biskup's men glean the code from that head of his."

"While I glean the code," Maksym corrected him, his eyes shining.

James smirked. None of Eric's Gods would be able to save him from Maksym.

~

The brick wall acted as a fortress around the estate, but nothing would keep them out tonight. James was back on his feet, and he felt better than he ought to. It was the drugs, James knew, and he hoped they'd keep him upright for as long as he needed. After tonight, he didn't care. He'd deal then with the pain and torture he was putting his body through.

He lowered his night-vision goggles and stood beside his brother. Deacon obviously wasn't taking any chances this time and he was keeping James right next to him—where he could grab him before he decided to run and make his own plan.

"Team One moving in," Deacon said, creeping forward.

Biskup's security force had eliminated the men on the fortress wall and had assumed their positions, using the radios to report in. So far James didn't think anyone inside had realized that had happened—but he could be wrong. They could be patiently waiting for them, ready to launch an attack.

Team One was going for the box on the left wing of the house. Deacon would swap out the wire at the exact same time Cami would change the wire in the box of the right wing. It was the same tactic they had planned to use when they were coming in to rescue James, he'd been told.

James had been given no role in this mission other than to stay on his feet. He didn't mind—he wasn't sure what else he was capable of. He'd have a few hours until the drugs began to wear off, but he hoped to be out by then. Hoped. They moved alongside an exterior wall of the house, slipping in underneath the security camera.

James' eyes flickered up to the sky. Stars twinkled above them, hundreds of them. *That's a better sign,* he thought.

They moved again, crouching in the shadows as they wound around the building. James focused on his breathing, remembering to keep it long and steady. He'd always done this, but it was even more important with an injured body.

It seemed like they ran forever, but it was just that they were moving slowly, and his body was so tired.

James had memorized the blueprints, and despite blacking out earlier and the cocktail of drugs he was on, he remembered them clearly. He knew exactly where they were, where the boxes were, and where Sorin's tower was.

Sorin.

The man who held the secrets of his past, and the key to his future. Sorin had to be eliminated—after James had spoken with him. There was no other way.

As they approached the box, James was surprised at the how forcefully his heart was beating in his chest. He wanted so desperately for this nightmare to be over. He had Eric. He had Lucian. There was just one more man to go.

James shook himself. *I need to treat this as just another mission.*

James held back the team at Deacon's instruction, and James watched on nervously as his brother approached the box.

"*In position,*" Deacon said.

"*Hold. ETA thirty seconds,*" Cami reported back.

James counted the seconds, as he was sure the other men were doing.

"*In position,*" Cami said, and James held his breath.

James had switched the wires at Eric's house in Amman, and even that had been a close thing. But to switch two wires at exactly the same time... *This could go horribly wrong,* James thought as his body tensed.

James' eyes darted around, looking for any threat. He didn't see anything.

Deacon counted down from three, and then there was silence.

When Samuel spoke, James exhaled.

"*We're in!*" Samuel said. "*Give me a few seconds... Stay in location...*"

Deacon mumbled a prayer of some kind as he ran back to where James and the men were waiting.

"Good job," James whispered and Deacon nodded.

"*I'm loading the surveillance...*" Samuel said. "*There's a woman in a bed in his tower,"* Samuel said and James wondered if that was his mother—Serena. *"He's there, in the adjacent room to the woman. He's with his head of security—a man named Kosti."*

James' body woke up. His legs moving fluidly, his breath easy.

I'm coming for you, Sorin.

50

SORIN

Sorin stood at the glass window, looking at the spot where he'd once seen Liam Smith, half expecting to see him again—staring back at him.

"Sorin, I can't express my concern enough. We need to leave, now. They have eliminated over one hundred of our men, and I can't contact Lucian or Christos. The plane is ready. If I give my command, the pilots will turn on the engines," Kosti said from behind him.

Sorin stood still, his decision made. "I'm not leaving. I've spent too much of my life searching for him to run from him now."

"Sorin," Kosti said with a sense of urgency. "I can't guarantee that I can protect you. I don't know how many men he has, and Liam Smith is no average soldier."

"I'm not leaving," Sorin repeated, turning on his heels.

Kosti stood tall, his back as straight as a broom, his broad shoulders squared. "He *will* come for you," Kosti said. "He knows that your men will continue to hunt him unless he ends this. With our men taken out, tonight is his best chance and he knows it. He won't wait for you to regroup and gather more men. He won't take the chance that he'll be able to find you again. Make no mistake, he's coming for you, and he's doing it tonight."

"I know he is," Sorin said, sitting gently on the windowsill. "Do you know that of all the things the Gods have shown me over the years—all of the visions—I've never once seen Liam Smith in one. Why do you think that is?"

Kosti looked around like he was on edge, like it wasn't a conversation he wanted to have right now. "I don't know, Sorin."

"Neither do I. I can't make sense of it," Sorin said, thoughtfully.

Kosti's cell phone rang. "Yes?" he answered before he took a darting step forward, grabbing Sorin by the shoulders. "Get away from the window," he said, moving him toward the wall.

He's here, Sorin thought, a giddy mix of excitement and fear invading his mind.

"Where?" Kosti asked. "Hold them there. I'll get Sorin down to the basement tunnels." Kosti hung up.

"I'm not going," Sorin said. "But I don't expect you to stay. Go now while you can."

Kosti's jaw fell open. "You're going to try and defend yourself against him? Have you lost your mind?"

Sorin raised one eyebrow. It was the first time Kosti had ever dared to speak in such a way. "I want to see him, Kosti. I want to meet the man who has managed to defy us for so long."

"This is suicide," Kosti said, exasperated.

"Perhaps. Perhaps not. Go now, before you can't." Sorin motioned toward the door.

Kosti stood, his feet firmly in place. "This is madness. Please reconsider this. You have an organization to run. Men to lead. They are going to need you now more than ever."

Sorin shook his head, slowly. "Don't you see? The damage has been done. It will take years—lifetimes—to rebuild the organization to what it was. Our men will have lost faith in us, and in their Gods. We promised them salvation, we promised them abundant blessings, and in a matter of months Liam Smith has destroyed all of that. To rebuild the organization is a challenge for someone else. I am too old, and too tired. It is my time to transcend to the Gods—if that is to be tonight."

"If that is to be? If he gets into this chamber, I promise you that *will* be your fate." Kosti changed tactics. "What about Serena? What about punishing her?"

"I will punish her, but not in the way I'd always thought I would," Sorin said. "Maybe that's why I never saw Liam in my visions," he said absently.

Kosti's cell phone rang again and as he listened to the voice on the other end, he closed his eyes. "Put another blockade in place. Call me if they break through that." Kosti ended the call and seemed to give his last ditch effort. "There is a war going on downstairs. We've lost control of the security system and they're breaking through every blockade my men have set. He's making his way up here, Sorin. This is your last chance to change your mind."

"I am at peace with my decision," Sorin said, going to stand behind the walnut desk that backed onto a roaring fireplace.

Kosti hissed through his teeth. "I will not stay, Sorin. You're on your own," the man said bitterly.

Sorin bowed his head. "You have served me well. I thank you for that."

Kosti turned and left, closing the large wooden door behind him.

"Cerah zalû," Sorin whispered as he opened one of the desk drawers.

The blade of a knife reflected the burning flames behind him. Sorin picked it up, running his finger along the beveled edge.

His eyes set on the door.

The door to Serena's room.

51

JAMES THOMAS

James was sprinting through the hallway when an explosion rocked the ground beneath him and he stumbled, crouching as he tried to keep his balance. He looked to Deacon who'd put a hand on the wall, steadying himself.

"They're blowing it up! They know they're losing, so they're going to blow the damn building up!" James shouted over the gunshots ringing through the air.

Deacon nodded in agreement.

James looked ahead. They were so close.

"Get out of here!" James said. "Take the men and get out of here!"

James was too close to leave now. He could see the stairs that led up to Sorin's tower. And Samuel had confirmed Sorin was still in there—he hadn't run even when his security had.

Loud bangs echoed in a sequence and debris fell from the bricks above them as the building shook. James shielded his head with one arm, his fingertips gripping the brick walls.

Deacon looked behind him—they had twenty men all looking at them for answers.

"Retreat!" James yelled, waving his left arm toward the tunnel they'd just run down.

The men turned and ran—they were nothing if not good listeners.

Deacon, however, stood there, gritting his teeth at James.

"They won't get out alive and you know it. Lead them out," James said, unfairly laying the guilt on Deacon.

It was a harsh strategy, but as James looked at the staircase once again, he seriously doubted his ability to get out before the building fell in. He was prepared to sacrifice his life—but not his brother's.

"We do this together!" Deacon said, his tone leaving no room for argument.

James looked over his shoulder. The men had run, disappeared from view. Deacon wasn't leaving, and there was nothing James could do about it other than to get in and out of Sorin's tower as quickly as possible.

Deacon must've had the same thought, because he ran ahead of James.

James ordered his legs into motion, ignoring the resistance of his muscles. Deacon was strides ahead when James saw a figure step out of the shadows and fired two shots, hitting Deacon square in the chest. His body fell backward and James screamed his name, watching in horror as his head slammed against the bricks.

His head injury, James thought as fear ripped through him. He looked at the man who had fired the shots.

Kosti.

Kosti turned his weapon on James, but James fired first. It was a running shot, and his body was tired. He missed the target but it made Kosti jolt back, giving James a second chance.

Focus, breathe.

James zeroed in on Kosti and fired. He'd been aiming for Kosti's forehead, assuming he was wearing protective gear. When the bullet landed in Kosti's neck it was good enough. A sickening, gurgling noise came from the man's throat as he clutched it. He fell to his knees, and then fell face down.

James ran to Deacon, dragging him up against the wall. He lifted his brother's T-Shirt, relieved to see the bullets were lodged in

Deacon's vest. The impact had winded him, but it hadn't killed him. James slipped his hand underneath the base of Deacon's skull. It was warm and sticky.

James' eyes flickered to the door that opened to Sorin's tower.

He propped Deacon up against the wall and brought the palm of his hand to Deacon's cheek. A sharp crack sounded through the tunnel.

Deacon's eyes sprung open.

"Deacon!" James said, watching as his brother's eyes tried to focus. James held up three fingers. "How many fingers, Deacon? How many fingers?" he repeated frantically.

Deacon squinted. "Three," he said groggily.

James exhaled with relief. "Stay here, I'll be back in a minute."

James stood, it taking him longer than usual to get to his feet. He looked each way down the tunnel. They were seemingly alone.

James inched up the stairs and toward the door. He raised his weapon to shoulder height.

He put his hand on the cast-iron doorknob, turning it slowly. He pressed his back up against the wall as he swung it open. He expected bullets to shoot through the door, but nothing greeted him. James peered around the doorframe. The room looked empty except for one bed in the center.

Cautiously, James took one step forward, and then another.

The room appeared vacant—except for the woman in the bed.

When their eyes met, her face crumpled, emotion overwhelming her. Her head shook violently, side to side.

James faltered.

What a hell of a reunion, he thought, as he moved closer toward the bed, never lowering his pistol.

"He's in there," she said, her voice faint and wheezing. James strained to hear her.

When he was next to the bed he saw the red, blood-soaked sheets beneath her wrists. Someone had recently slit them. James knew who that someone was.

"The door," she said, her eyes rolling backward as if pointing to the door behind the bed. "He's in there."

James looked at the door and then dropped his eyes to her wrists again. She was going to bleed out if the wounds weren't treated.

Her eyes followed his, and then she shook her head again. "Go." She coughed and blood trickled from the corner of her lips. "Save yourself... End it." Her eyes cleared, her words seeming to give her strength. She nodded.

James focused his mind.

Sorin.

That's who he was here for—no one else.

It was a cold attitude, but the only one he could afford to have right now. He needed to end this, and he needed to get Deacon and himself out.

James stalked toward the door. "Samuel?" he whispered.

"Copy. He's sitting behind a desk. He appears to be alone. There's a pistol in front of him but he's not holding it. It's like he's waiting for you."

"Copy." James said, turning the doorknob, pushing the door with his fingertips. It swung open without a creak.

"I've waited so many years for this moment," Sorin said slowly as James walked over the threshold, entering what appeared to be a private study.

James kept his pistol high, his finger on the trigger.

"It's not going to be very fulfilling for you," James said.

Sorin's lips twitched. "You look like you've seen better days."

"I've hit a rough patch lately. Things are looking up now, though," James said, keeping his eyes forward, but trying to take in as much of the room as possible.

He stopped a safe distance from the desk.

"I assume you met your mother on your way in?" Sorin's eyes were calculating.

"If she's really my mother," James said, "then, yes, I suppose I did. As you're well aware, I don't know who my family are."

Sorin's head tilted. "Would you like to know?"

"I don't care," James said. "I lived without them for this long, and I'm doing just fine."

"It must intrigue you, though, to know *why* we've been looking for you, yes?" Sorin laid his hands flat on the table, but James saw that his fingertips were casually inching toward the pistol.

"Perhaps, but I can live without knowing," James said.

But James had to admit that he did want to know—he'd always wanted to know about his past.

The room began to shudder like it was being rocked by an earthquake. A lamp fell off Sorin's desk smashing to the floor and the lights flickered, but neither man moved.

"Your mother, Serena, is my wife—something you likely know," Sorin said, breathing lightly. "Unfortunately, her soul is weak and she gave in to...temptation." When he said the last word, a hint of anger made its way into his voice as another tremor made James' feet slide.

Get on with the damn story, Sorin.

"You should've been my son. You would've been royalty within this organization... When you were born I was so happy, so excited to have a son to be my successor. I doted on you, bottle-fed you day and night. I changed your diapers...

"Did you know you were born with blue eyes? Lots of babies are, apparently. For thirteen weeks they stayed blue—but one day, while holding you in my arms, I noticed they were changing."

Sorin's voice lowered. "It was then that I questioned my wife. I'd heard the rumors from my staff and so I kept a close watch on her. I didn't see it initially—I didn't see the affair—nor did I see the revolution they were planning. Your mother, just like you, knew that the only way to secure her future was to eliminate me."

Sorin's fingers inched toward the pistol again. Movements so small that James could've easily missed them, but he didn't.

"I loved you. And even as your eyes continued to darken I wanted to believe that you were mine. But one morning I woke up and you were gone. Ripped away from me, so suddenly. I knew then that Serena had hidden you. We found your father the next day—hiding like a coward—but no matter where we looked, we couldn't find you.

I think your mother arranged for you to be shuffled from home to home, orphanage to orphanage, so that you were never in one place long enough to be discovered. Your deceitful mother is a smart woman—I have to give her that."

"So you decided to punish her for the rest of her life?" James asked.

"She betrayed the Gods," he said with sudden venom. "*They* punished her. I just enforced that punishment," Sorin said simply, and James thought he truly believed that. The man was more delusional than Eric.

"Your Gods are a fucking myth. You've brainwashed hundreds— thousands—of people for your own benefit. So that you can feel powerful and important. I've seen enough of what you do to people to know that no God would wish for that."

Another tremor ripped through the room. Books toppled from their shelves, to the ground, paintings fell from the walls, and a small crack opened not far from James' feet.

Sorin continued on, unfazed by James' criticism. "It's been a big week for you. You've met your mother, and you've also met your half-sister. A complete family reunion," Sorin said with a calculated smile. "She didn't tell you, did she? Marianne is very good at keeping secrets —better than any of us ever realized, her husband included."

James narrowed his eyes. *Marianne is my half-sister? How?*

"Sometimes life has the most peculiar way of working out, doesn't it? Lucian's wife died during childbirth on the same day Marianne was born. As part of Serena's punishment, I ripped her newborn baby from her arms and from her world—much like she'd done to me a few years earlier. Lucian raised Marianne as his own daughter and no one but myself, Lucian, and Serena knew."

It was a sick achievement that Sorin was clearly proud of, and the flickering lights cast a sinister shadow across his face, matching the man inside. The ground beneath James trembled again and he wasn't sure how long he could remain upright, but he needed to hear the rest of Sorin's story.

"However, when Marianne was studying nursing she also worked in a blood lab. I'm still not sure how she came to be suspicious of her parentage, but she decided to test some of our blood herself. She stole the vials from our storage unit and uncovered the secret we'd kept hidden from her... She was upset, of course, but after a while she seemed to settle down, and soon after that she was married. But perhaps she never got over it—I think now it was the turning point for her, when she first started to think about betraying us."

"Boys, you need to get out now. The building is falling in. Move, now!" Samuel said through his earwig.

Sorin couldn't have heard Samuel's warning, but he didn't need it. The room was crumbling around them.

A glint caught his eye and James realized Sorin's pistol had been a distraction—Sorin had never intended to use it, at least not as his first line of defense.

Everything happened so fast, but James saw it in slow-motion. His reflexes, however, were too slow—the knife came hurtling toward him and lodged in his left arm. A searing, slicing pain made his muscles cramp, but when James' eyes met Sorin's, he knew he only had a second to react.

Sorin had his pistol in his hand now and his finger on the trigger.

James pulled first, firing two bullets.

Sorin fired one just as a tremor opened up the crack in the floor and James stumbled backward, falling into the wall.

Red blotches began to seep through Sorin's gray suit, and the man blinked.

"Go to your fucking Gods," James said, bitterly, putting two more bullets into the man's chest.

Sorin gasped and fell forward onto his desk.

Relief washed over James and he fought to stay upright. The ground shook beneath him and his body was tired. So tired. He wanted to sit down and close his eyes. The lure was so strong.

Deacon.

Sorin might be dead, but it wasn't over yet—he still had to get his brother out.

He took a long, deep breath in until his lungs burned.

"Move, James! Move!"

James turned, immediately seeing Sorin's bullet lodged in the wall.

Close call, James thought distantly.

"Get out of there! Now!" Samuel continued to shout at him.

James looked at the knife protruding from his arm. He pulled a small coil of rope from his pocket. Normally it was best to leave the knife in to keep the blood loss at a minimum, but James knew that with the amount of running he was about to do, it would move around and further traumatize the wound. It had to come out.

James cursed as he pulled it out, throwing it to the floor. He tied the rope around his upper arm as best he could.

"Now!" Samuel screamed this time.

James pushed the door open, finding Deacon standing over Serena, trying to stop the bleeding, James assumed.

Deacon's head snapped up and he raised his pistol. His body sagged and he lowered his arms when he saw it was James.

"Done?" Deacon asked.

James nodded. He rushed to the woman's bed.

Deacon didn't say it, but James knew from the look on his face: *It's too late.*

Tears dripped from Serena's eyes. "I'm sorry... We gave you up only to protect you." Her voice was a faint, croaky whisper.

James nodded. He had no idea what to say, and he knew they were fast running out of time.

"Your father's name was Leonardo Carter." She inhaled and James heard the familiar death rattle.

Tears streamed down her cheeks now. Serena lifted her fingers like she was trying to reach him. James hesitated, but then took her thin, fragile hand.

The lights flickered as the building prepared to give way.

"Go," she said with a nod. "I am ready to die—I have been for a long time. Save yourself, and each other." She looked between the two brothers, her lips turning up in a smile.

James squeezed her hand as she closed her eyes, wheezing in a long, slow breath.

The windows shattered around them and James looked to Deacon.

He dropped Serena's hand, took one last look at his mother, and they turned and ran.

52

JAMES THOMAS

The ground moved beneath James' feet and each step was like an obstacle course. He hurdled over a fallen man in the hallway. He didn't recognize him. He kept running.

"Turn left at the next tunnel and then take a sharp right... You have to move faster!" James heard the strain in Samuel's normally calm voice.

Deacon was right beside him and James tried to push his body faster, but that familiar woozy feeling was creeping back in.

Just make it outside, James thought. *You can black out then.*

A crashing noise caused James to look over his shoulder—part of the ceiling had just fallen in. If it had landed on them....

The tunnel exit came so fast James almost ran past it. He skidded to a stop, his body screaming in complaint, and changed directions. Deacon was pulling him by his arm, supporting some of his weight.

The lights flickered and then went out, leaving them in total darkness. James couldn't see his own hands and he'd lost his night-vision goggles earlier in the night.

A small light came on and James realized Deacon was using the light on his phone. It was a pitiful light, but it was better than nothing. James pulled out his cell phone out, doing the same.

"Power's down. I can't do anything. Keep going," Samuel said.

They kept running. Deacon kept his eyes ahead, looking for any lone men still wanting to finish them off. James kept his eyes down, trying not to trip and fall.

His grip on his cell phone was loosening, and it was slipping in his hand. It was coated with blood, he noted absently. He swapped it into the other hand and kept running.

"Next left," Samuel instructed.

James had no idea where they were. He'd lost his sense of direction in the darkness and he couldn't recall the blueprints he'd memorized so well. The blueprints he'd been able to remember when they'd first come in.

His mind was too fuzzy, and he could only think of one thing now: get outside.

Deacon gave a loud grunt but kept running. James assumed something had fallen on him.

James pushed through the pain. He couldn't lag behind because he knew Deacon wouldn't leave without him. He'd drag James out and likely lose his own life in the process.

"Two more tunnels and you'll be on the first floor."

A piercing pain behind his eyes made James squint. He no longer had any idea what was causing the pain. His entire body was riddled with it.

Keep moving, James told himself.

They took the left as Samuel had instructed and this tunnel was faring worse than the others. Gaping holes lined the floor and James was amazed when neither of them fell into one.

"Next right. Go, go, go!"

Deacon tugged his arm, forcing James' body to take the right.

They turned a hair-pin corner and James ran into the Deacon's back when he came to an abrupt stop. They had light again, and it was coming from a ball of fiery flames.

"Samuel, reroute," Deacon said. "We're not going that way."

Samuel cursed. *"Okay, go back, take the left,"* he said as another shudder tore through the building.

James fell, unable to keep his balance. He put his hands out to break his fall, but the pain knocked the breath from his lungs.

Get up, James told himself as he scrambled onto his knees, and then onto his feet. Deacon was doing the same thing, having fallen too, but he was faster. He scooped one arm underneath James' armpit and they were back up and running.

They took the left and then another right, and then the floor disappeared beneath them, crumbling in.

"Damn!" Deacon screamed as they slid down a mountain of rubble.

It felt like someone had taken a razor to James back. He landed with a thud and heard something crack.

Deacon's arm was still locked around James' and his brother was groaning in pain. Both men wheezed in short breaths, and when James dared to open his eyes he saw darkness all around them.

"Get up! Get up! You're on the ground! This is good—move north, the building is standing, you're 30 feet from an exit. Go! Go!"

"Good?" Deacon said with a groan and James would've smiled if he could've. He rolled onto his side, trying to lever his body up.

Thirty feet. You can do this.

"Let's get the fuck out of here," Deacon said, now back on his feet and pulling James upright.

James blew out a breath and then grunted as he forced his body to move. It seemed like they'd run one hundred feet before Deacon opened a door and the fresh air hit his face.

James inhaled, drawing it deep into his lungs.

The gravel beneath his feet now made it harder to run but when they hit the soft, lush grass, James fell to his knees.

They were out.

53

CAMI

Cami shielded her ears with the palms of her hands as two loud bangs were followed by the scorching eruptions of fireballs. The whole building was on fire and collapsing in. Cami wasn't sure who had given the order, but someone within the organization had: if they couldn't capture them, kill them.

"Samuel, I can't see them. Where are they?" Cami said, the heat of the explosions stinging her skin.

"Keep going straight, you'll run right into them. They're on the grass."

"Come on!" Cami said to the men still standing behind her. For a team that had never worked together, the men had been a loyal bunch, fighting beside each other all night.

She ran forward, hearing their footsteps behind.

Her eyes searched desperately, sweeping over the manicured lawns.

Finally she saw two figures on the ground. She sprinted toward them.

Deacon was awake, his chest heaving, his body swaying as he was trying to tie a piece of his torn T-Shirt around James' arm.

"Damn, James Thomas, look at you," Cami said worriedly as she kneeled down beside Deacon. "I've got it."

She took over, instructing the men to attend to Deacon. The back of his neck was coated in blood and Cami's gut clenched as she thought of where it was coming from. The fact that he was awake and responsive, though, was a very good thing. "Shine a light here, please."

James was unresponsive—for the second time that night—and he'd gathered quite a few new wounds since she'd seen him last.

Cami tied the ripped piece of T-Shirt around James' arm, fastening it tight enough to reduce the blood flow. It was a nasty gash and it looked like a blade wound—a wound that, if it went through the muscle, would likely need surgery.

His left arm looked worse than his right, but both were red and sticky. Cami lifted what was left of his T-Shirt. His chest wounds were open. She muttered a curse—he was a mess.

When Cami tried to roll him over to check his back, he groaned, but his eyes stayed shut.

This isn't good.

She pressed the palm of her hand lightly over his torso, trying to locate the source of pain. He groaned again and his eyelids twitched when she pressed on his lower right ribs.

Really not good.

She heard the purring of an engine as one of their vans pulled up beside them. Cami shouted over the crackling of the blaze, instructing the men to lift him carefully.

"Sorry, James, this is going to hurt," she said as six men hauled him up, keeping his body as straight as possible.

James grunted and then sucked in a shallow breath as his body was lifted into the air.

"Get in the van, quick," she said, watching them as she spoke to Samuel. "Is the doc on standby?"

"Yes, he's at the safe house. How bad is James?"

"I don't know yet. Multiple wounds, a muscle that possibly requires surgical stitching, likely cracked ribs. And I haven't even looked at the wounds on his back, but his T-Shirt is stuck to his skin."

"Tsk," Samuel tutted, and Cami smiled at his disapproval. *"Well,*

he's alive. They're both alive. Let's just count our blessings. I'll speak to the doc and confirm a hospital in case he needs it."

"Thanks," Cami said, jumping into the back of the van. "I'll clean him up and treat what I can until we get there."

Deacon was propped up against the side of the van. "Give him some blood first. I don't know how much he's lost, but it's a lot."

Cami inserted a new intravenous line, hooked up bloods and fluids and then did what she could to clean up his arm wounds.

She crawled across to Deacon, looking him over.

"How are you doing?"

He held up his hand shakily. "My head is pounding. Just give me something for the pain. Otherwise I'm fine."

Cami drew up a dose and Deacon held out his arm. She pushed the needle through his skin, finding his vein the first time. She'd had a good teacher.

Their eyes met and Cami had so many questions about what had happened in the tower, but they were questions she didn't want to ask with Biskup's men around.

"It's all okay," Deacon said. His eyes dropped to James. "And he's going to be okay. But he's going to be fucking sore when he wakes up."

Cami grinned. Sore was better than dead.

She crawled back to James, using her hands and feet to keep her balance. She pulled out half the contents of the medical kit. She took the scissors and cut his T-shirt in half, and then cleaned his chest.

The text *Cerah zalû* lay emblazoned on James' chest.

The Gods had failed Eric when he'd needed them most. Cami wondered if Eric would still believe in them when James and Biskup were done with him.

Lucian and Sorin and the entire organization were gone—or at least Lucian would be soon. Sure, there would be offspring clusters of Saratani, recruits that were as zealous and passionate as Eric, recruits who wouldn't be able to let it go. But it had never really been the organization who had wanted James—it had been Sorin.

And now Sorin was dead, and Cami prayed that the nightmare was over for James.

They pulled up at the safe house and Cami coordinated the transfer of James inside. Deacon hobbled in with the support of another man. The doc was already busy—he had been for a good hour as Cami had sent vans back, loaded with injured men. They were lying on the carpet, on the couches, on the table, on the beds. It looked like a hospital tent in the middle of a war zone.

The doc's head snapped up as the men carried James in and he pulled his lips to the side. Cami gave him a summary of James' injuries—from what she'd been able to diagnose with a torch light in the back of a swerving van.

She then let the doc take over and went to the kitchen they'd stocked earlier. Half the contents of the refrigerator were already gone, but she grabbed two bottles of juice. She found Deacon sitting beside James now, watching the doc carefully.

"Tell Samuel we've got to take him in," the doc said. "I can't treat him here. I need a hospital—just for a few hours. I need to image him to check for internal bleeding and broken bones, and then I'll stitch up the arm muscle. We can bring him back after that."

Cami had been hoping that wasn't going to be the outcome, because although they thought it a small risk given that most of their enemies had been wiped out tonight, it still remained a risk to take him to a hospital. Deacon frowned and Cami knew he was thinking the same thing.

"I'll get a team together," Cami said.

A team that would stand guard over James' hospital room.

54

MAK ASHWOOD

Mak answered her cell phone on the first ring.

"Hey, Mak," Deacon said. "I've got good news. It's over. We've got Eric and Lucian captive, and Sorin is dead."

Mak exhaled the breath she felt like she'd been holding since James had said goodbye. "Is he okay?"

"James has seen better days, but he'll live. We've taken him to a hospital for a few hours so they can do a full assessment of his injuries and stitch up a wound. He's going to need a long, quiet recovery period, but he should be able to have that now."

Should be able to have that.

"Are you okay?" Mak asked.

"I'm all right. Cami's okay. I think everyone on the team has got a few wounds, but that's to be expected."

Mak noticed her hands were trembling and she wondered if it was all the anxiety she'd been holding in so tightly.

"What happens now?" Mak asked.

"Once James is back in the safe house and we're secure, I'll get you on a plane to Romania."

"Thank you," Mak said.

"Okay. Be ready to leave in a few hours."

"Sure." She paused. "Why did you capture Lucian, Deacon? Does Biskup want him as well?" Mak asked in a hushed whisper. Marianne was in the adjacent room.

"I kept him alive in case we need him. He'll live only until we confirm that we don't."

And then you'll kill him, Mak thought.

Mak cleared her throat. "Okay. What do you want me to tell Marianne?"

"I want her on the plane to Romania, too. The doc has got a lot of patients to treat and he could do with a nurse to assist." Deacon sighed. "From there I've got no idea what we're going to do with her. Samuel's found some overseas bank accounts that we think Marianne was hiding money in, so once we're sure she'll be safe, Samuel can use that money to buy her a home somewhere. She'll be able to start a new life with her children."

Mak smiled—they knew.

"I've got to go and organize a few things, but I'll call you soon with further details."

"Thank you, Deacon," Mak said. "Thank you for everything."

"You're welcome," he said before he hung up.

Mak took a minute to just be. To let the gravity of relief settle in. It was over.

Marianne stepped out into the hallway and Mak wondered how closely she'd been eavesdropping.

"That was Deacon," Mak said, lowering her voice, not sure where Kaela was. "Sorin is dead, and Eric and your father have been captured

Her lips began to tremble and she gripped onto the doorframe. Mak moved toward her, thinking the woman was going to collapse.

While Eric's imminent death likely didn't grieve her, Mak wondered how her father's would.

Marianne clearly tried to reel in her tears, but they came anyway in the form of small, trembling sobs. She covered her face with her hand.

Mak gently took her other hand, seriously worried the pregnant woman was going to collapse.

Mak didn't offer any vocal words of support, and Marianne didn't seem to need them. After a few moments she collected herself. "I can't believe it's over. I can't believe they did it."

Mak struggled to comprehend it as well. For a long time it seemed like it would never end, and now it suddenly had.

"Deacon asked if you would come with me to Romania. The doc needs a nurse," Mak said. It had been more of a demand than a request, but Mak thought there was no harm in rewording it.

"Sure," she said, the idea seeming to give her strength as she brushed away her tears. "Did James get the answers he wanted?" she asked, her face now impassive.

"I don't know," Mak said. "I suppose we'll find out soon."

Marianne nodded. "I'll pack up and get ready."

Mak looked across at the little girl curled up in a ball. Her father was an awful man, but she didn't know that. And she'd never see him again. Her life would never be the same, but Mak hoped that as she grew older, and one day learned the truth, she'd be grateful for the sacrifices her mother had made.

Mak left Marianne and went back to the couch. It took her only a few minutes to pack—she had little more than a small case of clothes and a bag of case notes. She then went to the kitchen and cleaned up, washing and drying all of the dishes. She kept herself busy until Deacon's call came. Her cell phone was never far from her fingers.

55

JAMES THOMAS

The rhythmic sound of the monitoring equipment was the first indication that he was still alive. His eyelids opened and then fell shut, several times. Finally his eyes focused and James looked around him. He was in a bed, and there were men sleeping on the floor all around him.

Safe house.

James sighed in relief. He wasn't bound to a bed, and Eric wasn't carving his chest. But where was Eric?

The monitor beeped faster as he tried to piece together the night. He remembered chasing Eric down the street, and then binding him. And then he remembered being at Lucian's estate, and the floor collapsing beneath them as they were running. He remembered falling. He remembered nothing after that. There were more than a few blanks in his mind.

"Hey."

James turned his head. He hadn't realized Cami was there. She gave him a beaming smile.

"Where's Eric?" James asked.

"Sleeping in a cell. You gave us strict instructions that no one was to wake him except you, so we've kept him sedated. You've been to the hospital and back."

"Right," James said, dazed.

"Do you remember what happened last night?"

James could tell that Cami wanted to say more, but was giving him the chance to remember himself.

"Most of it, I think... I know my father's name," James said and Cami's eyes creased as her smile broadened.

James had no doubt Samuel was already busy looking for intel on Leonardo Carter.

"Where's Mak?" James asked. He didn't think he'd ever wanted to hold her more than he did right now.

"She's on a plane, on her way here to Romania."

James nodded and then looked at the lines in his arms, noting what they were hooked up to. He wanted to get out of this bed—he wanted to see Eric.

"Ay, slow down," Cami said. "Doc says you have to stay in bed. You've got two cracked ribs, a bruised vertebra, a blade wound, two gunshot wounds, a carved chest and an array of other cuts and abrasions. Quite an impressive list, Thomas."

James looked at his mangled hands. Some of those wounds were from scaling down the warehouse building. He had no idea where the others had come from.

"Tough night at the office," he said drily.

James began to detach the lines, but Cami stopped him. "I'll do it, but don't tell the doc. He's going to be pissed."

James grinned at her. "I've always liked you, Cami."

Cami scoffed. "I'm not trying to enable you, but I know you're going to get out of bed regardless. With some help you might at least minimize the pain and damage to your body."

James winked as Deacon walked into the room.

"What is going on here?" Deacon asked.

"I'm going to see Eric," James said. He'd dreamed of this moment for months.

Deacon shot a disapproving look, but nevertheless helped Cami to get him out of bed.

"Better hurry, the doc's upstairs but he'll be in to check on you again soon," Deacon said.

James hobbled down to the garage, wincing with every step. Cami and Deacon lowered him into the backseat and Cami slid in beside him. Deacon drove.

James noted Deacon's freshly shaven head and the large white bandage across the base of his skull. James wondered if Deacon should even be driving, but he didn't comment—he just wanted to get to wherever they were going.

"Where exactly is he?" James asked.

"He's being heavily guarded in the basement of the second safe house we secured," Deacon said, veering out onto the street. "Maksym's in charge."

The building was only a few minutes' drive from the main safe house. The car came to a stop and James realized he didn't have a knife.

Maksym will definitely have one, he thought.

James waited until his escorts opened the door, helping him to his feet. His breaths were shallow and each one tormented his body. If Cami hadn't told him he'd cracked a few ribs, he would've known himself at this point.

James' feet moved slowly, but his mind was running at full speed.

Deacon unlocked the door and guided them to a set of narrow stairs. James looked at them fearfully, knowing the pain they would entail, but he also knew what was at the bottom: Eric. It was like a pot of gold dangling in front of him.

He took the steps one by one, pausing at the bottom to catch his breath.

"Let's go," James eventually said.

They passed Lucian first. He was supine in a steel cage—a makeshift cell.

In the second cage, Eric was bound and as pale as a corpse.

Maksym looked at James and chuckled. "You look fucking terrible."

James felt terrible, but it was irrelevant in that moment. "Have you got a knife?"

A smile stretched Maksym's lips. "Sure," he said, pulling out a pocket blade.

James took it and then stepped—hobbled—forward and into the cell.

James cut the fabric of Eric's shirt and then looked down at the man. The man that had caused him so much pain—the man that had almost taken his life.

James took a deep, satisfying breath as he brought the blade to Eric's collarbone, drawing it down, creating a ribbon of blood that followed James' hand.

He watched as Eric began to awake. His hands flinched, his eyelids twitched, his body jolted. James leaned over him so that when Eric woke up the first thing he would see was a pair of black eyes. Judging by his reaction, James knew he recognized them.

"You didn't think I'd let you die that easily, did you?" James said.

Eric's teeth began to saw against each other.

"Where are your Gods, Eric? Where are they now?"

"Fuck you." Eric spat the words out.

James grinned. "Sorin's dead—the Gods didn't save him. Lucian's as blind as a fucking bat and he'll soon be as dead as Sorin. But you..." James shook his head. "You're going to live for a while longer, and you're about to go on a little adventure. An adventure to Alexandr Biskup's house. Your new life is just beginning."

Eric growled and fought against the restraints.

"I told you that your death, when it came, would be very painful," James whispered as he dug the knife in deep, twisting it just like Eric had done to the sacrifice—Julia.

Eric sucked in a breath, screaming as his eyes rolled back in his head.

James finished the *V* carving, stopping just before Eric's jugular.

He left the tip of the blade there, teasing Eric.

Eric's eyes darted all around the room. James lifted the blade, leaned in, and whispered, "You don't get to die yet."

He wiped the blade clean on Eric's torso and then walked away, handing it back to Maksym.

James stopped at Lucian's cell. He was awake now—no doubt due to Eric's agonized cries.

"Are you praying to your Gods?" James asked and Lucian's head snapped toward him. Lucian didn't respond, but James had no doubt the man knew who was speaking to him.

"Unlock the door," James said to no one in particular, but one of Biskup's men stepped forward with the keys.

Lucian jolted upright and his hands gripped the edge of the bed, his fingers curling over the metal as James stepped in.

"Choosing Makaela Ashwood as a gift to Eric was your first mistake," James said. "Supporting Sorin's self-indulgent quest to punish his wife by attempting to kill me was your second."

Lucian's sightless eyes roved the room agitatedly. "It was the Gods. The Gods speak to us!"

James sneered. "Did the Gods tell you to take a woman's child from her arms and raise her as your own, denying her any chance of knowing her mother?"

Silence.

"I didn't think so," James said. "Tell me, because I'm curious to know... If your Gods punish the family members of someone who betrays them, who were the Gods going to punish? You? Or Sorin?"

"I am her father," Lucian said. "The Gods will punish me."

James grinned. "The Gods won't punish you. But we will."

"I can give you information," Lucian said quickly. "I'll trade it for a clean death—a bullet straight to the heart."

James looked at Lucian's blank eyes. "You're not in a position to be making deals," he said. "But I'll make you one: tell me the information and then I'll decide whether or not to give you a clean death." Silence. "It's a good deal, Lucian—you should take it."

It didn't take long for Lucian to start talking. "Have you asked yourself why Sorin held on to his anger all these years? Why the betrayal hurt him so dearly? It was as much *who* betrayed him as it was *how* he was betrayed."

"Get on with it, Lucian," James said. He was out of patience and his vision was blurring.

"Leonardo—your father—was Sorin's best friend. His business partner. His closest confidant. They were not related by blood, but in every sense they were brothers—much like you and the Ranger appear to be. Imagine if the Ranger had an affair with your wife and planned to destroy your organization... Perhaps then you'd make the same choices as Sorin, no?"

"No, Lucian, I wouldn't," James said, turning to leave, needing a wall or some kind of support to keep him upright.

"Please! Please! One clean bullet, please!"

James kept walking, stepping out of the cell. He looked over his shoulder. "Maksym, finish him... Finish him however you like," James said.

James slowly hobbled back up the stairs, smiling as Lucian's screams echoed loud in his ears.

James had his eyes closed, resting. He didn't hear her walk in, but he knew she was there.

"Good evening," James said, opening his eyes and forcing himself to smile.

"You're okay," Mak's voice cracked and she seemed to do her own sweeping assessment of his injuries.

James held out his hand and she rushed forward, but stopped at the side of the bed. She sat on the very edge, carefully.

James smiled. "I'm okay. You won't hurt me," he said. "I'll heal...in a few months time."

It could've been worse—a lot worse. James knew it, and so did she.

She went to take his hand and then hesitated when she saw his torn-up skin. He took hers instead, holding it in his lap, brushing his thumb over her knuckles.

"Biskup's arriving shortly to take Eric. It's finally over, Mak," James said.

"I don't know how to thank you. There aren't words for how grateful I am for what you've done for me, and my family," Mak said and James saw that she was fighting back the tears. "Is it over for you, now, too?" Mak asked.

"Yeah, it is... I met my mother," James said, recalling the memories. "I mean, I'd probably need a DNA test to confirm it, but everything seems that she is—was—my mother."

Mak frowned, and then bit her lip. "Did you speak to her?"

"Very briefly. There wasn't a lot of time," James said casually even though the situation had been anything but. "She told me my father's name and Samuel's run a few reports. He found my birth certificate... my birth name is Evan Carter." The name was unfamiliar to him, and he couldn't associate with it. He much preferred the name James Thomas.

James continued. "And, as it turned out, I'd already met my half-sister."

Her eyes widened. "Really? When?"

James glanced over her shoulder, then returned his gaze to her eyes. "When she helped me escape."

Mak's face reflected her thoughts, and then her mouth formed an O. "Marianne? How?"

"They were my first thoughts, too," James said. "Marianne is Serena and Sorin's daughter—Lucian raised her, but he's not her father."

"Wow," Mak said, "I did not see that coming... So, you're dating your half-sister's husband's wife, right?"

James wet his lips, grinning. "You'll have to ask the Gods about that one."

"That is wrong on so many levels," Mak said, shaking her head, but the corner of her lips turned up. "How do you feel about seeing your mother—meeting her—after all these years?"

"I don't know... I haven't had a lot of time to process it, I suppose. But I didn't feel much when I looked at her. I don't know her, and I've never had a mother, so I didn't look at her like that. Sister Francine..." The words lodged in his throat. "She was more of a mother."

Sister Francine's death was also something he'd have to force himself to deal with at some point, but for now he just wanted to heal and repair his relationship with Mak—those were his priorities.

Mak squeezed his hand softly and when he searched her eyes, he didn't find any of the things he'd always feared. Even when he'd finally told her about Paris, her reaction had been one of sadness and grief rather than the shame and disgust he'd expected to see.

I should've told you.

"How long will you stay here?" Mak asked with a heavy voice.

"A few days, maybe. You can go back to New York tonight, Mak. Go and spend some time with your family. I think it will be good for you. And I'm sure Maya would like to see you."

Mak nodded, her eyes cast down.

He lifted her chin. "Take as much time as you need... Call me when you're ready to talk."

She exhaled a shaky breath. "I love you, James, I just need—"

"I know," he said, gently. "I understand... And I think you should talk to someone about Eric, about Tom's death and Maya's kidnapping. You've been through multiple traumatic experiences, and I think it will help. We have a few contacts that we use for our staff— they're on our payroll, as such. We've already given their details to Maya, and Samuel's going to send them to your phone, too. Make an appointment."

"Okay. I will," she said with glistening eyes.

She leaned in and he brushed his lips over hers. His body heated, his skin sung. She deepened the kiss, and he closed his eyes, committing it to memory. When she pulled away, he felt part of him leave with her.

James' eyes sprung open as a loud bang pierced his sleep.

"Sorry!" someone yelled and James exhaled in relief, assuming they'd just dropped something.

It took him a minute to realize who was standing beside his bed, hooking up a fresh bag of fluids.

"Don't worry, I didn't put anything in it," Marianne said with a look that indicated she was joking, but the fleeting thought had crossed his mind, too.

He mustered a grin. "Good to know."

Marianne pressed her lips together, perhaps searching for the words.

"Anything you'd like to tell me?" James raised one eyebrow.

She finished securing the bag and took a seat in the chair beside his bed. "I didn't know whether to tell you or not. I didn't know if us being half-siblings could somehow be used against me, and I'd already taken so many risks."

James nodded. "Fair enough. Is that the same reason you didn't tell us about your pregnancy?"

She nodded heavily, not seeming surprised that he knew.

"We don't hurt innocent people, Marianne. And we definitely don't hurt people who are helping us," James said.

It was a very surreal feeling to know that he was looking at, and having a conversation with, his half-sister. As a child, he'd so often wondered if he'd ever meet his family—and now that Marianne sat beside him, he didn't really know what to say.

"For what it's worth," James said. "I think you were very brave to defy Eric and the organization."

She gave a small smile. "It runs in the family. We got it from our mother."

James wondered how much Marianne knew about Serena, and how much time Marianne had spent with her. They were conversations he hoped to have one day, but as it was he could barely keep his eyes open.

"You should rest," she said, standing.

"Deacon is going to arrange an apartment for you in New York,"

James said. "It'll be best, and easier for us, for you to be in New York. There might be some small clusters or offspring of the organization that aren't thrilled about what you did. We'll monitor things for a few months at least, and then when we deem it safe you can decide what you want to do from there."

"Thank you, James," Marianne said. She turned to leave but stopped. "We'll talk again soon...if you want to."

"I do," James said, giving a small smile.

The warehouse creaked as the cool night breeze blew through it. James sat on a couch that someone had dragged in.

"Biskup will be here in a few minutes," Deacon said, coming to sit beside him. "I've just woken Eric up. I think he was relieved to see it was me with a needle and not you with a knife."

"His relief is going to be very short-lived," James said, but there was something else on his mind. "The night that I was captured, did you doubt that you could get to Mak?" James turned to his brother, watching him carefully.

"Why are you asking me this now?" Deacon said, lines creasing his forehead.

"Because we haven't had a chance to talk about what happened, and I want to know," James said.

"Yes," Deacon eventually admitted. "It was too close. There was a moment when I thought that I wasn't going to get to her. We couldn't get clear shots at the men hustling her out, and I was scared that if we took the shots we'd kill her instead of them."

Even now the thought of Eric's men taking her was bone-chilling. James shook out the thoughts—unable to bear thinking them. Thoughts that were Deacon's reality.

James looked his brother in the eye. "You don't deserve the pain this life has brought you, Deacon. Your life should've been so different," James said.

"I think that every day." He shrugged. "But it is the way it is. I don't know why life works the way it does, and maybe we're not supposed to know. Maybe there is a bigger plan for all of us."

James heard the doubt in his voice. "You don't believe that."

"Yet I keep telling myself that every day. Otherwise what is the point of going on with life? I was spared for a reason, surely, so I want to know what it was. If I get to the end of my life and I still don't know, then I'll be really pissed—that's all I can tell you."

Their conversation was cut short when Biskup strolled into the room.

"Gentlemen, what a fine evening this is!"

Deacon stood to greet him, but James didn't. He was in too much pain, and he didn't have it in him to make pleasantries this evening.

"You both look like hell," Biskup said, grinning. His eyes turned serious. "Where is he?"

"I'll take you down," Deacon said and James nodded.

Biskup followed Deacon, his long, black coat flowing behind him.

James listened, but he didn't hear anything. Finally footsteps sounded as Biskup and Deacon returned.

Biskup sat down on a crate opposite the couch. He motioned for one of his men to come over. The man passed Biskup a bottle of whisky and three glasses.

"Tonight we celebrate," Biskup said, his face joyous. "A job very well done, boys. If I need help again, I know who to call."

James looked to Deacon, who didn't attempt to hide his true feelings.

Biskup chuckled, and then poured three glasses neat.

He passed one to each of the brothers.

James was on a cocktail of medications right now, but he wasn't going to refuse the celebratory drink.

They clinked glasses and as James brought the drink to his lips, Eric's scream roared through the warehouse.

Revenge had never tasted so good.

EPILOGUE

JAMES THOMAS

James dropped his bag by the kitchen island. He had five minutes before he had to leave for the airport. He searched the fridge for a snack. After months of living in makeshift camps and safe houses, it had taken an adjustment period to get used to living back at Thomas Security.

But now his life was back to normal—running the company, living quietly, staying out of trouble. And it was dull. Agonizingly dull. Even all of their client cases were stable. He had one upcoming trip to Tokyo in a few weeks—to finish paying the last of his debts—but that was his only foreseeable adventure.

However, it wasn't the action he missed. Nor was it the adrenaline. It was the woman he loved.

The woman who had moved into another apartment—one he'd had no say in. The woman who had no security team except a bodyguard—Cami. And one with whom he'd had very little contact with for four weeks and counting.

James pulled out a container of chicken and fried rice that he'd cooked a few nights ago. *Dull,* he thought. *Even my food is dull.*

One might've assumed James had been lonely all of his life, particularly the years spent in orphanages. And while that was true for short periods of time, he'd usually been content. He hadn't known any different. He hadn't known what it was like to truly love someone. But now, despite the company of Deacon, Samuel, and Cami, he was unbearably lonely.

James put the container in the microwave, watching it spin, thinking he should take a step back before the microwaves fried his brain. He snorted, and stayed where he was—it was much more likely something was going to kill him before a few microwaves did him over. However, with the organization destroyed, and Pavel Sokolov eliminated, his future had never been more secure. Sure, there were still Russian enemies, and other men from his past, but the worst had been dealt with.

James was still watching the container spin when a knock at the door broke through his idle thoughts. He paused. No one who lived in this building bothered to knock before letting themselves in, though occasionally senior staff did turn up unannounced. *Maybe it's Lenny,* James thought.

The microwave beeped, but James ignored it, walking to the foyer. His heart skipped a beat when he saw his guest.

"Hi," he said, opening the door.

"Happy fortieth birthday!" Mak held out a small gift-wrapped package. Her eyes darted side to side. "You're looking at it like it's a bomb," she said.

"Um, sorry, I'm just surprised," James said, smiling. He accepted the gift, clueless as to what it might be. "Come in," he said, stepping aside and closing the door behind her.

A subtle hint of citrus-fresh perfume trailed her like a wake and James yearned for her. To hold her—even if just for a second.

She walked into the kitchen and her chest rose with tension. "You're very hard to buy for, because you don't want for anything, so I hope you like it."

On the contrary, he thought. *I want for one thing—you.*

"Should I open it now?" James said. He wasn't used to receiving gifts.

Marianne had stopped by earlier this morning, but they were hardly at a gift-giving stage in their relationship. And Samuel had organized a huge cake for James' birthday, which they'd devoured in Samuel's office, but that was as far as they went with gifts. He'd grown so use to celebrating James Thomas' birthday that it didn't feel right to celebrate today—Evan's birthday: 12 December.

Mak smiled, wiggling her eyebrows up and down. James chuckled and then undid the wrapping.

Inside a velvet pouch was an intricate silver pocket watch.

"In our family it's a tradition that the baby boys get a watch with their name engraved on it. Obviously I don't know what the traditions were in your family, or if you even had them, but my brothers still have their pocket watches displayed in their homes," she said. She seemed to search his eyes, but he didn't know what she was searching for.

"Thank you," he said, stunned by the thoughtfulness of the gift. He turned it over, brushing his thumb over the engraving. His name, and his birth date. He'd never been given such beautiful gift.

"Thank you, it's perfect," he said, trying to keep his composure.

The microwave beeped again and James cleared the settings—he was grateful for even the slightest distraction. He kept the pocket watch in his hand, not wanting to let go of it.

"So," Mak started, pressing her lips together, her eyes were unfocused as she ran a hand through her hair, mindlessly, as she seemed to search for the right words. "This past month without you has been...more difficult than I could've ever imagined." She took another deep breath. "I keep thinking about us, and the issues that stand between us, and I still can't find a resolution."

James' pulse quickened.

What is she saying?

"I want you to tell me the truth about who you are and the things you've done"—she cleared her throat—"even the less-than-admirable things."

"You know the worst, Mak. I meant that when I said it."

"And I believe you. But I need to know everything in between, too. I know that you can't tell me things about the cases you worked on, anything related to the CIA, and that's okay—I don't need to know that. I do want to know all of *you*, though. No lies, no secrets. What's the point now, anyway? I know enough about you now that any of your remaining enemies would have a field day torturing me for information, so why hide it?"

James nodded, and took a small step forward, and then another, closing the space between them. "I'll tell you everything about me," James said leaning in, drawn to her. "I'll give you all of me."

He wouldn't repeat the mistakes of the past. He'd tell her about himself, and not just the parts he wanted her to know.

He took her hand and felt a small tremble in it.

"I promise," James said, looking deep into her eyes. "We'll take things slow. Go back to the beginning. It'll be the way it should've been the first time."

"There won't be a third chance, James," she said quietly.

"I know," he said quickly. He didn't need to be told. "I don't want to live without you, Mak. I always thought that I was happiest on the field, amongst the action—that that was where I belonged, what I was born for. And while I do enjoy it, it's not what makes me happy. You do. Our life together brought me more joy than anything else in my life has. Without you, it's so bleak. There are more things about my past that you won't like, but you do know the worst of it."

She knew about Paris, and she knew he was capable of such things as removing a man's face—they were definitely his least *admirable* qualities. Although, he wasn't going to promise her that he'd never do the latter again.

She rolled her bottom lip between her teeth and James' eyes dropped to them.

"How do we move forward?" she asked. "I want this to work, but some things have to change. I struggle with you making decisions for me—decisions like choosing my apartment without consulting me, however good your intentions."

James nodded. "I get it. And unless it's a life-or-death situation, we'll make decisions together... We'll talk it through, negotiate. Compromise." He raised an eyebrow.

Mak looked like she was trying to hide a smile.

"We can make this work, Mak. I know we can. It won't be smooth sailing every day, but we'll have many more good days than bad. I want to spend the rest of my life with you."

She looked up through her long lashes, her lips just inches from his now.

"I want that, too," she said, quietly, but without hesitation.

Her chest rose and James closed his eyes as her lips parted. He put a hand on the small of her back, bringing her body flush against his. The kiss was soft, tender, innocent, and perfect. And it left him completely breathless. He pulled back, bringing her head to his chest, kissing the crown of her head.

"I love you, James," she said, her voice muffled against his sweater. She tightened her arms around him, and he felt pure contentment.

Every night since his escape he'd gone to bed longing to hold her —praying to hold her again. Someone very kind had answered his prayers.

Eventually, James pulled back, but he didn't let go.

"So," she said, and then stopped, her eyes finding his bag. "Were you going somewhere?"

James was surprised she hadn't seen the bag when she'd walked in. He would've seen it, but old habits die hard. And he didn't think now was a good time for a lecture in paying attention to her surroundings.

"Uh, yeah, I was. I'm pretty sure I've missed my flight," James said with a beaming grin.

"Why didn't you say something?" she asked, smiling.

"It doesn't matter, it was a personal trip. I ..." he stumbled. "I was going to Paris. I was going to visit his grave," James said.

He questioned again whether he should give the baby a name, instead of continuing to call him "Him." He hadn't yet come up with the answer.

"Come with me," James said.

"Now?" Her eyes widened.

"Why not? Did you have plans this weekend?"

"No, not really... I have a prison visit at Riker's on Sunday after-noon, but that's it," she said.

Plenty of time, James thought. "We'll fly overnight, spend the day in Paris, and I'll have you back before lunch on Sunday," James said.

He'd never intended to take anyone to the grave—he hadn't even been sure if he would go there himself until this morning—but now he couldn't think of anyone he'd rather take with him. "We'll go past your apartment on the way to the airport and you can grab what you need. Please, come with me."

Her lips turned into a smile. "Okay."

James drew his cell phone and messaged Samuel to organize a jet. Samuel's response was quick.

Two options: 1) A small plane can be ready in forty-five minutes, no airhostess. 2) Larger plane ready in 1.5 hours, airhostess.

James typed his response: *Small plane. Thanks.*

James picked up his bag, swung it over his shoulder and held out his hand. He couldn't stop smiling.

The engines were humming when they arrived in the hangar. James parked the car and noticed Mak peering out of the windows, and then she looked at the plane.

"We're not taking a security team?" she asked, giving him a look that indicated she was excited by the prospect.

"No, right now the risk is low in general—plus no one will be looking for us where we'll be going," James said. "When we first started dating, I already knew that someone was hunting me. Actu-ally, that's what I'd been doing in London—following up on a lead— and that's why I was on your flight back to New York. Needless to say I was being extremely cautious when we first started dating."

Mak narrowed her eyes. "And by 'following up on a lead' you mean what, exactly?"

"I mean extracting information via physical means," James said.

"That's a polite way of putting it," she said, raising an eyebrow. She looked at the plane again. "Okay, let's go."

"I'll be a good bodyguard, I promise. Come on," he said, getting out of the car and retrieving their bags from the trunk.

He held Mak's hand as they walked toward the stairs. He checked in with the pilot when they boarded and then searched the small refrigerator for some refreshments. He felt Mak's eyes on him. She was the only person he liked watching him.

He grabbed a pillow from the overhead storage. "Come and sit here," he said, relaxing down on the couch. She sat beside him just as the plane began its taxi.

James buckled her in, taking her already tense hands. This was the first time he'd been on a plane with her and could actually distract her the way he'd wanted to.

"Relax," he whispered, angling his body toward her. He ran his hand up her leg, resting it high on her thigh. Her breath hitched and James didn't think it had anything to do with her aviation-related anxiety.

James felt that invisible force pulling him in. She opened her lips for him, and her mouth tasted like a sweet mint. James moaned as her tongue wrapped around his, caressing it.

His hand moved up to her waist, and then her ribs. He stopped there. He wanted to take things slow, in every sense. He didn't want a moment of their time rushed.

She cupped his face and as James lowered her back onto the pillow, their mouths never separated. Their bodies clung to each other. James' thumb brushed against the side of her breast and he stopped himself again. He wasn't going to have sex with her an hour after they'd resolved to try and make things work, nor was he going to have sex with her on this plane. The door to the cockpit was closed, and James knew the pilot wouldn't come out for several hours yet. But still, it wasn't appropriate—especially not for how James wanted to pleasure her, not for how he wanted to hear her scream his name.

James brushed her hair off of her cheek, gazing down at her.

"I'm happy you're here with me," James said. "I've been back to Paris a few times—for work purposes—since everything happened, and all of those times I've been filled with dread. It's easier with you here."

"Because I'm a good distraction?" she joked.

"I won't lie and say that's not part of it," he said, smirking. "But it's more than that, it's having you here, by my side... I'm glad you know about Paris, Mak. I'm glad I can share it with you, despite how horrific it is."

"I don't believe you would've done it if you'd known, James. No part of that sits well in my soul. Even now I can see the anguish on your face when you're thinking about it."

James shifted her so that he could lie down on his back—still mindful of his healing wounds—and then she tucked into his side, curling up in his arms. She drew circles on his abdomen with her fingertips and James closed his eyes, concentrating on her touch. He felt the lure of sleep calling him and he let it take him. He had everything he wanted.

~

"Do you think we should stop and buy some flowers?" James asked as he drove down the road. "I don't really want to leave them there, though. It's unlikely anyone would stumble across the grave..." He swallowed. "But still."

Mak placed a hand on his leg. "You don't need to take flowers." She smiled at him and he was grateful for the support. The closer they got the more the self-loathing kicked in, but Mak continued to look at him the same way she always had, and that helped to ease his tortured mind.

"How did you find this place?" she asked.

The grass was a vibrant green and small shrubs bunched together in clusters. Quaint village homes were staggered over the country-side, but James was yet to see anyone. They hadn't even passed another vehicle in the last twenty minutes. It was one of the reasons he'd chosen this site: it was quiet and peaceful.

"I'd been to this area before, passing through on a mission, and thought it was beautiful," James said, activating his indicator despite the lack of traffic. He turned onto a thin, winding road.

"It's breathtaking," Mak said, her voice mesmerized.

They were almost there, and James' pulse quickened. If Mak hadn't been in the car he wondered if he would've turned around at this point.

But he didn't—not today. He kept his foot on the accelerator as the old home came into view. When he parked at the front, Mak's jaw dropped.

"You buried him at someone's house?" she asked in a hushed whisper.

A slight laugh slipped through his lips. "I buried him at my house."

"Oh," she said. "That's okay, then." She leaned forward, looking through the windscreen. "You probably need to do some minor reno-vations at some point."

James chuckled. There was a good possibility that if he didn't repair the large cracks in the walls that the house would fall down, but he figured he had a few years yet.

Mak's expression sobered. "Are you okay?"

"Not really," James said. "But I need to do this."

He looked at the door handle, but he didn't get out. Mak must've seen his hesitation and she opened her door, leaving him in the car alone.

He watched her walk away, but even in the remote countryside, at a secluded property, that made him anxious so he sighed and went after her.

He locked the car and took Mak's hand when he caught up to her. She weaved her fingers through this, and gave it a small squeeze.

"Which way?" she asked.

"Through here," James said, forcing himself to put one foot in front of the other.

He led her behind the farmhouse and through the back garden. He opened the old gate that led to the countryside behind it. He'd purchased the land as part of the home package.

Flashbacks of the only other time he'd come here surfaced in his mind. He'd cradled the fetus in a thick blanket in his arms, carrying him down this very path. He blocked the images before he couldn't take another step forward.

They kept walking, farther and farther away from the house until James could no longer see it when he looked over his shoulder. He looked for the markings he'd carved into the trees, using them as signposts. When they came to a part of the ground that was covered in purple flowers, James knew he was in the right spot. He led Mak through them, stopping four foot away from a boulder that James had painstakingly pushed into position.

He set his eyes on the green grass between him and the boulder.

I'm so sorry.

"He's there," James said with a voice so thick he could hardly make out the words he'd spoken. He pointed to the concealed grave.

Mak gave a sigh that sounded like a small cry. She put a hand on his back and rested her head against his arm. James wrapped his arm around her shoulder, holding her for strength.

He stood, motionless, staring at the grave. He hadn't realized how much time had passed until he looked up to the now ink-blue sky—night was setting in.

"Do you think he knows how sorry I am?" James asked.

"I don't know if he does," Mak said. "But I do. You're a good man, James Thomas—your mistakes can't take that away from you. And they can't take you away from me, either."

James drew in a long breath, never more grateful to have Mak by his side. James took a shaky step forward, kneeled down, and placed his hand on the grass, over his son, letting it rest there.

I'll come back again soon. I promise.

Slowly, on weak legs, he stood and gave a small, stiff nod.

"Let's go home," James said.

He held Mak's hand as they walked back through the fields, but his eyes remained fixed upward, gazing at the twinkling blanket above—he'd finally found peace within the stars.

//

ALSO BY BROOKE SIVENDRA

THE JAMES THOMAS SERIES

#1 - ESCANTA

#2 - SARATANI

#3 - SARQUIS

#4 - LUCIAN

#5 - SORIN

#0.5 - THE FAVOR

The complete James Thomas series is available now. THE FAVOR is a novella, and Brooke recommends reading it after SORIN.

THE SOUL SERIES

#1 - The Secrets of Their Souls

#2 - The Ghosts of Their Pasts

#3 - The Blood of Their Sins

A GIFT FROM BROOKE

Brooke is giving away the first book of the Soul Series, *The Secrets of Their Souls*, for **FREE**. All you need to do is sign up here:

http://brookesivendra.com/tsots-download/

Enjoy!

DID YOU ENJOY THIS BOOK?

As a writer, it is critically important to get reviews.

Why?

You probably weigh reviews highly when making a decision whether to try a new author—I definitely do.

So, if you've enjoyed this book and would love to spread the word, I would be so grateful if you could leave an honest review (as short or as long as you like) where you bought it.

Thank you so much,
Brooke

ABOUT THE AUTHOR

Brooke Sivendra lives in Adelaide, Australia with her husband and two furry children—Milly, a Rhodesian Ridgeback, and Lara, a massive Great Dane who is fifty pounds heavier than Brooke and thinks she is a lap dog!

Brooke has a degree in Nuclear Medicine and worked in the field of medical research before launching her first business at the age of twenty-six. This business grew to be Australia's premier online shopping directory, and Brooke recently sold it to focus on her writing.

You can connect with Brooke at any of the channels listed below, and she personally responds to every comment and email.

Website: www.brookesivendra.com
Email: brooke@brookesivendra.com
Facebook: http://www.facebook.com/bsivendra
Instagram: http://www.instagram.com/brookesivendra
Twitter: www.twitter.com/brookesivendra

CPSIA information can be obtained
at www.ICGtesting.com
Printed in the USA
LVOW03s1723080218
565809LV00004B/1016/P